OUT OF THE
SHALLOWS

INTO THE DEEP #2

SAMANTHA YOUNG

Out of the Shallows
Copyright © 2014 Samantha Young

Edited by Jennifer Sommersby Young

Cover stock image by Vitaly Valua
(http://www.valuavitaly.com)

Cover design by Samantha Young

Interior Design by Angela McLaurin, Fictional Formats
(https://www.facebook.com/FictionalFormats)

Other Contemporary Novels by Samantha Young

Into the Deep

On Dublin Street Series:
On Dublin Street
Until Fountain Bridge (a novella)
Down London Road
Castle Hill (a novella)
Before Jamaica Lane

OUT OF THE
SḤALLOWS

Chapter One

Lanton, August 2013

The heady scent of flowers filled the room. These days it clung to everything. Even after I washed my hands a dozen times, they still smelled as if I'd doused them in floral perfume.

"That's pretty."

I turned from the arrangement of red roses and white lilies to find Claudia gesturing to it. I glanced back at the flowers. "I think I'm getting the hang of it. Finally."

"Whose it for?"

"It's Hub's. For his wife. Their fifteenth anniversary."

Claudia nodded. "Heart of mush underneath that bear-like exterior, huh?"

I grinned. Hub owned the local diner in my small hometown of Lanton, Indiana. He was a huge guy with an even huger beard and gruff demeanor, and I could see why non-locals might find him slightly intimidating. But Claud was right. Hub was all heart. "He placed this order over a month ago. That is not a man who forgets his anniversary."

My friend smiled and then gestured behind her into the store front of my mother's florist shop. "I rearranged the shop window like you asked."

Delia's was the only florist in town, and although Lanton wasn't huge, she kept fairly busy. She'd had a mold issue in the back room where I was working on floral arrangements, but after spending money my parents really couldn't afford to spend to fix it, Delia's was up and running again.

If only I could be one hundred percent positive that Delia, my actual mom, was up and running too.

"Thanks. If I don't tell you enough, I really appreciate you being here." Once Claudia had finished at the University of Edinburgh, she'd rushed back to the States, suitcase in tow, and moved in with my parents and me. She'd been here the whole summer, helping us out during one of the worst times of my family's life.

"You can stop saying that now. I might have to hurt you if you don't."

I smirked. "Fine."

Claudia frowned as she glanced around us. "Uh… where is Delia Mom, anyway?"

Mom was at the cemetery. It was becoming a regular hang out for her. I found myself hunching back over the arrangement as I murmured, "Where else?"

"Ah. Okay." Claudia sighed. "So, Lowe called me this morning."

I didn't answer.

"He says he's tried calling you."

Shrugging with more nonchalance than I felt, I said, "I know. I just… I haven't spoken to Jake, so I don't think it's right if I speak to Lowe."

"Lowe's your friend."

"No, Lowe is Jake's friend. I've hurt Jake enough without

confiding in his friend when I won't confide in him."

I reached for more filler foliage. Claudia's hand curled around mine, stopping me. "The arrangement is done."

Turning to her, I said, "I get the feeling you want to talk."

"Charley, school starts back up in a week. Are you ready?"

"No. But I'm trying to be."

"We're going back to the old apartment, and it's senior year so we'll have tons on our plates to keep us busy. You'll get to see Alex again, too. This will be good."

I looked away, worrying my lip between my teeth. After a moment of silence, I said softly, "Do you really think they're okay for me to go? Mom still visits the cemetery every day and Dad… he's still mad at me."

Claudia's eyes were filled with sympathy but I could also see determination in them. "Maybe Delia is still visiting the cemetery but that doesn't mean she's not good. She's much better, Charley. She can cope on her own here now. And Jim… he loves you. He'll come around when you come around."

"Don't," I warned, definitely not wanting to walk into *that* territory.

She held her hands up in surrender. "I won't. But are you ever planning on talking to Jake again?"

I glowered at her. "What is this? Piss-Off-Charley Day?"

"No, this is 'It's time to get back to normal and start facing up to the decisions you've made these last few months Day.' Such as the one you made regarding a certain Jacob Caplin?"

A familiar pain sliced across my chest, but I refused to give into it. Instead I brushed past Claud to grab a broom and started on the back room floor. "Then no, I don't plan on talking to Jake again. It's over. We're just going to leave it at that."

Claudia inhaled sharply. "You're just going to leave him hanging, wondering where it all went wrong?" She sounded horrified. Guilt crashed over me.

I shoved it forcefully aside. "We've hurt each other too much. How can we possibly come back from that?"

"You could try."

"Like you're trying with Beck?"

Her elegant brows drew together. "That's different."

"Claudia—"

"But I'll drop it. For now."

Somewhere along the way I think people got the wrong impression about me. I think *I* got the wrong impression about me. I don't know if it was that time I shoved my sister out of the way of a moving vehicle, taking the impact instead, and I got the nickname Supergirl. Or maybe it's my general cockiness.

Whatever it is, I think people think I'm this fearless, brave, independent young woman who couldn't give a shit what other people think.

I really couldn't give a shit what *other* people think.

But I care what my parents think of me. And I'm afraid of losing them.

So not fearless. So not brave. And I guess not nearly as independent as I used to think I was.

When you're a kid, your whole happiness is wrapped up in your parents. A hug from them, a kiss on the forehead, a piggyback ride, their laughter, their kind words, their affection, their love... it took away a hurt knee, or a classmate's name-calling, or the death of a beloved pet. As long as I knew my parents loved me, that I made them proud, and that I had their respect, I'd been all right.

That feeling never really goes away, though. It's amazing how easy it is for a parent to make you feel like a little kid all over again.

That's how I'd been feeling around my family for months now… like a kid craving my parents' love and respect. Lately, for the past few months, I felt like they were nothing but disappointed in me. Especially my dad.

Later that day, after Mom came back from the cemetery and helped Claudia and I finish out the day, we went home to make dinner. My dad, a mechanic, owned a local auto shop. He got in from work not too much later and soon we were seated around the dining table.

A familiar silence fell.

The clinking of cutlery off plates, glasses against cutlery, the rustle of napkins, the crunch of bread, it amplified the quiet. We didn't have a whole lot to say to each other these days.

I was surprised when Dad asked, "You thought any more on taking that exam you need to pass to get into law school?"

I looked over at Claudia, her eyes rounded at Dad's question. I shocked her by replying, "I'm taking the LSATs this fall, Dad."

Claudia's eyes bugged out. "You are?"

She had taken the LSATs in June and passed, but she was under the impression that I was done with pursuing law school.

Feeling my parents' gazes burning into my cheeks, I nodded. "I am. As long as I take them in time for February results, I can apply to start law school next fall."

"I'm pleased to hear it. I'm sure Claudia will help you study," Dad said.

Our eyes met and for the first time in months, Dad's were almost tender. He was genuinely pleased. To him I was making the right decision.

I didn't know if it was the right decision to apply for law school instead of applying to the police academy like I wanted to. That was probably why I hadn't mentioned anything to Claudia about my decision—I didn't want someone talking me out of it. The truth was I'd made the decision based on what was best for my family.

"So am I." Glancing over at Mom, I saw tears shining in her eyes as she smiled at me.

Yeah, totally the best decision for my family.

It gave them peace of mind, and they needed that more than I needed to be a cop.

Claudia bravely queried, "Are you sure that's what *you* want, Charley?"

"Of course." I gave her a tight smile.

Dinner was less awkward than usual after that. Mom and Dad actually engaged in conversation and afterward, instead of shooing me off when I attempted to help clean up, Mom let me.

I followed her into the kitchen and piled the plates near the trash. As I began scraping off the leftovers Mom said, "I'm proud of this decision, Charlotte."

I glanced over at her. "Yeah?"

She smiled, her eyes misting. They did that a lot these days. Mom had never been a big crier before… well, before… but she welled up at the slightest thing now. "I have to admit it's been playing in the back of my mind these last few months—you going off to the academy after graduation. Going into the police. It's not like I haven't always known you could take care of yourself. Even when you pushed Andie out of the way of Finnegan's SUV, I worried for about half a second until I saw you. Your leg covered in a cast, bruises all over, and you grinned at us when we walked into that hospital room. All cocky. If that had been Andie, it would've shaken her up more. She was a mess after it happened. She followed you around for weeks. It drove you nuts."

Just like that, a lump formed in my own throat and I turned away, trying to swallow past the collection of mounting tears. "I remember," I whispered.

"I didn't want you to be a cop. But before this summer, I felt guilty for pressuring you into not going for it. I didn't want to spend the rest of my life waiting for a phone call in the night to tell me that my daughter had been killed just doing her job. But more than that, I didn't want my kid to resent me for holding her back. For not supporting her.

"But then Andie..." She pushed away from the counter and walked toward me. She stopped and reached out to take my hand. "I know it's selfish to ask you to give up the academy. I know it. I don't know if you really want to take the LSATs or if you're just saying it to please your dad and me. If I were a stronger woman, I'd tell you to go for it. Go for your dream. But I'm not. I'm happy you're not applying to the academy. I'm sorry, but that's the truth. Please don't hate me."

"I get it. That's why I'm not doing it."

"Do you really want to be a lawyer, though? Because you don't have to be."

I grinned wryly. "I can't give Dad what he really wants. For the first time in my life, I've disappointed him—"

"Charley—"

"No, Mom, you know it's true. I wish I were stronger too. But I'm not, so this is all I can give right now. He's always wanted me to be a lawyer. I'm sitting the LSATs."

Mom's grip on my hand tightened. "One day we'll be us again."

God, I hoped so because right now I really missed my dad and I *really* missed Andie.

The tears spilled down my cheeks and I turned away, trying to focus on the dishes. Mom gave me space.

Just as her footsteps disappeared out of the kitchen, my phone buzzed in my pocket. My stomach flipped unpleasantly at the name on the screen.

Another missed call from Jake.

That would be one a day since I'd left Edinburgh.

Like clockwork the text message came after it.

You know the drill...

Despite the fact that I never answered his calls, Jake kept trying, hoping for the day I'd change my mind. Six weeks ago, when it became clear I wasn't going to answer his calls or texts, he'd sent me a message asking me to at least let him know I was all right. So I did. Every day since, he'd wanted to know at least that.

Brushing the remaining tears from my cheeks, I replied.

I'm okay.

I never asked him if he was okay. There was so much guilt weighing on me, I was taking the coward's way out with Jake. I'd hurt him. I knew that. I just didn't want to hear him say it.

Shoving my phone back in my pocket, I thought how ironic it was that only a few short months ago, I'd made him work his ass off to make up for the way he broke up with me when he was seventeen. Over four years later I'd hurt him just as badly. I'd promised myself I'd never hurt anyone the way Jake hurt me.

What a difference a few months can make.

Chapter Two

Edinburgh, February 2013

"...you against my fallow heart. There'll be no sympathy from me, my friend. I lost you out in the shallows..."

For the past twenty minutes I'd been successfully working on a tutorial project, my laptop open on the table, beer beside it, while my friends sat around me listening to indie rock band The Stolen.

We were in Milk, a bar on the Cowgate, an area of Edinburgh where my fellow Americans and I were living while doing a year abroad at the University of Edinburgh.

Luckily for me, I was the kind of girl who could drown out a live rock band and a noisy crowd in order to complete classwork I forgot was due the next day. I could've stayed back at my apartment, but I had unpleasant business to take care of there later so I was avoiding having to spend any more time there than necessary.

This hadn't been a problem until my friend Lowe, lead vocalist of the band began singing my favorite song, "Lonely Boy." Since the moment I'd heard it months ago during their first set in Scotland, it'd struck a chord. And every time I heard it, it pulled me in.

I turned my head from my laptop screen to look up at the small stage. Lowe, a hot, smart musician with tattoos, a lip ring, and messy dark hair, caught my movement and focused on me, his eyes smiling over the top of his rimless glasses.

I gave a small smile back and picked up my beer, listening to his song.

Lowe told us that he was never more honest than he was when he wrote a song. In response, my boyfriend Jake had joked about me writing a song for him. The joke fell flat because the truth was I *wasn't* being open enough with him. I was keeping a part of myself from Jake. Tonight was supposed to be a step forward for us—a big step for me, but one I felt I had to take if we had any hope of holding onto a relationship.

I'd been feeling nervous but okay about it. Until Lowe and his freaking song.

As if he'd guessed where my mind had wandered, Jake rested his chin on my shoulder. He wrapped his arms around my waist and drew me against his chest. "Where are you right now?" he asked, his lips tickling my ear.

I shivered and turned my head slightly so his lips touched my cheek. "I'm right here."

"Why does this song get to you?"

I jerked, staring into his gorgeous face in surprise.

Jake smiled slightly, his dark eyes warm and knowing. "I pay attention."

"You're a know-it-all."

His white teeth flashed. "Only when it comes to you. When a subject really interests me, I give it my unwavering focus."

"Are you saying you're an expert on me?"

His eyes lowered and I felt his grip loosen. "Hopefully one day you'll let me be."

Not knowing how to answer, I looked back at the stage. For the last few days, since we'd started a physical relationship, the uneasiness that existed beneath the surface had only increased. It wasn't borne of not wanting one another. Far from it. No, I was holding out on an emotional level and Jake was trying to be patient, which wasn't his strong suit.

All in all, it had created a sense of fragility between us.

I relaxed against his hold, brushing my fingers over his knuckles.

"Beck, show us your pecs!" a pretty brunette at the next table shouted over the music. I smirked at the scowl my girl Claudia shot her way.

Beck was Jake's best friend. He was also now one of Claudia's best friends. As lead guitarist, Beck stood at the front of the stage with Lowe. He was absurdly attractive, tall and blond, with lethal gray eyes and an even more lethal smile. Beck was everything you'd expect from a rock band, with his sleeve tattoos on one arm, lazy-ass sense of style, and a way with women. He oozed sex and charisma more than anyone I'd ever met in my life, but I knew there was more to him than the whole bad-boy thing he played up. I knew this because I'd seen how different he was around Claudia. He wanted to be devoted to her in a way he wouldn't even admit to himself, which was probably why he was eye-fucking the brunette at the next table.

Catching the look, Claudia downed her drink and turned away from the band. Rowena, our Scottish friend who we suspected was sleeping with the bassist, Denver, brushed her bright purple hair out of her eyes to exchange a worried glance with me.

Claudia was erratic around Beck.

I knew she was attracted to him, but I had my suspicion, as did every person in our group with the possible exception of Beck, that Claudia was in love. However, one minute she pretended to be fine about his manwhorish ways, and the next she looked like she wanted to find a corner to cry in.

I nudged her arm and she looked up at me with sad, stunning green eyes. Did I mention she was the most beautiful girl I'd ever met in real life and one of the coolest, funniest, kindest girls to boot? Did I mention Beck was an idiot?

"Do you want to go?"

She glanced back at the stage, glowered (which, in all honesty, I preferred to the sad puppy-dog look), and turned to me. "Yeah, if you're ready."

"You're leaving?" Jake leaned into me again.

"It's either that or I kill your best friend."

Jake looked over at Beck and gave a slight shake of his head. "He needs to pull his head out of his ass."

"Yup. Before then, though, I'm going to head back to the apartment with Claud."

"Want me to come?"

I heaved a shaky sigh. Time to admit what I was up to tonight. "I actually have a thing tonight. A telling-Mom-and-Dad-about-me-and-you thing…"

Jake's eyebrows rose. "Did I hear that right over the music?"

I cupped his face in my hands, feeling the slight bristle prickle my skin. Playfully, I rubbed my nose against his, smirking. "You might want to watch what you say next. I'm feeling a little nervous right now. I might back out."

In answer, I felt the soft press of Jake's mouth against mine. My lashes fluttered closed and my lips parted for his soft, sweet kiss. My mouth tingled as he drew back.

"I'm also telling them about the academy."

For that, I got another kiss, but instead of drawing back

afterward, Jake pulled me into a hug. I melted against his strong chest, my hands resting on the hard muscles of his back. He smelled great, and the strength in his arms as they held me to him made me feel safe.

In that moment all my worries disappeared. I felt the traitorous compulsion to open my mouth and whisper those three little words.

"You ready to go?" Claudia's loud question stopped me in the nick of time.

Pulling reluctantly out of Jake's hold, I said, "Wish me luck."

"You don't need it." He brushed my cheek with his thumb. "Thanks for doing this for me. It means a lot."

My throat clogged with emotion so I flashed a cheeky grin to cover it. "I'm doing it for *us*." I stood and shoved my laptop and notes into my backpack.

Jake's hand curled around my thigh and I glanced down to see him staring up at me, unable to hide the uncertainty in his eyes. "You'll call me afterward?"

"If it's not too late." I bent down and pressed a quick kiss to his mouth. "See you tomorrow."

I said goodbye to Rowena as Claudia moved through the busy room toward the barroom. When I turned back to wave goodbye to the guys, I got a chin nod from Lowe but nothing from Beck. He was too busy watching Claudia leave, a little furrow between his brows.

She hadn't bothered to say goodbye to him and at this point, I didn't blame her.

Outside the bar, Claudia wrapped her arms around herself, her long dark hair blowing wildly behind her. She had a remote expression on her face I didn't like. Not one bit. Ignoring my own nerves over the conversation I was about to have with my parents, I strode forward and linked my arm through hers.

She smiled absentmindedly at me as we walked toward the apartment.

"So," I said, "last weekend you and Beck seemed fine. You seemed to have come to terms with how things are between you, and you were nervously excited about taking him with us to Barcelona to meet your father."

Claudia's parents were wealthy, self-indulgent, neglectful socialites from Coronado. They had no time for their daughter. Over Christmas break, Claudia found out why her dad was particularly indifferent. Turns out he wasn't her real father. Her real father was a British artist called Dustin Tweedie. In an effort to make some kind of amends, Claud's mom had tracked him down. He lived in Barcelona and Claud's mom was going to pay for Claudia to fly out there this spring to meet him—with Jake, Beck, and me in tow for moral support.

Claudia tightened her grip. "I was. But that was last weekend."

"What happened between then and now?"

"I wrote an email to Dustin two days ago." She wouldn't look at me, and anger burned hotly in my blood at the sight of her throat working against emotion. "I still haven't heard anything back."

Having no idea what it felt like to be the recipient of not one, not two, but three indifferent parents, I really didn't know what to say. "It's only been two days."

Two of our neighbors called out to us and we waved back. As soon as they were gone, Claudia shrugged. "Does it matter? I should just face it now. He won't want me coming out there and interrupting his life." Her laugh sounded hollow. I hated it. She wasn't meant for bitter. "Let's face it, Charley. I'm missing whatever that thing is that makes men care."

Stunned, I stopped outside our courtyard gate. "That's not true."

She pulled away. "I can't even look at you. You would never let them make you feel like this."

"Uh, hullo." I waved my hand in front of her face. "Were you not here these past few months, watching me wallow in self-pity over a certain handsome young man with the surname Caplin?"

She snorted but still wouldn't meet my eyes.

"Claud, we're allowed to have bad days, okay? Today is a bad day for you. That's all. This shit with your parents is not going to change you. Please don't let it."

"And Beck?"

I cared about Beck, I did. And I know he cared deeply for Claudia, but right now it wasn't enough for her and I felt like we'd had this conversation one too many times. "I think maybe you had the right idea last week."

"Cutting him out a little?" She shrugged. "He got all broody about it and I caved."

"Well, this time, don't cave."

She shot me a droll look as we walked toward our building. "Oh really? It's that easy."

"Okay, maybe not. Maybe you just need a distraction."

"A distraction?"

"Yeah." I thought of the one thing that had distracted me while Jake was dating Melissa. I grinned. "You need Lowe."

"Um, I like the guy and all, but I am not sleeping with Lowe."

"I'm not talking about sex." I gave her my most serious look. "Believe it or not, Lowe is an incredibly insightful, compassionate, patient guy. He's a really good friend to have on your side."

"Jesus, does Jake know you're half in love with his friend?"

"I am not in love with Lowe. He was just there when I needed him. You should hang out with him. Seriously. Oh, and don't say shit like that in front of Jake."

She grinned mischievously and the uneasiness I felt dissipated. This was more like Claudia. "Does Mr. Caplin have a jealous streak?"

"Yes. It's almost as wide as mine," I grumbled.

"And you're positive my hanging out with Lowe won't incite *your* jealousy?"

I considered it, letting her walk into the apartment ahead of me. It wasn't too long ago I'd had a crush on Lowe, but that's all it was or ever would be. What I felt for Jake… it burned in my very depths. No one had ever come close to making me feel what I felt for him.

He was my missing puzzle piece.

"Nope," I finally concluded. "He's sexy as sin and I like him, but he doesn't come close to Jacob."

"Aww, *Jacob*," she teased.

"Please don't start calling him that."

"Oh, I believe you started it."

"Great. He'll kill me."

Claudia laughed, coming to a stop outside her door. Her laughter melted into a smile. "Thanks for making me feel better."

"You're my family. I hurt when you hurt."

Tears shimmered in her eyes. "Dude!" She shook her head as she unlocked her door. "This mascara is not waterproof!"

The door slammed shut in my face and I burst out laughing. "Good night, then!" I moved slowly to unlock my own door.

Once inside, I felt the butterflies come back to me with a vengeance. Fighting through the nerves, I hurried to set up my laptop on my desk, plugging into the hardline Internet connection. My Skype page opened and I sat on the narrow bed in front of my desk to wait.

Eight years ago I earned the nickname "Supergirl" from my entire town. When the people of Lanton, Indiana, heard the name

Charlotte Redford, that's the first word that popped into their heads. However, I've never felt as brave as people tell me I am. I certainly didn't feel brave as I waited to face my kryptonite—my parents.

There was nothing I hated more than disappointing Jim and Delia Redford. My parents had always been loving and supportive, and my sister Andie and I almost felt like we owed it to them to be good, obliging kids. But my mom and dad hated the idea of me becoming a cop from the moment I mentioned it to them. I think they might've been okay with it if they thought I had any intention of settling for a deputy job in Lanton. There wasn't a whole lot of crime in my hometown. But nope. They knew I had every intention of hightailing it to the Chicago Police Academy in the hope that I would one day join the illustrious ranks of the Chicago PD. My sister's fiancé, Rick, happened to be a detective in the city. And I wanted to specialize—possibly work the homicide division—so I understood their reservations, their desire for me to go to law school instead.

It was Jake who pushed me to realize I was sick of compromising for them…

Four days ago

"Is it possible to die of sex exhaustion?" I panted, collapsing in a sprawl across Jake's sweat-dampened chest.

He lazily stroked my spine. "I'm thinking yes."

"That was…" I groaned at the feel of him inside me.

"Mind-blowing?" he offered with a suspicious amount of smugness. "Told you it would be."

I bit his shoulder gently. "Cocky."

"I dare you to leave teeth marks." Jake cupped my ass. "I'd love explaining it to people."

"What people?" I mumbled. "You're inside the only person who should be seeing you shirtless, mister."

He chuckled and I burrowed deeper against the sound in his throat. "The guys and I don't really care about walking around the apartment shirtless."

Despite my exhaustion, I found the energy to jerk away from him, my hands pressed to his chest as I scowled down at him. "In other words, you'd love to explain those marks to Lowe."

Inured to my glower, Jake tucked my long hair behind my ear before following the wavy strand of platinum down over my breast. "It would make a point."

"A point he is well aware of. The traitor dumped me in your hands last night."

Jake offered me an unrepentant grin. "That's true."

Before I could respond, he took me by surprise, wrapping his arms tightly around me as he sat up. Our lips almost brushed as he brought us chest to chest. Sensing I wasn't going anywhere anytime soon, I shifted off my knees and wrapped my legs around his waist. Jake's eyes darkened with the movement.

"No way," I said. "You can't possibly…"

"Not yet." He crushed me against him, whispering the words across my mouth. "Anyway, we have stuff to talk about."

I instantly wanted to pull away but Jake cupped his hand around my nape, forcing me to look at him. I jerked against his hold.

"Good, we'll start with that," he muttered darkly. "Why do you keep pulling away from me?"

"I told you I don't like it when you hold me by the neck. It's not a big deal." It was *so* a big deal. And Jake knew it was. He just didn't know why.

The truth was he used to hold me like that when he wanted my entire focus. It was kind of intense and more than kind of sexual, and I thought it was something he just did with me. However, I'd once witnessed him holding his ex-girlfriend Melissa in the same way, and as stupid as I knew it was, it bothered me. A lot.

"I don't believe you."

"Next question," I sighed, tugging his hand off my neck.

Jake didn't look happy but he relented. "When are you thinking about telling your parents about us?"

"Well," I wriggled on him with a cheeky grin, "I was thinking we should uncover the plot of some evil mastermind and you can save the world first. There's no way they won't be happy for us after that. It would be petty."

Kneading the muscles in my lower back, he said, "I'm trying to be serious and I can't do that when you're sitting on me naked, acting cute."

"Then I guess my work here is done." I kissed him hard. Jake's arms turned to steel around me as he hauled me closer, deepening the kiss with a groan that reverberated through me in such a delicious way…

I wrapped my arms around him. Jake broke our kiss, grabbing my upper arms to push me gently back.

He scowled at me. "Play fair."

I slumped. "Why should I? You're not."

"How is trying to have a conversation with my girlfriend not playing fair?" He narrowed his eyes. "How did I become the chick in this scenario?"

Laughing, I ran my fingers through his hair, loving the way his lashes lowered over his eyes in pleasure at my touch. "You did that all by yourself."

"I'm being serious." He turned to kiss my wrist. "I'm not asking you to tell your parents. I'm just asking you if you're planning on doing it at some point. We can't," he exhaled heavily, eyes locking with mine, "we can't move forward until you tell them."

"I know. I will. Just… it's hard. Give me time."

"And while you're at it, tell them about the police academy." He crushed me close again, his breath hot on my lips. "Please. This is your life, Charley. Live it how you want to. Four years ago, you were solid in your decision. I don't know if it was because of me, if I made you doubt yourself somehow, made you doubt your ability to make the right choices…" He tilted his head back, looking at me with such belief and love, I wanted to melt all over him. "Stop compromising who you are. They'll love you. They'll understand."

As the chat-request bubble popped up on my laptop screen, I sucked in a deep breath and kept Jake's words with me as I clicked the answer button.

Chapter Three

West Lafayette, August 2013

Although I'd been worried about leaving Mom and Dad when our relationship (my relationship with my dad, really) was in limbo, I could breathe a little easier now that Claudia and I had settled into our old apartment in West Lafayette. The apartment was in a picturesque red-brick building with whitewashed balconies. It looked over a green, and had a communal pool and gym. The apartment itself was big, contemporary, and we each had a good-sized bedroom and bathroom to ourselves. It cost Claudia's parents a small fortune in rent every month. However, they could afford it and Claudia couldn't give a crap if she milked them for all they had, considering money was the only currency they offered up in terms of affection.

"Well, I think I'm finally unpacked," I announced, walking into the open plan living room and kitchen area. Claudia was playing Carrie Underwood on her laptop while she—"Why are you rearranging the furniture?"

She stood from pushing the sofa, wiping sweat from her brow. "New year, new everything." She grinned as if that was an answer.

"Watch your back, okay?" I said, eyeing the brown leather couch dubiously. "It's not exactly a poodle you're pushing around there."

"I'm fine. I'm done." She strode into the kitchen and pulled two bottles of water from the fridge, throwing one my way. I caught it as she said, "Did you check in with your parents?"

She knew too well I had. "They're going to Chicago this weekend. That usually does them some good. I just wish things weren't still so strained between us. I was hoping it would miraculously return to normal before I left for school."

"Maybe if you'd go with them to Chicago once and a while…"

"Don't," I snapped.

"Okay, shutting up."

Turning the tables on her, I said, "Speaking of parents… have you spoken to any of yours?"

Claudia's expression soured. "My mom. She's been calling more since Barcelona."

Surprised by the seeming show of parental concern, I said, "That's good?"

My friend raised an unimpressed eyebrow. "We'll see."

"Cautious as she goes. Smart." I glanced around at the exceptionally clean and tidy living space, knowing it wouldn't stay that way for long once classes started. "So… are we meeting Alex and Sharon tonight or are you planning on something else for the 'new year, new everything' attitude you got going on?"

She made a face at my sarcasm. "Be like that if you want, but I actually got the idea from you. You said you wanted a fresh start. Well, you're absolutely right. We're starting over almost from scratch. I have a plan—now you need one."

"And what exactly is yours?"

"Life is for living, right?" Claudia grinned, her green eyes glittering. "I'm finally going to ask Will out."

"The hot TA?" Will McPherson was a TA in our second-year criminology class. Claudia had crushed on him. "Do you think he'll still be there?"

Her face fell. "I did not think of that."

I turned away to hide my smile. "He could still be here. Don't lose hope. Your plan to distract yourself from the fact that you're in love with Beck could still work out."

"Don't, or I'll whip out my Jake card."

I flinched at his name. "Fine. Your plan: ask out Will. My plan: pass the LSATs."

"Unimaginative, but if it's what you want, I will help you attain it."

"I appreciate it. Now get your butt in the shower. We're meeting Alex and Sharon in an hour at The Brewhouse."

"An hour?" She tugged on a lock of silky, black hair. "It takes me an hour just to blow my hair out."

"Then you better get a move on, Pocahontas."

The Brewhouse was a bar close to campus that was a little slack on the ID thing. A lot of the campus bars were but The Brewhouse hosted live bands on the weekend. Claudia complained all the time that there were never any country singers booked to play. I pointed out that the usual clientele weren't really country people.

As soon as we walked in, I saw Alex and Sharon. My eyes met Alex's and an overwhelming sense of home washed over me. When I'd hurried back from Scotland months ago to be with my parents, Alex was there for me. He returned to Lanton from Purdue. Once the worst was over, he still came home on the weekends to see me.

However, he'd taken off this summer with Sharon and they'd gone traveling around Europe. I'd missed him. I'd missed his support and how he withheld judgment.

All I really wanted to do was throw myself into his arms and hug him tight.

However, as nice as Sharon was, she was a little cagey of me being affectionate with her boyfriend considering he was my ex, and I understood enough to keep my distance when she was around.

Alex, however, was clueless that way.

He grinned at me, got up out of his chair, and strode across the bar with determination. Next thing I knew I was crushed in his bear hug.

I hugged him back, squeezing my eyes shut and taking in the familiar smell of his sandalwood and musk cologne.

"It's good to see you, Charley," he said quietly.

"You too."

"Don't I get a hug?"

Alex let me go, smiling at Claudia over my shoulder. "Always."

They hugged as Sharon approached. She was a five-foot nothing, cute-as-a-button blond who had a nice thing to say about everybody. Bubbly and sweet, she was my complete opposite. She reached out to hug me and I hugged her back. "How are you?" she asked as she pulled away.

"Getting there," I answered honestly enough. "How are you? How was Europe?"

Her blue eyes lit up. "So amazing! We have so many great stories to tell you guys."

We settled down at their table with drinks, noting that the stage was set up for a band tonight. "Who's playing?" I asked.

Alex shrugged. "No clue. More interestingly… did I hear a rumor you're taking the LSATs?"

Glancing over at Claudia, I saw her looking away innocently. I sighed, turning back to Alex. "Yes, you heard correctly."

"I'm glad to hear it." He threw me a boyish grin.

"I thought you might be." When we were together, Alex had fervently pushed me toward law school. He hated the idea of me becoming a cop as much as my parents had.

"Testing, testing!"

Our attention was drawn to Duke, a thirty-something bartender who'd worked The Brewhouse for years. No one really knew anything about him, a fact he played up to deliberately, often referring to himself as "mystery bartender guy," which kind of took the cool out of the enigma. Duke stood on stage, tapping the mic. Satisfied, he gestured behind him. "For those not in the know, every Friday and Saturday night it's live music night here at The Brewhouse. So if you're looking for a quiet drink, you might want to try The Turtle down the street. But I promise you the jukebox selection there is as *slow* as the service." He grinned waiting for laughs. They did not come. "Anyhoo, tonight I'd like to welcome to the stage some local boys—neighbors, really, from the Windy City. They've been making a name for themselves touring bars across the Midwest this summer. Please give a warm welcome to The Stolen."

What the…

I stopped breathing as Lowe, Beck, Matt, and Denver made their way on stage.

What the…

Lowe lifted his guitar over his shoulder and sidled up to the mic. He looked the same, rimless glasses, lip ring, tattoos. Except not having seen him for five months made him more attractive. I'd missed him and the guys. Lowe's eyes swept the bar and as soon as they hit our table, his shoulders seemed to lose some of their tension.

Our eyes locked and he smiled. "Thanks for having us at The Brewhouse. It's nice to be here. We've got some friends in the audience, so tonight is for them. Charley, Claudia, The Stolen missed you this summer."

Beck's eyes were on Claudia as the band started and when I turned to question her, I found her staring right back at him in total surprise. Okay, then, so she didn't know we were going to be hijacked tonight, either.

"These are your friends you met in Edinburgh?" Alex said, confusion and curiosity in his tone.

Claudia tore her gaze from Beck's. "Yeah. I told Beck months and months ago that they should play here. Obviously he didn't forget."

Sharon's brow wrinkled. "I thought they went to Northwestern."

"They do," I answered, willing my heart rate to slow. If The Stolen was here, then…

"It's a bit of a trek just for one gig."

"Uh…" Claudia gripped my arm hard and gestured toward the bar with her head. "That's because this isn't about a gig."

My heart was full-on galloping, trying to burst out of my chest.

Jake.

I braced myself against my chair as he strode through the crowd toward our table. His eyes were on me but his face held no expression whatsoever.

Honestly, I felt like the world dropped from beneath me.

He stopped at the table, towering over me and all we could do was stare at each other. I drank in everything about him. His hair was a little longer, like when we were kids, and he needed a shave. His skin seemed paler than usual and he looked tired.

I wanted to stand up, wrap my arms around him, and feel and smell him all around me. Every muscle in my body ached with how much I missed him and I didn't know if I should cry or curse or scream. Until that moment I hadn't realized how much I truly, deeply *missed* him.

He was so much a part of me.

"Jake." Alex stood, holding out his hand. "Long time, man."

Giving nothing away, Jake shook Alex's hand. "Alex."

"Uh," Alex looked down at Sharon, "this is my girl, Sharon. Sharon, this is Jake."

She stretched out her hand with a congenial smile. "Nice to meet you."

"You too," he replied quietly, shaking her hand.

"Jake." Claudia's chair scraped back and she rounded the table. She walked right into him, hugging him tight.

Jake cracked as he enveloped her, his eyes squeezing shut as they hugged.

I blinked away tears.

He was sad.

I'd made him sad.

And I should've known that I wouldn't get off that easy.

"Can we take a walk, Charley?" he asked loudly over the music.

Looking back up at him, I saw Claudia had shuffled away to give us space. Jake's expression was unreadable again.

I nodded and got up, leaving with him after giving Alex and Claud a look of reassurance.

We strolled outside into the warm evening air, the sound of The Stolen disappearing behind us. I glanced back at The Brewhouse, part of me hating the guys for taking a gig here and the other part of me a little more in love with them for doing this for Jake. He'd needed support and they were right there with him.

God, it was a wonder they didn't all hate me for what I was doing to him.

Silence was thick between us as we walked down the sidewalk, passing other college kids enjoying their last weekend of freedom before classes started. The tension between us was palpable and the pull…

Jake walked beside me but he'd given me plenty of space, as if he was afraid to touch me. My body felt drawn to his, eager to pull him closer. I felt like I was physically fighting to keep the space between us.

Five months.

What guy comes back after five months?

I hated myself.

Jake exhaled loudly. "First, how is everyone?"

Not surprised he led with that, I said, "Better, thank you."

He rubbed a hand over his head. He did that whenever he was unsure or uncomfortable. "I should explain something. When Andie… I kept my distance not only because you asked, but because it was the right thing to do. It wasn't about me and I know having me there would've upset your parents. Not to mention it might stir things up in Lanton, with my history with the town and I… you and your parents didn't need that on top of everything else. So me not turning up to push the issues between us was about that—it wasn't about me giving up. And you knew that. You knew you could break up with me and not have to deal with the fallout and the questions because if I turned up, I was a selfish dick. Yet, if I didn't turn up, I was the dick who didn't care enough to fight, so for you it was a win-win." He shot me a searing look, his soulful eyes making me so breathless with pain,

I had to turn away. "For me... I've been waiting five months. Five months of hell, waiting for you to leave Lanton. Now you have and now I'm here."

I felt sick. It was my turn to exhale. Shakily. "My being here hasn't really changed anything, Jake."

He huffed, "See, maybe that's the problem. I don't know what the situation is now. I don't know why you pushed me away. I don't know why you broke up with me because you didn't even give me a reason... *over the phone*. I want to know why. How did we go from being perfect to being nothing?"

I didn't have any answers that wouldn't make me sound like a crazy person. Instead, I pulled on the attitude that had gotten me through our first breakup. "Can't you just be angry with me, resent me, hate me, and then leave it at that?"

"Oh, I'm angry," he said. "But I also love you, so the answer to that question is no."

I sucked in my breath and looked away, willing the tears to fuck off. "I'm angry at me too. Okay? I haven't been able to face you because I've been dealing with a lot of other stuff. You're just not a part of that equation anymore."

"That's still not an answer. And I can see how upset you are right now, so I'm not believing the whole unaffected shit you're trying to pull." Suddenly, I felt his hand wrap around my wrist. I jerked away instinctively, knowing if I let him touch me, I'd break in an instant. Catching sight of the hurt in his eyes gutted me. "You could stop acting like this. You could just be honest and tell me what the hell is going through your head."

"I've chosen them," I said abruptly, wanting this conversation to be over. "That's what I said to you when we broke up, and I meant it. When I pushed you away, that was me choosing my family over you.

That's *all* this is."

The muscle in his jaw flexed. "Why does it have to be an either-or situation? We can work on bringing them around. That was the plan all along."

"It's not anymore." I made myself meet his eyes, forcing all the conviction I could into mine. "I hurt them for you, Jake. I put you first and now I've damaged my relationship with them. Maybe irreparably. I have to try to fix that, so…" I shrugged unhappily, every part of my body screaming at my mouth not say it. "You and I are over."

He lowered his gaze from mine as he rubbed a hand over the scruff on his jaw. I felt a little punch to my gut as I realized his hand was trembling slightly.

"Jake?"

A couple of kids pushed past us and Jake took that opportunity to turn his back on me, staring out across the street with his hands locked tight behind his head.

I gave him his space but waiting on his reaction was excruciating.

Finally he turned back to me. The anger in his eyes was there for all to see but his words were careful, controlled. "I thought if I came here and you had to face me, then you'd see what a colossal mistake this is. But that's not going to happen, is it?"

"No…" I shrugged helplessly. "I'm sorry."

"So that's it?" he said, and I found myself growing confused by the anger and pain in his eyes and the calmness of his tone. "We're no longer fighting for us?"

I waited until an approaching couple had passed out of earshot before I said, "We've hurt each other. Maybe we could get past that, but right now I have to work on myself and my relationship with my parents. You and I are a lot, Jake. You know we are. We're drama. I can't deal with that. Plus, I'm taking the LSATs this year so I'll be too busy—"

"You're what?" he said, surprise written all over his face.

I ignored the stab of disappointment I felt. I wasn't interested in analyzing whether it came from him or from within myself. "I'm not going to be a cop."

Jake stared at me silently for a few seconds. There was a confused and wary aspect in his eyes as he gestured to me. "You really aren't you right now, are you?"

Frowning, I looked away. "I'm me. I'm just not yesterday's me."

For a while we didn't say anything. My body was eager to get away from him. Somehow around Jake, I felt stripped bare in front of a mirror and I wasn't too fond of the reflection staring back at me.

"Can we still be friends? Your parents were all right when we were friends."

Now it was my turn to be surprised. "You want to stay in my life? After what I've put you through these last five months?"

That little tick of muscle in his jaw and the glitter in his eyes gave away his anger, but the words tumbling out of his mouth belied it. "You forgave me once. I'm forgiving you. I want us to be friends. You don't have to shut me out of your life, Charley."

I knew it would be easier to do just that. Last time it had been too hard to be around him and just be friends.

Yet now that I had him in front of me again, I couldn't find the words to deny him. It would be easier this time. He went to Northwestern, I went to Purdue. We were almost three hours apart. Our friendship would fizzle out on its own without me having to be the one to sever the undeniable connection between us. Time and distance would do that.

"Okay," I agreed.

We walked for a little while before deciding to make our way back to the bar. I asked about his family, about school, about his summer touring with The Stolen. His one-word answers didn't exactly scream, "Let's be friends," which made me even more bewildered by his attitude about our breakup.

He was visibly upset, clearly pissed off, and yet his words were strangely calm and accepting.

I had no idea what was going on.

Stepping into the bar, I saw the stage was empty. The band had finished their set and the jukebox was playing Arcade Fire.

My Claudia radar found her pressed into the near right corner of the bar. Beck had his hands on the wall at either side of Claudia's head, his own head bent toward her. By their body language and the look on Claudia's face, I'd say they were arguing. Their reunion apparently was going as well as Jake's and mine had.

"Charley!"

I walked toward the shout of my name, smiling at Lowe as he stood up from the table the guys were sharing with Alex and Sharon. I hugged Lowe, taken aback by how happy he was to see me. Denver and Matt equally so, their hugs just as long and tight. In all honesty, I'd been preparing myself for their defection. It would've made sense if they'd taken Jake's side in this whole thing.

I did notice a look passing between Lowe and Jake, however, and Lowe got a little quiet with me after that. Matt and Denver, not so much.

"You should've seen the tail I picked up this summer, Charley." Matt smirked, as he leaned back in his chair.

I smirked right back. "Tail?"

"I could've said worse. That was me censorizing myself."

Denver snorted. "You need to stop with the weed, Matt. It truly is killing your brain cells. And your vocabulary."

I laughed. It was like we'd never been apart. "I take it the mini-tour went well."

Denver nodded. "It was great. We got permission to film in a lot of the bars and our live sets are getting a lot of exposure on YouTube. We're just waiting for a label to see it."

I frowned, turning to Lowe. "No luck on the demos you sent out?"

Lowe shook his head and took a drink, his eyes on the table and not on me.

I sighed.

Great.

I opened my mouth to speak to Alex, knowing I'd get eye contact out of him, when Claudia's shriek filled the bar. "Asshole!"

We all turned around, watching as she shoved a pissed-off Beck aside and stormed toward the exit.

I instantly pushed my chair back at the same time Alex held out Claudia's purse. I gave him a grim *thanks* and glanced around at the guys, carefully avoiding Jake's gaze. "I've got to go. Bye, guys. It was nice to see you."

It was wrong that I was glad Claudia and Beck had a fight that got me out of there. I knew it was wrong. But still… I was grateful.

Chapter Four

Edinburgh, February 2013

"You look wiped," Jake said, his expression sympathetic as he stood to press a soft kiss to my lips. "Did the tutorial go okay?"

I slipped into the seat opposite him as he sat back at the table. "I didn't even have to say a word," I grumbled, stifling a yawn. "I don't know why I bothered."

He shot me a mock frown as he gestured to a nearby waiter. "Why, to accumulate great knowledge, of course."

I grinned at his faux uppity accent. "Oh, is that what I'm spending all this money on?"

"That, and a little piece of paper that proves you've spent thousands and thousands of dollars on an education *Good Will Hunting* got for a dollar fifty in late charges at his public library."

Rolling my eyes, I gave the waiter my coffee order and turned back to my boyfriend. "You've seen that movie way too many times."

Jake looked at me like I was nuts. "There's no such thing."

"I guess not." It was a pretty damn good movie. "How was class?"

"Uh-uh." Jake shook his head. "None of that. How did last night with your parents go?"

Before I could tell him of the discussion that had left me bone weary, my phone rang. With a sigh, I pulled it out and winced at the caller ID. "You're about to find out," I mumbled. "My sister. I'll be a sec."

Jake nodded, eyes curious, and I stood, answering my phone. "Hey, Andie," I said quietly, moving through the small café to an empty spot in the corner.

"Don't you 'Hey, Andie' me," my big sister snapped. "I just got off the phone with Mom and Dad. When were you going to tell me you were back with Jake?"

"Today. I was planning on telling you today."

"Oh, now I feel better," she replied. "It's not like you haven't been dating him for the past two months!"

"Five weeks."

"Yeah, that makes it better."

"Andie, please—"

"No, listen. I can't let you make such a huge mistake. What the hell are you thinking?"

My blood heated. "You can't *let* me?"

"Don't get snotty. Charley, you're not thinking clearly around this guy. Don't you remember what he did to you? Don't you remember how heartbroken you were?"

Trying not to get mad in a public place, I bit my nails into my palm. "I'm not a silly child, Andie. I'm perfectly capable of making rational decisions—"

"But—"

"No 'buts.' He was seventeen and he made a mistake. I'm giving him a second chance. It would be nice if you'd support me on this."

"Support you?" Andie's voice had quieted. "Supergirl, all I ever do is support you. However—and note that was not a 'but'—I can't support this decision. I *don't* think you're in a position to think rationally around Jake."

Not at all happy with her reaction, I felt queasy as well as angry. "Stop being condescending. You have no idea what you're talking about."

"Your whole family doesn't agree with this, Charley. Doesn't that tell you something? Mom told me how last night's conversation went down."

Yeah, that had not gone... well.

Last night

Mom and Dad stared at me with completely bemused expressions.

I shifted uncomfortably on my bed, watching the Skype screen.

Finally, I said quietly, "Well?"

I'd just told them about Jake and the police academy in one big rambling speech.

"I don't even..." Mom shook her head, dazed. "I don't even know where to begin."

My dad stood abruptly so I lost sight of most of him. He disappeared off screen and I stared after him in disappointment.

Mom looked in his direction and from the way she swallowed, I knew my dad was all kinds of mad.

"Mom?" I whispered.

Before she could say anything, Dad was back on screen, slamming down on his chair and glowering at me. And Jim Redford gave good glower. "Are you crazy?"

"Jim," Mom admonished.

"I'm sorry I had to tell you like this," I hurried to explain, "but I need you to know what's going on with me. I need you to support me."

"Support you?" Mom narrowed her eyes. "Support you? All we ever do is support you and up until now, you've never given us reason to doubt your decisions. But getting—"

"Back together with that boy is a mistake," Dad finished for her, his voice rising in temper. "And the police thing? I can't believe that one hasn't got to do with the other. A few months ago you were settled about going to law school. He comes back in the picture and suddenly you want to be a damn homicide detective all over again. It's morbid, Charley!"

Despite the severity of the situation, I struggled not to laugh. He didn't mean it to be funny, but it kind of was. Especially considering I hadn't mentioned anything about becoming a homicide detective. Clearly, our discussion about it when I was sixteen had never left my father. And I knew it was purely because he worried about me.

"Dad, Jake has nothing to do with my decision to apply to the academy. I've always wanted to be a cop—I just didn't want to disappoint you and Mom."

"Then don't," he grumbled.

I snorted. "Dad, I've got to do what makes me happy. That's all you and Mom have ever said I should do."

"Since when," Mom snapped, "does happiness and mortal danger go hand in hand?"

I released a beleaguered sigh. "Since when did becoming a police officer become such a big deal? Rick is one."

"Rick's not my daughter," Dad growled. "I've done everything in my power to keep my kids safe, but you seem intent on thwarting me."

"Thwarting?" I teased.

Mom gave me a look. "This is not the time to be a smart-ass."

"When you were five, I caught you trying to turn a coyote into a pet," Dad reminded me.

"He was wounded," I argued. "He needed my help."

"He was a coyote!"

"Jim." Mom rubbed his shoulder. "Chill."

I raised an eyebrow. "Chill?"

They glared at me.

"Dad—"

"When you were ten, you almost drowned in the creek trying to save Lacey—"

"Technically, Lacey almost drowned."

"If Roger Pearson hadn't been walking his dog nearby, the two of you would've gone under! And let's not forget the time you shoved your sister out of the way of a moving vehicle!"

"Oh, so you would've preferred that I let her get hit!" I shouted back, wondering where the hell all of this was coming from.

"I want—" My dad took a deep breath and when he spoke again, his voice had lowered. "I want my kid to be safe. Don't get me wrong, Charlotte, I am so proud of who you are. But that doesn't mean I don't worry myself sick over what situation you're going to put yourself into because you've got it in your damn head you have to save people."

"I don't have that in my head," I promised. "But I was raised by two people who taught me that you don't stand idly by when someone needs help."

My parents were quiet for a moment. Then Mom said, "There's

helping when a situation arises, and then there's looking for that situation. That's what being a cop is."

"No, I disagree. It's being there to help when a situation arises. It's who I am."

"And Jake?" Dad said, his words brittle. "Is he who you are? Because last time I checked, he was a selfish coward who broke my daughter's heart."

My defenses rose at his insult. "Don't talk about him that way," I said, quiet but stern. "I won't listen to it."

"You need to think." Dad leaned toward the camera, his hazel eyes almost pleading. "Just… promise me you'll take some time away from him to really think."

"I don't need to."

"Charley—"

"Are you going to support me or not?"

My parents looked at each other, something grim passing between them. Finally, my dad looked at the camera. "I won't ever have that boy in this house again and we are not done discussing law school."

I knew that look on my father's face. I knew it because it was the same look I got when I wouldn't budge. My chest ached and I felt the stinging burn of tears behind my eyes.

For the first time in my life, my parents had really hurt me.

"You always told me people deserve a second chance."

"Charley—"

"If I don't have your support, we have nothing left to talk about." I snapped the laptop shut, trembling.

There had never been discord between my parents and me. The ugly burden of it rested on my shoulders and I hoped that it wasn't preparing for a long stay there.

I tightened my grip around my cell as Andie waited on my reply. "Yeah, it didn't go great, but I'll tell you what I told them. If you don't support me, don't bother calling me."

"You're putting him before your family?" Andie's voice was so quiet with anger, I barely heard her question. My skin prickled with unease. "After everything he did? After all the support Mom and Dad have given you. You're just spitting in their faces with this… and, although I get that you want to be a cop, you could take their feelings into consideration. At least you shouldn't have just dropped those two bombs on them at the same time." She was silent a moment. "When did you get this selfish?"

"Selfish?" I whispered in disbelief that my sister, one of my best friends, was talking to me this way. "Is that what you think?"

"I think yesterday I respected my little sister. I think today I feel disillusioned."

"Disillusioned?" I guffawed, feeling my blood heat. "I haven't committed a crime here, Andie. I'm just asking you to trust me."

"I don't with this."

My fingers clenched around the phone. "When did *I* get so selfish? When did you get so self-righteous? Mom and Dad weren't thrilled with the idea of Rick at first, remember? The guy is ten years your senior. Did I say anything? No. I supported you."

"That's completely different. Rick never broke my heart and left my family to pick up the pieces."

"You know, you're the one person I thought I could count on to be there for me through this. It isn't easy. I'm trying to work things through with Jake, and I'm finally taking the reins of my future despite Mom and Dad's concerns about it, and I need my big sister."

"No, you *want* me to tell you that it's all right to steamroll your way through life without taking other people's feelings into consideration."

"Andie, it's *my* life. My heart. *My* career."

"And I'm telling you, if you don't dump that loser, he's going to break your heart and ruin your future."

"Fuck you," I bit out before I could stop myself.

There was silence on the other end of the line. All I could hear was the sound of my blood rushing in my ears.

Finally… "No, Charley, fuck you," she whispered back, the hurt evident in her voice. "And don't bother calling me until he's out of your life and you're you again."

She hung up.

I stared at the wall in front of me, trembling.

I'd just burned my Andie bridge… for Jake.

But she was wrong. Right? My family was wrong.

They just were.

Right?

I jerked in fright as two strong arms wrapped around my waist, but I relaxed as Jake held me against his chest. His lips burned on my cheek. "You okay?"

No, I wasn't okay. My sister was no longer talking to me. We'd had the biggest fight of our lives and I wished I had some guarantee that Jake was worth it. Was any guy worth losing Andie over? I was afraid if I dug deep enough, the answer would put Jake and I in an even more precarious position. Yet, Andie's attitude… she'd never made me feel like a bad person before and I didn't think that was fair. I hadn't done anything wrong. Exhausted, I said, "I don't know."

"They'll come around," he promised, his voice soothing. "They're Redfords. They don't know how to be anything but cool."

I slid my arms over his. "I hope that's true." I turned around, dipping my head back to look into Jake's soulful eyes. "I'm fighting between being hurt that they can't trust me about this and really grateful they care enough to be mad at me."

Without me having to say so, Jake knew I was thinking about Claudia and her parents' neglect. "Yeah, I get it. Maybe, though, you should tell them you're hurt rather than blowing up at them."

Wrinkling my nose, I looked away sheepishly. "You caught that?"

"Yup. You do that last night too?"

"Maybe…"

"It's that fire in your blood," he grinned wickedly. "I do love it but sometimes it gets you into trouble—and not the good kind." Jake grabbed my hand and led me back toward our table.

"There's a good kind of trouble?"

He lifted my bag and held it out to me, a sexy glint in his eyes. "Why don't we go back to my place and find out?"

And just like that, Jake lifted me out of the bleakness, if only for a moment. Yeah, I had high hopes he was worth it, all right. I giggled, sliding my arm around his waist as he wrapped his around my shoulders. "I walked into that one."

The sight before us brought me to an abrupt halt. Jake stumbled into my back, catching my elbows to steady me.

I grinned at the sight of Claudia and Lowe sitting at the guys' kitchen table. So. My friend had decided to take my advice after all. "Hey."

Claudia caught my look and made a face. "I was supposed to be meeting Beck," she explained. "But I'm guessing he tripped and fell inside another groupie because he isn't here."

Lowe laughed, a deep, sexy sound. His eyes glittered in amusement and I felt a rush of anticipation at the thought of something happening between these two. So Claudia was too hung up on Beck to notice Lowe. That could change once they started hanging out more. I'd just have to make sure they had reason to spend time together. Alone.

As if Jake read my mind, he pulled me against him and murmured in my ear, "No."

Spoilsport.

"You seem in a better mood." I raised an eyebrow at Claud, ignoring Jake's warning.

She shook her head, giving me a little smile that said she wasn't mad at my attempts at matchmaking. "I got that email I was waiting on."

"And?" I held my breath.

Claudia's eyes lit up. "It's all good. I'll tell you about it later."

Relief moved through me. I couldn't be happier for Claudia that her real dad had gotten back in touch. I was curious to know what he'd said, but I knew it was something she was keeping private.

And then an idea hit me.

"You should go out for a drink. Relax about it now. Maybe Lowe could take you."

Jake gently nudged me toward the door with a huff of exasperation. "Charley and I will be in my room. Do not disturb."

"Too much information," Lowe muttered into his coffee.

"That's your definition of too much information?" I heard Claudia say as I followed Jake down the hall. "You have a lot to learn."

"Was that an invitation?" he purred back.

I shot Jake a triumphant look but he shook his head sternly and pulled me inside, locking the door behind us.

He turned to me, completely serious. "Beck would lose it if anything happened between Claudia and Lowe."

"But you heard him."

"That's just Lowe. He'd flirt with a houseplant. What he would not do is touch Claudia. He knows how Beck feels about her."

"You know, I'm starting not to care about Beck's feelings when it comes to Claud. He's messing with her. He doesn't want to date her but he gets pissed when some other guy does. No. That does not fly in Charley World, Jake. I've advised Claudia to move on."

Jake gently pulled me close. "And you're probably right. But don't pit best friend against best friend."

Feeling bad, I played with a button on his shirt. "I'm sorry. That's not cool, I know."

"Anyway, Lowe wouldn't touch Claud."

"Why not?" I glowered. "She's smart and funny and prettier than all his groupies put together."

I felt him shake with laughter. "Sheath the claws, sweetheart. I know your girl rocks but Lowe and Beck are tight. He wouldn't do that to Beck, no matter how much of a dick Beck's being."

"Uh, he did it to you with me when *you* were being a dick."

Jake tensed and I knew it was exactly the wrong thing to say. He released me and wandered toward his desk. Turning on his computer, he spoke without looking at me. "That was different. Lowe isn't as tight with me as he is with Beck. And it was you."

I was almost afraid to ask. "What was me?"

He gave me a sharp look. "Come on, you must know Lowe really likes you. You're not just some girl to him."

"If you know Lowe likes me, why do you rub us in his face?"

"I'm not."

"The comment about the teeth marks. The comment just now. 'Do not disturb.'"

"I'm just being me, I'm being us. I'm not going to stop being us. Plus, this way he'll get over it quicker."

"You were definitely far more concerned about protecting Melissa's feelings."

"That was different." His face clouded at the mention of his ex. "Lowe wasn't in a relationship with you. You didn't tell each other you loved one another."

Realizing I was digging myself deeper into unstable territory, I tried to stumble out the way I came in. "I'm just saying, I think there's animosity between you two I don't understand."

"He tried to fuck you," Jake snapped.

My cheeks flushed. "I think you'll find that it was a little more complicated than that. He's a good guy. He was there for me. All I want is the same for Claudia."

Jake groaned and buried his head in hands. "Baby, I hear what you're saying but please pick someone else. Not for my sake, not for Lowe's sake, but for Beck's." He glanced over his shoulder at me. "He doesn't get to hold her captive while he messes around with other girls. I get it. I do. Advise her to move on, cut him out, whatever… just don't… He's got his issues but me and The Stolen are his only real family. Lowe is like his brother. Don't do anything to mess that up for him."

I softened. "You sure are giving me a lot of credit if you're truly worried I could make something happen between Claudia and Lowe."

Suddenly looking very boyish, Jake said, "I believe you can do anything you put your mind to, Charley Redford. You're a force to be reckoned with."

His words cast stillness over me, my eyes drinking in all that he was. "Totally worth it," I murmured.

"What?"

I grinned. "Get on the bed. You just won bonus sex."

His low chuckle tickled me in all my good-for-nothing places as my sweater fell to the ground. Standing, Jake unbuttoned his shirt, his fingers stalling on one at the sound of a ringing coming from his computer. He frowned at the interruption and glanced down at the screen.

"Shit, it's my mom." He hurriedly rebuttoned.

"You're going to answer it?"

"I forgot I said I'd take her call tonight. If I don't answer, she'll keep calling."

"Crap!" I yanked my sweater on just in time.

"Mom," Jake greeted innocently into the camera.

"Jake, sweetheart, how are you?"

"Fantastic. Charley's here." He gestured for me to come to him.

Even though Jake said his family was cool about us being back together, after the chat with mine, butterflies invaded my belly as I walked slowly to the screen. Jake's mom hadn't changed an iota since I last saw her almost four years ago.

"Hi, Mrs. Caplin."

Her eyes lit up. "Charley, it's so good to see you. I was so happy when Jake told me you two were back together."

My butterflies slowly abated at her sincerity. "Good to see you too. How are you?"

"I'm well, sweetheart, thank you. And you? You're even prettier than I remember. Your hair is so much lighter. I like it. How are Jim and Delia? Are they well? How are the florist and the auto shop?"

"Mom, slow down." Jake laughed as he pulled me onto his lap.

46

"I just got her back. Don't scare her away with the Spanish Inquisition."

"I know, I'm sorry." She grinned unrepentantly. It reminded me of her son. "I can't wait for you both to get back here. You have to come to Chicago, Charley. Stay the weekend. We'll have a big family dinner. I know Lukas is looking forward to seeing you again."

I relaxed deeper into Jake, the stress of my parents' disapproval eased under the warmth of Jake's mother's acceptance. "I would love that, Mrs. C."

Chapter Five
West Lafayette, September 2013

After Claudia's "asshole" outburst at The Brewhouse I chased after her. When I caught up to her she was hurrying down the street with the invisible smoke of her fiery rage pouring out of her.

"What happened?" I asked as I shoved her purse at her.

She snatched it off me, her nostrils flaring. "You first," she snapped.

So I told her what had gone down between Jake and me. The resultant glower of her disapproval was nothing new. "And was he cool with that?"

I shrugged, not knowing what was going on with him. "I think so. It was weird. He wants to be friends."

"Yeah, because that worked out so great for you last time. He didn't put up more of a fight?"

"He was angry… but no."

"That doesn't make sense."

Face carefully blank, I said, "We've both hurt each other. Maybe he gets that we don't work."

I received a grunt in response.

"So that asshole thing? What did Beck say?"

She started fuming again. "It's like he just assumed I was going to fall all over him."

"What did he say?"

"He said, and I quote, 'This ignoring me shit? I'm done with it. You made your point but life is short, babe, and I want to spend what time I've got with you. I missed you like crazy this summer.'"

I knew it would be wrong of me to say I actually thought that was kind of sweet so I kept my trap shut and listened to her tirade continue.

"And I said 'until you get bored with me and end up nailing your groupies again.' And he said, 'I'm never going to get bored of you.' Pfft!" she made a face. "So I said 'Yeah, well, I'm bored of this conversation.' I told him I didn't trust him. I told him I want a guy who loves me enough to put his own bullshit aside. I said he blew it."

"What did he say?" I was almost too afraid to ask. This confrontation between Beck and Claudia had been a long time coming. It didn't surprise me that it had ended the way it had.

Claudia's face fell, and her voice lowered as she replied, "He said that he was sorry and he wanted a second chance... a second chance to prove how he felt about me. A second chance to make me feel as special as I am."

"That all sounds... good?"

"I told him it was all just bullshit words, and I know how good he is at lying to get what he wants."

"And...?"

"Oh, he was pissed. He said he'd always tried to treat me with care and that I should trust him. I said I didn't. He said I was being impossible. I said, 'Screw you, I'm moving on,' to which he replied, 'If you actually took a chance and screwed me, babe, the only moving on you'd be doing is with me. Forever.' So I called him an asshole and got out of there."

I was silent a moment before peeking at my friend out of the corner of my eye. "You were equally turned on as you were pissed, though, right?"

"So turned on I could kill him," she snapped. "Arrogant asshole."

We didn't say anything else on the subject and two weeks later we still hadn't discussed it further. We hadn't talked about any part of that night. I hadn't heard from Jake and I was trying not to think about that. I threw myself into my work and sometimes it helped. That's why, while I laid on my stomach in our living room, surrounded by papers and textbooks, I nearly came out of my skin when my phone rang and it was Jake calling.

I could've ignored it but without really thinking about it, I answered and closed my eyes at the sound of his deep, rich voice on the other end of the line. He asked me how I was. I said I was fine. Studying a lot. And also that the apartment smelled of homemade soup all the time because Claudia was experimenting in the kitchen.

It was awkward and stilted… and painful… and I was thankful when Claudia got home because I had an excuse to get off the phone.

"I've got a date with the TA!" Claudia yelled as she stepped into the apartment.

I heard Jake groan on the other end of the line.

"Claudia's home," I said dryly.

"What she said… is that the kind of thing I have to tell Beck?"

"I don't know. I'm not privy to the bro code."

"Shit," Jake muttered and I took that to mean under the bro code, he was obligated to tell Beck what he'd heard.

Claudia appeared in the doorway grinning, her eyes widening at the sight of me. "Oops, sorry, you're on the phone."

I smiled at her and said to Jake, "That's my cue to go, I guess."

"Wait. I'm, uh… I was actually calling to invite you to Lowe's birthday party. It's at the end of this month. We're in off-campus housing together but Beck has friends at Bobb. One of the halls on campus. They're letting us throw the party there. It would really mean a lot if you and Claudia would come."

See him again? So soon? "Uh… I don't know…"

"You should come. It'll be—wait. Lowe wants to talk to you."

I sat up, not knowing what to make of the invite and if I was perhaps reading too much into it to think that this was some kind of plan of Jake's to get me back.

"Charley," Lowe's warm voice sounded in my ear. "You've got to come to my party."

More than a little taken aback he was inviting me after his weirdness in the bar two weekends ago, I said, "Are you sure?"

"Of course. This summer wasn't the same without you and Claud. Don't make my birthday suck without you."

"Let me just ask Claudia." I covered my phone with my hand and turned to my expectant friend.

"What's going on?"

"Lowe and Jake are inviting us to Lowe's birthday party at Northwestern at the end of the month. You in?"

She bit her lip. "Are you?"

I shrugged.

And then, Claudia nodded. "Tell them we'll be there."

Feeling nervous at the mere thought of seeing Jake I said, "You sure?"

"Positive."

I put the phone back to my ear. "We'll be there."

"Great. I'll text you the details. See you then."

"Bye."

"Here's Jake. Bye, Charley." After some rustling, Jake was back on the phone. "Charley."

"Hey. I better go, but I guess we'll see you in a few weeks."

"Great." And he did sound like he thought it was great. It felt like a fist was squeezing my heart. "We'll talk later."

Yeah, because that's what friends do and I'm an idiot. "Later."

Once I'd hung up, I made a face at Claudia. "You think that was wise?"

"You could've said no."

"Well, you could stop making soup," I growled.

Claudia snorted. "Way to focus your anger elsewhere." She wrinkled her nose. "It does kind of smell in here, though, huh." She threw her bag down and collapsed on the couch. "So, Jake's calling you?"

"Well, I am the idiot who said we could be friends." I shoved my papers aside. "I just didn't think he'd actually enforce said friendship."

"He seems to be dealing with your break up quite well…"

I glared at her. "Yeah? So?"

"How do you feel about that?"

"Right now? I'm thinking I want to throw your soup on you."

She laughed. "I'm just saying… you seem kind of pissed that he's doing okay."

"Not pissed," I huffed. "Confused. I'm a little hurt it's not killing him like it's killing me, okay. I think he's as upset as I am, but then he acts like he's not."

"A bit like what you're doing?"

My mouth fell open.

Claudia smirked.

I threw a cushion at her. "If I want a rational conversation, I'll call Alex."

Chuckling, Claudia got up off the couch and started for the kitchen. "Let's have soup."

"Let's talk about the TA," I called after her.

She smiled at me over her shoulder. "I found him. He's a grad student now. So hot. He said yes within an instant of me asking him out. Apparently he wanted to ask me out sophomore year, but he didn't think I was interested. I have got to get less subtle, Charley."

"Oh yeah, because you're a real shrinking violet."

Two seconds later, an oven glove smacked my head.

"Subtle." I threw it back in her general direction as I opened up my textbook.

Northwestern University, two weeks later...

Bobb was part of Bobb-McCulloch Halls on the north campus of Northwestern. It was a plain brick building that wouldn't have been very inviting if not for the stream of students flowing in and out and the far-off beat of music coming from somewhere inside.

"This might not be such a good idea." I stared nervously at the building.

"We could just go back to the hotel," Claudia suggested as she stood by my side.

It was amazing how quickly the last few weeks had flown by. I spent my days studying, answering random texts from Jake, talking on the phone to Mom and having one-worded conversations with Dad, and holing myself up in the apartment. Alex would stop by sometimes and ask me to come out for drinks, but I was steadfast on my path to reclusiveness. While I did all this, Claudia studied, ignored phone calls from her parents and Beck, and went on a few dates with Will the TA. Unusually for Claudia, she didn't talk about the dates and I didn't ask.

I'd spent the interim weeks between the invitation and the actual party worrying about seeing Jake again and I had no doubt by how quiet Claudia was on the subject that she was anxious about facing Beck. She had major reservations, but I knew she put them aside for me because it was my first time back in Chicago since... well, since everything.

I felt guilty being there for this party when I should've been there long ago for a different reason altogether.

I looked at my friend, grateful for her support. "The hotel?"

The guys had invited us to stay at their apartment while we were in the city, but Claudia and I both thought it was safer to get a hotel room.

She smirked at me. "What? We've gotten pretty good at running from shit."

"True. But this we can face up to."

Once inside we followed the posters directing us toward the party. Not that we needed the posters. The music and kids with plastic cups in their hands were like flashing arrows.

We walked through the corridors in silence, the music growing steadily louder. We passed a couple of open dorm rooms, a few people mingling inside, as we neared the central point of the party.

Gazing into the large common room, I saw a whole bunch of people I didn't know, drinking and chatting.

I felt Claudia's hand curl around my wrist and tighten. "You were right," she said just loud enough for me to hear over The Killers. "Maybe we shouldn't have come."

She sounded pained, her eyes locked on something to our left. I followed her gaze.

It took me a moment to register what I was seeing.

And when I finally did, I felt like I was back at that first party in Edinburgh, seeing Jake across the room for the first time in four years.

In the corner, past a group of college girls, was Jake. He was sitting on a table that had been set up with plastic cups of beer and standing in between his legs was a tall, curvy redhead. She had one hand on his shoulder, her other hand clutching a plastic cup, as she grinned down at him. He wasn't touching her, but their proximity and his body language more than made up for it. I knew he was flirting in the way his dark eyes danced, in the half smile he gave her as they talked.

"Charley?" Claudia gripped my wrist. "We can go, babe."

It was unfair of me, right? To feel betrayed. To feel the blade of jealousy score across my chest. To feel the burn of his loss in my gut. I only had myself to blame. Six months ago he was mine.

I'd given him away.

"Oh shit," Claudia said, "it just got worse."

I blinked, tugging my eyes from the car crash that was my relationship with Jake, only to find my focus zeroing in on the beautiful brunette walking toward me.

Melissa.

Yup. It just got worse.

I flinched at the sympathy in her eyes as she came to a stop before us. "Claudia, Charley." She gave us a pinched smile.

"Hey," Claudia answered, her tone wary.

I gave Melissa a nod, not sure I was able to speak past the burning lump in my throat. It took everything within me not to look over Melissa's shoulder at Jake and the redhead.

Melissa looked over her shoulder for me. When she looked back at me, her expression was unreadable. "Jake told me you guys broke up."

Another score across my chest. I only just stopped myself from touching it, to see if there was an actual wound.

Jake was friends with his ex? He was confiding in her? Since when?

Her eyes softened, like she'd caught something in my expression that tugged at her compassion.

I quickly wiped my face clean of emotion.

"This is just what he does," she said, gesturing behind her. "When he's hurting. Specifically when he's hurting over you."

Why was she telling me this? What did she expect me to say? That I was sorry Jake turned into an assholey manwhore when his heart was broken?

So I didn't say anything at all.

Melissa shifted uncomfortably. "Just try not to be too pissed at him. He really loved you."

He really *loved* me? Lov*ed*.

By some strength of will, I didn't let her know that hearing those words was like taking a bullet.

"Why do you care?" Claudia suddenly stepped toward her, her eyes glittering with suspicion. "He dumped you for Charley, so why would you give a crap about him or Charley?"

Melissa shrugged. "Time heals, I guess. And I don't care about Charley. I care about Jake."

The uncharitable thought that perhaps Melissa was hoping history was about to repeat itself raced across my mind. Maybe she thought Jake would whore around for a while and then end up running back to her.

Apparently that occurred to Claudia. "He'll never care about you the way he cares about her, so do yourself a favor and get over it."

Jake's ex looked like she'd been punched. She stared at Claudia incredulously before looking to me for help. All I could do was stare back at her, stunned Claudia had enough bitch in her to say that. Melissa shook her head and wandered back into the crowd.

"You do realize I'm to blame for her heartbreak," I said to Claudia.

"Yeah? Well, that right there wasn't her being nice, Charley. That was her kicking you when you were down. Oh look, Charley catches her ex-boyfriend flirting with another girl and is obviously gutted by it. Why don't I stick another knife in her by telling her Jake is my friend again and I clearly have plans to go after him once he's done sampling the redhead."

I smirked sadly at her. "I don't even need to tap into my rage. I've got you to do that for me."

"Well, ye-uh," Claudia said, still looking agitated.

"Claudia." I grabbed her hand. "I've got no right to be mad at him." *Right?*

My friend's eyes misted over. "It doesn't mean it doesn't hurt you."

I blinked at the rush of tears heading straight for my own eyes and turned around so I had my back to the room and to Jake. "It's self-inflicted. Doesn't count."

She sighed but let it go.

"Guys, you made it!"

Looking over my shoulder, I saw Lowe grinning broadly as he made his way across the room. I was immediately enfolded in his hug and I found my arms tightening around him without even meaning to.

Tears stung my nose. "Happy birthday."

His own arms tightened and when he pulled back, he searched my face in concern. "Babe," he murmured.

Not wanting to make his birthday about Jake and me, I forced out a smile and stepped back to let Claudia greet him.

"Happy birthday, Lowe," she chirped a little too cheerily as she hugged him. "Great party!" She looked across the room where a beer pong table had been set up. "Oh, I see Matt." Sure enough Matt lounged against the wall, talking to some chick with his eyes glued to the table. *Way to show your interest, Matt.* "Why don't you take Charley to get a drink while I go say hi."

Lowe frowned as he watched her walk away and then I saw him stiffen when he caught sight of Jake across the room, still flirting with the redhead. Lowe looked back at me and I did my best to keep my face blank. I got the impression he wasn't buying what I was selling. "Let's get you that drink."

I grabbed hold of the hand he held out. He led me into one of the quieter dorm rooms.

"Beck's friends with three of the guys that room here. They opened their dorm rooms to us for the party." He grinned over his shoulder at me as he led me toward a desk littered with beer. "How he talked them into that, I have no idea."

"Here." I held out a small gift-wrapped box.

His eyes lit up as he took it. "You didn't have to get me anything."

I shrugged. "It's just a little thing."

"A *wee* thing, Row would say."

I flinched at the mention of our Scottish friend Rowena. "I haven't spoken to her at all since I left Edinburgh." Another thing to feel guilty about. "Have you guys?"

He nodded as he unwrapped the box. "She actually joined us for a couple of weeks this summer. She's fine. And she gets that you've got a lot going on."

"Still, I'll email her when I get back to Purdue."

Lowe opened the box and lifted out the small item inside. He turned it over and his eyes flew to mine.

"I saw it and thought of you." I gestured to the guitar pick in his hand, my eyes on the words written across it: *Play It Fucking Loud.*

"Bob Dylan," he answered quietly. "You remembered."

Back in Edinburgh, back when I was with Jake, back when everything was good, we'd all sat around the kitchen one afternoon, talking about everything and nothing. We'd gotten onto the subject of favorite quotes, and Lowe had talked about the reported incident when Bob Dylan was playing in Manchester and someone in the crowd called him "Judas" for playing electric guitar. In response Dylan told his band to "play it fucking loud." Lowe said he got it—Dylan's anger, yeah, but mostly his conviction in himself and his music.

"Girls remember shit." I shrugged it off.

Lowe surprised me by cupping my cheek and leaning into me. My breath stuttered and warning bells chimed in my head. "You make it really difficult, you know that," he said softly, his eyes on my mouth.

"Lowe…"

His gaze flicked to my eyes. "Thank you."

"You're welcome," I whispered.

He dropped his hand and took a step back. For a second or two he just stared at the pick before pulling his wallet out and sliding the pick safely inside. Once he tucked the wallet away, he handed me a beer.

"I've got to admit, I've been kind of pissed at you."

I shouldn't have been surprised by the comment, but still, I was taken aback by how much I didn't like that Lowe had been angry with me.

"The way you treated Jake…"

"It was bad, I know." I took a sip of my drink. "I told him sorry. I don't know how else to apologize. I handled everything… well, I didn't handle it. I let it all just crumple around me."

Lowe sighed. "I've got to ask… I was there. When you walked in and saw Jake with that sophomore just now… I saw your face, Charley."

My eyes flew to him. "So?"

"Well, are you okay?"

"I'm fine," I lied. "Obviously breaking up was the right thing to do."

"Charley, I know you're lying."

"I can't be with him. Okay? Simple as that," I hissed, all the hurt pouring out of me. "It doesn't mean I'm not in pain. Or that I don't care. So yeah… you saw my face when I saw my ex-boyfriend clearly getting ready to bed down with a leggy redhead. Did I look like I'd been slapped? Because that's how I felt just then. Now… not so much. See, I can move on, knowing how easily it is for him to be a typical guy and start fucking his way through the sorority houses, if he hasn't already."

Lowe looked suddenly panicked. "Charley, that's not what's happening here. Just talk to Jake—"

"No, I'm done. I don't want to talk about him anymore." I took a shuddering breath, trying to calm my throbbing pulse. "Let's just go enjoy the party."

He didn't look so sure.

"C'mon." I started heading to the door with my beer. "You can introduce me to people I won't remember in the morning."

Chapter Six

Edinburgh, March 2013

It was the first day of March and spring was technically a few weeks away. Could've fooled me.

As I stepped out of Old College onto South Bridge, an icy wind blew through me. I shuddered, hurrying to button my coat while trying to juggle my bag and notes.

That morning I'd woken up with the same concerns that I'd been waking up with for the past few weeks. I worried about my family. I hadn't spoken to Andie since that fateful phone call and once my dad found out about it, he also refused to talk to me until I apologized to my sister. Since I wouldn't apologize, it was turning into a long and very silent stalemate that weighed on me more and more each day. The only one talking to me was Mom and even then it was strained.

After catching a glimpse of Melissa in Old College for the first time in weeks, I found myself feeling guilty for not worrying more about her. I wondered if she was doing okay these days.

"Need a hand?"

I glanced up at the familiar voice and straight into Beck's striking light gray eyes. "What are you doing here?"

"I just finished class. I was heading back to the apartment." He took my bag and notes while I finished fastening my coat. As he slipped my notes into my bag, he smiled. "Walk with me?"

When Beck wasn't winning Brooding Hero of the Year and messing with my best friend's heart, he was actually the most laid-back, nonjudgmental person I had ever met. He was soothing and funny and kind, and I loved hanging out with him. Unfortunately, I was actually heading in the opposite direction. "I'm meeting Claudia at the Library Bar for coffee."

His expression lightened at the mention of Claud. "I'll come with. I haven't seen her in a few days. She's been busy with school."

I nodded but didn't say anything. The truth was Claudia was taking my advice and trying to wean herself off Beck in the hopes of getting over him.

"You and Jake seem good?" Beck looked down at me, his hands shoved in the pockets of his jeans, the fabric of his T-shirt flapping in the wind. He wore a long-sleeved thermal under it, but still…

"Aren't you freezing?"

"It wasn't this cold yesterday." He shrugged. "I've stopped guessing how to dress for the weather here."

"True." It *was* a perpetual guessing game. One second it was chilly but the sun was out; the next second brought torrential rain and winds.

"So you and Jake?"

I so did not want to discuss my relationship with Jake's best friend. "We're good."

He nudged me. "You're not going to break his heart, are you?" His voice was teasing but I knew better.

"Are you going to break Claudia's?"

A muscle in his jaw ticked. "Fair enough."

"Hey, here's a question that won't get either of us punched: do you know how Melissa is doing these days?"

Beck raised an eyebrow. "Melissa?"

"Melissa. You know, dark hair, legs forever, one hundred percent drop-dead gorgeous and one hundred percent nicer than me."

He grinned. "She may be nicer, but she is way less fun."

I smirked at him. "As much as I enjoy getting my ego stroked, I'm serious. Do you know if she's doing okay?"

"Melissa's a nice girl but we're not close. We never were. She's one of the few people who doesn't understand that underneath this roguish charm is a heart of 80 percent gold."

"Come on, don't undervalue yourself. It's at least 82 percent."

Laughing, Beck wrapped an arm around my shoulders, pulling me into his side. "This is why I was rooting for *you*."

"Well, I appreciate that." I hugged him back but frowned up into his gorgeous face. "So you really wouldn't know if she's okay?"

Beck pulled out his phone, fingers flying over the keys. "I texted Maggie. She should know. They're friends."

"Maggie, my roommate Maggie?"

Catching my hesitant tone, Beck gave a reassuring smile. "I wouldn't go there. I do have *some* control over who I sleep with."

"That's good to know, I guess," I said, sounding a little doubtful. The last thing I wanted was Claudia returning to the apartment one night to find Beck stumbling out of Maggie's room. I think that might just be the straw that would break the camel's back. About to stick my nose in and ruin our pleasant camaraderie, Beck's next question halted me.

"So, why do you want to know if Melissa is okay?"

I shrugged, feeling that familiar gnawing guilt. "I'd think that was obvious."

As we climbed the steps to the student union, Beck fell silent. Once inside, he turned to me, a small smile playing on his lips. "Jake is right. You and Claudia are not like other women."

I arched an eyebrow. "I'm taking that as a compliment since I happen to know for a fact that Claudia and I are freaking awesome."

Something sad flashed in Beck's eyes as he smirked back at me. "I'm not to going to argue with that."

I wish I had a magic potion to shove down his throat and make him see that whatever was stopping him from taking a chance on Claudia didn't compare to how bad the regret would be later. I sighed inwardly and followed his tall body upstairs to the Library Bar.

I almost slammed into him when he drew to an abrupt halt just inside the doorway. I peered around him. "What's up?" I followed his confused gaze across the room.

Claudia was cozied up in a booth with Lowe. Her laptop was open in front of her but they were sitting turned into one another, laughing about something.

The muscle under my hand tensed and I glanced down to see Beck's fists tightening.

"They're just friends," I assured him.

Sure, the way they were sitting suggested otherwise but I had assurances not only from Lowe that he wouldn't go there, but from Claudia also. Only yesterday she told me how much fun it was to hang out with a guy and not have to worry about any sexual tension.

The chemistry wasn't there for them, which was a little disappointing, but the whole point was for Claud to have someone who would distract her from Beck, and Lowe was doing the job.

"I didn't say a word." Beck glowered down at me.

And just like that, I had Broody Hero of the Year on my hands. "You need to work on your poker face. It sucks." I strode away before he could reply.

"Hey there, hot stuff," I said as I slid into the booth.

Lowe grinned. "Hey, yourself."

"Oh, as pretty as you are, babe, I was talking to Claudia."

Claudia smiled and opened her mouth to reply only to freeze at the sight of Beck with me. "Oh. Hey."

He nodded as he slid in beside me.

"Hey, man," Lowe said, something akin to excitement in his eyes. "Guess what Claud's doing for us?"

"I have no idea," he replied in a tone that suggested he couldn't give a shit.

I kicked him in the shin, eliciting a grunt.

Claudia narrowed her eyes. "Who spit in your bean curd?"

"What the hell does that even mean?"

I tried not to smile, deliberately avoiding Lowe's eyes because I knew he'd make me laugh.

"It means," Claudia gave a long-suffering sigh, "what's your problem?"

"I don't have a problem. I just sat down." Beck pulled his buzzing phone from his pocket, glaring at Claudia. He looked at the screen. "According to Maggie, Melissa is doing okay. She's even got a date this weekend."

A little weight lifted off my shoulders. "That's good to hear."

Claudia caught my eye. "Feel better?"

"Much," I admitted. "You know I hate guilt."

Relaxing, I had a drink with my friends, listening to Beck and Claudia snipe at each other. They were on the cusp of giving me back the tension I'd just gotten rid of, so I decided it was time to leave.

"I need to go too." Lowe slid out of the booth at my announcement. "I have stuff to do. Claudia, if you and Beck can stop griping for five seconds, why don't you show him the plans for this summer?"

Claudia's green eyes filled with something like panic.

"Go ahead," Beck said, clearly not in the mood to leave her company. "Do you want another coffee?"

Instead of answering, my friend looked to me for help.

I needed to get her out of this somehow. I looked at Beck, but any excuse that might've been making its way from brain to tongue melted upon seeing the puppy-dog look on his face.

Crap. No wonder she has such a hard time resisting him.

I looked back at Claudia and shrugged. "I'll catch you guys later."

Seriously. Where was my willpower? If I couldn't harden my heart enough against Beck to keep them apart, how the hell was *she* supposed to?

Lowe and I hit the top of the steps off Chamber Street that led to my apartment. We were about to descend them when I started at the sight of Jake coming up them.

His head down, hands jammed into his jacket pockets, he was listening to whatever band was singing through his earphones. A rush of longing ripped through me. My heart soaked in what little it could see of his familiar face; my eyes drank in his broad shoulders and long legs.

I missed him.

Even when I was with him I missed him. What we had wasn't what we'd had before. At this point I only had myself to blame for that.

Lowe chuckled beside me as we waited for Jake to reach us. "I never had a chance, did I?" he joked.

I made a face. "I'm that obvious?"

"Only when he's not looking," he said, seeing way more than he should.

Perceptive pain in my ass.

Jake looked up, faltering on a step. At first he didn't seem sure how to react to the sight of me with Lowe, but he quickly shrugged it off, bestowing a gorgeous smile on me. He pulled his earphones out. "Hey, you," he said, coming to a stop at the top of the stairs. He leaned down to kiss me, his lips soft. He smelled great.

"Hey," I whispered back, unable to speak any louder over the force of my emotions. It still surprised me that my feelings for him had the ability to bowl me over without warning.

"Hey, man." Jake nodded congenially at Lowe. I was relieved.

Lowe seemed to be too. He gave Jake a small smile and nod. "Well, I better get back to the apartment. I have an essay due in two days and we have a gig tonight."

"Good luck." I waved goodbye and watched him take the steps two at a time.

"I was coming to get you." Jake tightened his arm around my waist, and I found myself swiftly falling into his eyes. "I called Beck and he mentioned you were worried about Melissa?"

I shook my head. "It's fine. Just guilt. But apparently she's doing okay."

His dark eyes looked troubled. "I'm glad she's okay. But you have nothing to feel guilty about."

I could see his own guilt in his eyes and instantly felt bad for bringing Melissa up. "Ja—"

My ringtone blasted, cutting me off. Giving Jake a look of

apology, I dropped his hand and dug through my bag.

My pulse sped up at the sight of the caller ID. My dad.

Relieved more than I could say but still angry and hurt that he hadn't called in ages, I hesitantly answered.

"Where are you?" he asked abruptly.

Disappointed by his tone, I huffed, "Last time I checked, I was in Scotland."

"Smart-ass," Dad grumbled, the edge chipped off his tone. "What I meant is where exactly are you, right now? Because I'm standing in your apartment after your roommate stupidly let me in without checking my identification first. Does that happen a lot? Because maybe while I'm here, I should hold a stranger awareness meeting with you girls."

I didn't hear anything after "I'm standing in your apartment…"

"I'll be right there." I hung up, eyes wide on Jake's curious expression. "My dad is here."

Jake's eyebrows squished together. "*Here*, here?"

"Yup." I turned and started down the steps.

"Hey, I'm coming too." Jake hurried to catch me.

Marching into the courtyard of my building, I threw over my shoulder, "Do you think that's wise?"

"I think he's here for a reason and I think *we* need to reassure him." His hand curled around my arm. "Would you slow down—as in, calm down?"

My breathing was way too fast. "I can't." I pushed my building door open and rushed the stairs. "My dad has flown all the way across the ocean to come talk to me. That's not a good sign, Jake. My parents don't exactly have the kind of money where plane tickets aren't a luxury." I stopped in the middle of the first floor and Jake immediately wrapped his arms around me.

"It's going to be okay," he promised. "I'm here. I'm not going anywhere."

"I don't want you to get punched."

"If I get punched, I get punched. It's no less than what I deserve."

"I couldn't have said it better myself."

I gasped at the sound of my dad's voice, wrenching back from Jake to gaze up onto the next landing. My dad stood above us, huge, intimidating, and not at all happy to see me in Jake's arms.

"Before anyone says another word," Jake said, "let's get inside."

My dad threw him a disgusted look but turned and headed back upstairs toward the apartment.

There was a great deal of pounding going on in my chest as Jake and I followed.

Dad stood in the middle of the kitchen. His dark hair, speckled with gray, was mussed, and he had day-old bristle on his cheeks. He looked exhausted.

"Your roommate left," Dad's voice rumbled. "We'll have privacy to talk as soon as *he* leaves."

I braced for the battle to come, the nerves suddenly disappearing as indignation moved through me. Dad was the one intruding on our lives. He'd flown clear across an ocean to have this out without even telling me, after having shut me out for days.

I was *not* a child.

"Jake stays."

Dad opened his mouth to argue and I held up a hand to stop him.

"Jake stays," I insisted.

Jake was treated to a look that would fell a mountain lion. "Fine," Dad snapped.

"Can I get you anything?" I gestured to the kitchen.

"Coffee."

"Jake?"

Jake gave me a small smile but shook his head.

I brushed past my dad to prepare his coffee. "I can't believe you flew all the way over here. I take it Mom knows."

"Of course she knows. I had to dip into our savings."

"You didn't *have* to do anything."

"My daughter is in the middle of making two momentous decisions in her life and she wasn't even in the same country as I was. Of course I needed to do this."

"If you're here to talk, Dad, then we'll talk. But if you're here to tell me what a giant mistake I'm making without hearing me out, then you might as well leave now." I shot him a look. "Which would be crap because I haven't seen you in two months."

Dad's eyes softened. "Can I get a hug?"

I nodded, suddenly feeling like a little girl, trying not to cry. Abandoning the coffee, I strode over to him and sank into his tight embrace. No one gave good hug like Jim Redford.

He held on to me longer than usual and I let him because I knew there was a possibility we were about to have a huge falling-out.

When I pulled back, I shot a look over his shoulder at Jake. His eyes were downcast.

"Jake," I whispered his name without even meaning to, drawing his gaze to me and causing Dad to pull away.

Dad looked at Jake. "You're not what I want for her. She's strong and she's brave. She deserves to be with a man equal to that."

"Dad—"

"No, Charley, don't." Jake cut me off. When he looked into my dad's face, his expression was unbending and resolute. "I admit I

71

wasn't that for her when we were younger. But I'm not that guy anymore, Mr. Redford. I don't like that guy any more than you do, and I've not just promised Charley that he's gone for good, I've promised myself."

"That's just talk, Jake. I'm only interested in actions."

Instantly defensive, I stomped back to the coffee. "What do you want him to do? Don a mask and fight crime?"

"Can we do this without your usual smart-ass commentary?" Dad glared at me.

"Nope." I shoved a mug at him. "Somewhere you and Mom have lost sight of who I am. Just because my parents have decided to rewrite my whole personality doesn't mean that the rewrites are going to stick."

"This is nuts." Dad shook his head, his tone calm despite his words. "You can't throw away law school for a job that's dangerous and underpaid. And you can't erase the months of shit you went through trying to get over him."

"Let me ask you a question, Dad." I leaned back against the counter. "Did you honestly think talking to me in person was going to... what... convince me to think your way?"

"No, I came here to see what it is that's going on in your life that would suddenly cause you to make these massive decisions, decisions that impact your entire future. It's not just about me worrying about you and Jake; it's me completely exasperated by your attitude toward your sister and this notion of you becoming a cop. Your recent actions and decisions ring with immaturity and frankly, Charley, that was something I never thought I could accuse you of."

"That's because she's not," Jake argued.

Dad ignored him. "You've got this childish, naïve, rose-colored view that being a cop is a great thing—you wear a uniform people will respect, you save lives, fight crime. And that makes life worth it—"

"Bullshit," Jake uttered quietly, his features taut with anger.

"Jake…" I moved toward him but Dad reached out an arm to stop me.

"No," Dad said. "I'd love to hear this."

"How dare you stand there and condescend to her," Jake continued, calm, despite the flints of anger in his eyes. "You might think Charley taking me back is a bad idea, but stop letting that color every single thing you know about her. You *know* her. How can you say she's living in some fantasy world about being a cop? Do you want to know the real reason she wants to be a cop? Because it's who she is. She can't stand by and watch people suffer. She can't witness something wrong and not want to do something to make it right. What about your nephew—Ethan? Murdered and no one was brought to justice. She knows being a cop isn't easy, she even knows it can be thankless, but she still wants to do it. For her—for Ethan and all the people like him."

I couldn't even find the words to describe how grateful I was. Jake had said all I'd been trying to say for years. I'd failed to find the words to explain it to my parents, but Jake knew me so well, he'd succeeded where I hadn't.

Dad looked stunned. Slowly, he turned to me. "This is about Ethan? You never told me that."

"You never wanted to hear it."

Processing, Dad sipped his coffee. He looked at me over the rim of the mug and lowered it to ask, "Since when do you let Jake fight your battles?"

Grinning, my eyes met Jake's. "I never asked him to. But I've got to say, it's nice to have him on my side."

Jake smiled back at me and I felt our connection strengthen for the first time since we'd started dating again.

"Alex certainly would never have faced off with me," Dad mused, watching Jake carefully. I tensed at the mention of Alex.

Jake frowned. "What?"

Dad's gaze switched between us, noting the sudden tension. "You haven't told him yet?" he asked me.

I narrowed my eyes. "Are you deliberately being a troublemaker?"

"Alex?" Jake said.

That was so not a conversation I could have with him right then. "Jake, I promise we'll talk about it but right now, I'm taking my crazy father to lunch."

There was uncertainty on his face, but Jake nodded. "Call me."

"Just as soon as I've convinced this person who looks like my dad but doesn't act like him that I'm a grown-up and I can make my own choices, I'll come over to see you."

Dad snorted. I ignored him.

Sitting across from my dad in my favorite Tex-Mex restaurant, I shook my head. "I still can't believe you spent all that money to come here and lecture me."

"It wasn't about lecturing you, Charley." Dad leaned back in his seat, his expression grave. "It was about being a parent who's worried about his kid and not being able to think about anything else until I saw for myself she was okay."

Tears burned the back of my eyes. "Dad," I mumbled, blinking rapidly.

"I still don't like Jake, but I've got to admit, I like everything he said in that apartment. I like how he sees you." His face darkened. "But that doesn't mean I accept him as part of your life. Just because the boy is good with words doesn't change his past actions."

"Dad…" I tried to gather my patience. "Please, just give him a chance."

"I can't promise that." He shook his head stubbornly. "I'm just here to see my kid and try to convince her to do the right thing. Starting with calling Andie and apologizing."

"I can't promise that." I threw his words back at him. "I don't think I should be the one apologizing."

Dad sighed. "And this from someone who wants me to treat her as an adult."

I closed my eyes, feeling my patience slipping. "Let's just eat dinner," I muttered. Seemed neither of us was willing to compromise. I'd just have to hope for some kind of miracle to happen while he was in Edinburgh. A miracle that would finally show Jake in a favorable light and bring my family on board with our relationship.

I wasn't holding my breath.

Chapter Seven
Northwestern, September 2013

No matter how much I was willing myself to be unaffected, to be calm, I wasn't. Bolstering my courage, I threw back my shoulders and prepared to reenter the common room where Jake had some redheaded sophomore hanging all over him.

Instead of facing Jake, however, I walked smack bang into a hard chest.

"There she is." Beck wrapped his arms around me and I hugged him back. I felt his lips brush my ear. "Can you please talk to your best friend?"

I pulled back, frowning. "Hi, Beck, it's good to see you too, *after six months*, since the last time didn't really count."

He blanched. "Sorry. It's good to see you. It really is. I'm just a little distracted at the moment." He glanced to his left, where Claudia stood laughing with Denver, Matt, and a couple of guys I didn't recognize. "She won't even look at me."

"Whatever you do, don't start flirting with another girl."

It was his turn to frown. "Wasn't planning on it. Any other suggestions?"

I felt Lowe's hand at my back. "Don't put Charley in the middle, Beck. The middle is a fucked-up place to be."

"I'm not. I'm just running out of ideas."

Honestly, it was frustrating watching two people who were supposed to be together mess it up so royally. I had a hard time keeping my nose out of it. But my nose tried.

Beck searched my face as I stared back at him, steadfast in my stoicism. His eyes narrowed. "Is she really dating someone?"

I shrugged.

"Charley. Please."

"Yes."

A pained look crossed his gorgeous face. "Is it serious?"

"She doesn't talk about it."

"What does that mean exactly?"

I shot a look Claudia's way to make sure she wasn't aware I was talking to Beck and about to betray the girl code. "It means when you see her on her own, stop her and make her listen."

"Just stop her and make her listen? I don't know if you remember but last time that happened, I got verbally bitch-slapped in public."

"Yeah." I smiled, remembering it. "But you also made your point and you got to her. She can't not listen if you're constantly there trying to talk to her."

"Valid point," Lowe added.

Beck smirked at us both, his eyes softening when they met mine. "Thanks, Charley."

"Just don't tell her we had this conversation."

"Secret to the grave."

Just like that he disappeared stealthily into the crowds like a love ninja.

Despite my own situation, I couldn't help but laugh. "I'm finding this side of Beck incredibly endearing."

Lowe snorted, guiding me farther into the room. "You don't have to live with him."

I raised an eyebrow.

"I love Claudia, I do, she's a great girl, but brooding Beck is a pain in my ass. We already had Jake to put up with. Now there are two."

"Did I hear my name?"

My shoulders tensed at the sound of Jake's voice. My whole body tensed when I turned to find him standing before me. There was no redhead now, but the specter of her remained.

Lowe's fingers flexed on my lower back and I had to admit it was easier to deal with this crapshoot of a situation with him supporting me.

"Hey." Jake said. "It's good to see you."

"Let's find more beer." I ignored him, turning my whole body into Lowe. "I definitely need more."

He shot Jake an unreadable look out of the corner of his eye. "Sure," he said and we moved through the crowd, away from my ex and his stunned, hurt expression.

Over the subsequent hour or so, I had a couple more beers, chatted with Matt and Denver, watched Beck stare broodingly at Claudia, witnessed Claudia bestow a beyond murderous look his way when he intercepted a cute guy trying to give her a drink, and then I started dancing with a strange guy. His name was Toby or Tony or Troy or something and he liked my hair.

Something he told me a number of times before I said yes to a dance.

All I really wanted was to forget everything. I didn't want to acknowledge that I was aware of Jake every single minute of the evening. Jake was popular and every time I turned around, he was hanging out with someone new. We didn't make eye contact once.

It was like we were complete strangers.

I was barely even aware of the fact that a slow song had come on, or that I was dancing in Toby/Tony/Troy's arms when I heard Lowe say in voice that brooked no argument, "I'm cutting in."

Toby/Tony/Troy was forcefully removed from my vicinity and suddenly I was dancing with Lowe, except he'd pressed me back so I wasn't smooshed up to him like I had been with my previous partner.

"Problem, officer?"

He laughed and shook his head at me. "Can you not be cute right now?"

The smirk died from my lips at his comment. Jake sometimes said that to me when I used humor as a deflection. If Lowe noticed the change in me, he didn't say so.

"Why are you dancing with that guy, Charley? That's not you."

"Uh, do you not remember Halloween last year?"

He blinked. "Jesus, we've known each other a year. How did that happen?"

"I imagine it had something to do with the world turning for almost 365 days."

Lowe's lips twitched. "You really are a smart-ass."

I saluted him. "Top of my class."

"I'm being serious." He gave me a little shake. "I don't want you doing anything stupid because Jake hurt you tonight."

"Hurt?" I said, suffusing just the right amount of boredom into my tone. "I'm not hurt anymore, Lowe. I feel better. Any doubts I had… poof!" I gestured an explosion with my hand. "I've been replaced." I shrugged. Beer did help with convincing deception. "That means we weren't meant to be. I was right in the first place. Makes moving on now very easy to do."

I was too busy congratulating myself on sounding like I meant it to notice Lowe was now searching the room with an anxious expression on his face.

A couple of beers later I wandered through the main rec room and away from Denver, Matt, and a bunch of people I didn't know. I searched the room as I left, not seeing Jake, Lowe, Beck, or Claudia. I frowned. Only a few minutes ago I'd seen Lowe practically making out with some brunette in the corner, and Claudia had been flirting with a random guy as Beck watched on, seething.

I wondered where they'd all disappeared.

"Hey..." I stopped a girl wearing a Northwestern hoodie. "Nearest bathroom?"

"Down the hall to your left. Third door down, I think."

I thanked her and walked out into the corridor, thinking after I'd used the restroom it might be time to grab Claudia and get out of there. Bemoaning the disastrous decision we'd made to come here, I wasn't really paying attention to the fact that the third door down didn't have signage on it.

I thrust the door open and froze at the scene in front of me.

I was in a dorm room, a dorm room in which Beck had a girl pressed up against the wall, kissing her with a passionate intensity that actually made my cheeks heat. It took me a second to recognize the girl, and I must've made some kind of strangled noise because it broke the scene up.

Claudia pushed Beck away, her eyes bright, her tan complexion tinged with a flush.

Stunned by this development, I stammered out an apology for interrupting.

My best friend shook her head frantically. "You're not interrupting anything." She brushed past Beck who grabbed her wrist to stall her. Claudia tugged out of his hold, glowering at him. His eyes narrowed and he turned away, staring at the wall, the muscle in his jaw flexing.

Claudia gave me a look that screamed, "Don't you dare ask," and rushed out the door behind me.

Well, this was uncomfortable.

I watched Beck as he blew out air between his lips and hung his head.

Sympathy opened my mouth. "Beck."

He looked at me over his shoulder, appearing so disheartened I actually forgot my own woes for a moment.

"Be patient," I told him. "Keep doing what you're doing. Claudia just needs to know that she can piss you off, try your patience and drive you a little crazy, and you'll still be there at the end of the day."

Something in his eyes flickered, something a little like hope. "Yeah?"

"Yeah."

His face darkened. "But the TA?"

"She's not in love with *him*." I shrugged and took a step toward the door. "Why do you think she's so scared of *you*?"

"You shouldn't really be telling me this stuff, should you?"

"No. If Claudia finds out, I'm on her shit list, so I'm taking a risk."

Beck laughed softly. "Well, I appreciate it."

I smiled back at him and turned around to resume my search for the bathroom, still a little stunned. I shouldn't have been surprised to walk in on Claudia and Beck making out, and I guess I wasn't. The truth was it wasn't the fact that they'd kissed that had me reeling—it was the kiss itself. It wasn't just the kiss of two people who were attracted to one another; it was the kiss of two people who *needed* one another. There was desperation in it, a longing so intense, it had been palpable to even me.

It was the kind of kiss I'd once shared with Jake.

Feeling even lower than I had been before, I walked down the hall, wondering if the bathroom was perhaps right, rather than left.

I was approaching an open dorm room door when two familiar voices made me stop in my tracks.

"I'm trying to tell you that you're fucking up," I heard Lowe snap.

"I know what I'm doing," Jake replied, sounding irritated.

Curious, and yes, hoping to overhear my name, I pressed back against the wall and held my breath.

"Jake, I'm confused. I thought you got me to throw this thing, invite her here, so you could talk to her, patch things up. Who the fuck is the redhead?"

My mouth dropped open. They'd orchestrated this party just to get me here? What? Since when did Jake and Lowe work together on anything... especially something involving me?

"The redhead doesn't matter. The whole point of tonight was to get Charley and me in the same room and show her what life is going to be like for us if we're not together. Practically strangers at a party. I know Charley. She's hating this as much as I am. We're possessive of each other. We need to be in each other's lives, know what's going on with each other. Sooner, rather than later, she's going to realize what a mistake this is. But not if she's three hours away. It was only when we started hanging out again in Edinburgh that not being together was too hard."

He was… manipulating me?

I just stopped myself from gasping out loud.

Jake wasn't over me. This wasn't… what the hell was this?

"I hate to tell you this but your plan is backfiring. She thinks you've moved on so she's moving on. She thinks this proves that she was right to break up with you."

"What? What are you talking about?"

I'd done a lot of cowardly things these last few months, but walking away from this wasn't going to be one of them. Nobody, *nobody* manipulated me, and got away with it!

With anger burning in my blood, I stormed into the dorm room Jake and Lowe had chosen to have their little tête-a-tête. They both blanched when they turned to see who was interrupting them.

My eyes must have registered my feelings of betrayal when they met Lowe's because he flinched. "Charley, it's not—"

"Since when do you align yourself with him?" I snapped, gesturing to Jake. "You got together to manipulate me? Are you high?"

He shrugged helplessly. "I was trying to help two friends out. I wasn't trying to hurt you." Lowe shook his head, looking between Jake and me. "It was a mistake to get involved and I'm now uninvolving myself." He was still shaking his head as he walked past, not meeting my fiery gaze.

As soon as he was gone, Jake took a step toward me, holding up his hands in placation. "Don't be pissed. I was just trying to fix us."

"No." I stepped back. "You were playing games, and I thought we were done with that."

"Charley," he stared at me, looking incredulous, "did you honestly just expect me to give up, walk away, after everything? I didn't know what else to do. You wouldn't have come here if I said I just wanted to hang out, talk, try to actually work out our problems instead of running from them. You're the one acting like a child here. I just picked up where you left off."

I couldn't actually dispute any of that, which made me even more pissed, hurt, defensive, scared and... confused.

I started to shiver. "I... I can't do this." I turned away.

I hadn't taken two steps when I felt his hand wrap around my wrist. Jake tugged me, forcefully, pulling me around so I stumbled into his chest. His lips crashed down on mine, his kiss hungry, desperate, angry...

For a moment I forgot everything else but the hard pressure of his mouth on mine, the smell of his cologne, the feel of his body. I was surrounded.

Drowning.

And I let it happen.

His lips moved from my mouth to my chin, along my jaw, as his hand slid up my waist, his thumb just grazing my breast. I sighed, my body arching into his. I was hot. Hot and wanting. Nothing else mattered but the way I felt when he touched me.

His voice was ragged in my ear. "I've missed you so much. I love you so fucking much." He squeezed my waist and pulled me closer, his mouth reaching for mine again but those three little words had broken through the spell of lust created by Jake's proximity and the four beers I'd had.

"Stop," I whispered, pushing gently on his chest.

Instead of stopping, Jake kissed me again.

I pushed harder, breaking contact. "Jake, stop!"

He stumbled back, frustration and something else in his face. Panic? "Charley—"

"No." I moved away from him, holding a hand out to ward him off. "This was a mistake. We're..." I trailed off, not really knowing what to say as I tried to catch my breath.

We stared at each other in tense silence.

That's when I came to the hardest decision of my life.

I felt like someone had stuck burning needles into every muscle in my body, and all I could feel was torturous pain, and I didn't know why it was necessary. What point it had? Why it had to be that way? I started to imagine that perhaps those needles were my family, and horribly in that moment I resented the hell out of them. "We're done for good. We can't be friends and we can't be this. Lose my number, Jake."

He looked grief-stricken. "You can't be serious?"

The tears slipped down my cheeks now and I brushed them hastily away. "Deadly. I won't answer if you call."

"Why?" he shook his head, his own resentment building his gorgeous eyes. "Just tell me why. A real answer this time."

"I told you why. You didn't listen."

And just like that, I turned and walked out.

It was hard to make sense of something to someone else when you had a hard time figuring out if it really made sense to yourself. But I wasn't crazy.

The truth was I'd made a promise. This was me keeping it.

Chapter Eight
Edinburgh, March 2013

I left Dad at his hotel talking to Mom on the phone, reassuring her that he was all right, I was all right, and that we were… talking things out. Although I still didn't feel one hundred percent certain that we'd reached an understanding, I hoped we would by the time he left.

For now, I headed to my boyfriend's apartment.

Something had shifted inside me when Jake sprung to my defense. It didn't seem like much, but in reality, knowing he had my back was a huge step toward me trusting him. The old Jake was too determined to keep on my dad's good side to ever interfere in any small parental disputes I might have had. He'd once sat quietly in the corner of the living room while my mom and dad refused to listen to me about being a cop.

He'd changed.

Anxious to see him, I hurried up to his apartment.

"Jake's not here," Beck said as I followed him into the kitchen.

Sitting at the kitchen table were Claudia and Lowe. I smiled at my girl. "Have you seen him?"

Claud shook her head. "Nope. But—"

"She's been too busy planning our summer tour," Beck interrupted, offering me a can of soda.

"No, thanks." I raised an eyebrow at Claudia. "Summer tour?"

Lowe grinned. "It's what we were talking about at Teviot. Claudia is amazing. She's already helped us book eight gigs for the summer, and she thinks we can turn it into a state tour. It could get us noticed."

"Isn't that expensive?"

Lowe shrugged. "We're pooling our resources. And these are paying gigs." He nudged Claudia. "Now I just have to convince Claud to be our manager and come on tour with us."

"If she doesn't want to, she doesn't have to," Beck said, trying—and failing—to sound casual.

I studied them carefully, wondering what I was missing. "Well… that sounds great. And you should think about it, Claudia. It might be a lot of fun to tour with them."

Claudia shrugged. "I don't know. Anyway, back to the matter at hand. Jake is—"

"A sappy, overachieving, broody little son of a bitch and you could do much better." Beck grinned up at me.

I made a face at him and had just turned back to Claudia when I got a text.

You should know I'm in the kitchen of this blond chick I'm kind of in love with. If you see her, tell her I miss her and to get her ass back here.

"Jake is waiting for you—"

"In our apartment," I finished for Claud, waving my phone at her.

I wondered why Jake had gone back to my place when he knew I was hanging out with my dad. It occurred to me that perhaps he was concerned my dad might've said something to change my mind about our relationship. I longed for the days when we could stop reassuring each other about our mutual commitment.

When I got to the apartment, Jake was in the kitchen with Maggie. I tried to be polite to her, but I was in a hurry to talk to my boyfriend so I offered a quick *hello* and *goodbye* as I dragged Jake into my room.

"Eager, are we?"

"I just wanted you to know that we're okay. Despite my dad and everything."

Instantly, Jake's eyebrows puckered. "Speaking of your father… I really want to hear how things went with your dad tonight, but I have to know something that's been bugging me since he mentioned it… Alex?"

I'd actually forgotten my dad had mentioned Alex's name. Shit.

Now for the truth. I had no idea how Jake would react to it.

Alex Roster was one of my best friends. But for a while… he was more than that.

I took a deep breath. "The guy, the one I dated for ten months freshman year of college… it was Alex."

Jake tensed and then he gently pushed me away. "Alex was *the* guy?"

Sensing this was going somewhere bad, I hurried to explain. "After you left, everything was different. We'd both changed and we grew close. We're really good friends. At college we decided to give it another go. It worked for a while but I couldn't give him what he wanted and he couldn't give me what I needed." I shrugged. "We broke up, but we've stayed friends. He's been seeing his girlfriend Sharon for ages. They're happy together and—"

"Ten months?" Jake interrupted. He'd paled. "You fucked him?"

he whispered hoarsely.

"Jake…" I felt betrayed by the question. "That's not even fair. You probably fucked an entire sorority house while we were broken up."

"They weren't goddamn Alex Roster!" he yelled, brushing past me.

I watched on as he wore out my carpet, pacing back and forth.

"All that time we were dating, you said you had no feelings for him and you were lying to me?"

I'd expected him to not like the news, but I hadn't expected him to be so angry and hurt. "No, I wasn't lying. I didn't have feelings for him then," I promised. "Like I said, Brett's death changed us. You breaking my heart changed me. You left, Jake. Alex stayed."

Jake jerked to a stop, like I'd hit him. "Is that how it's going to be forever? You winning an argument for the rest of our lives by throwing *that* in my face?"

"I threw it in your face for this particular argument because it has relevance. You wanted to know how I ended up dating Alex."

"For ten months?" He shook his head in disbelief and slumped down on the bed. "God, the thought of you with him…" Jake closed his eyes. "The thought of you with anyone else…" His dark, tumultuous gaze met mine. "You were in love with him?"

"No." I sat next to him. "That's the reason we broke up. He told me he loved me but I didn't love him. We weren't right for each other, Jake. He didn't want me to be a cop, and I'm pretty sure he thinks I'm a little crazy. He drove himself nuts worrying about me. And he… he was too concerned with how everything looked to everyone else. And…" I curled my hand around Jake's neck, drawing our faces closer. "It was never passionate between us. It was just nice. And you have no idea how heartbreaking 'just nice' is when you know what 'beautiful' tastes like."

"Yes, I do," Jake whispered against my lips before closing his eyes again. He leaned his forehead against mine as he reached for my free hand. "This is how you felt watching me with Melissa?"

"Yes," I whispered back.

Jake's expression crumbled and suddenly he was cupping my face in his hands, his anguished eyes blazing into mine. "I am so sorry. I am so sorry I hurt you over and over again."

"Jake…" I folded into him, wrapped my arms tightly around him as his enclosed around me.

"Every day," he said softly, "I'm going to spend every day making it up to you."

I sat in his arms for a while as he rocked us gently.

Finally Jake broke the silence. "Your dad? How did it go tonight?"

"You're having dinner with us tomorrow," I said, making the decision on the spot. No way would Dad change his mind about Jake if he didn't spend time with him. I pulled back to look at Jake.

"Okay."

"Yeah?"

"Yes."

"Tonight," I abruptly tugged up the hem of his T-shirt. Without questioning, Jake raised his arms and let me pull it off. "When you defended me," I threw his shirt on my chair and slowly drew my own sweater up over my head, "it felt amazing. I don't need anyone to fight for me, Jake." I pressed a soft kiss to his waiting mouth, coasting my fingertips across his chest, my thumbs brushing his nipples, my touch making him shudder. "But I have to admit that I like that you want to."

"Always," he said, arching his neck for me as my lips trailed kisses along his jaw and down his throat.

I caressed his abs with my hands, soft, gentle touches that accelerated his breathing. I flicked my tongue over his nipple and his hands clamped around my arms in reaction. "Let me." I looked up at him.

His eyes burned with lust. "Torture me?"

I shook my head. "That implies you won't to get play too. I'm just asking you to let me play first."

Jake nodded, his excitement evident. "Whatever you want, baby. I've missed you."

Kissing my way down his stomach, I felt my own skin start to heat and the pulse between my legs throb at the increase in Jake's breathing. When I reached the low-slung waistband of his jeans, I traced the skin just above with my tongue, excited by the low, deep growl emanating from Jake's throat.

His erection strained against his zipper.

"Let me help you with that." I smiled up at him mischievously. "It looks painful."

The look on his face almost broke me. His features were taut, his eyes fogged with desire, and everything in me wanted to answer it— just rip off his jeans and mine and jump him.

Patience was something I needed to practice.

Jake watched me, his intensity making me shiver with anticipation as I unzipped his jeans and pulled at the waistband and of his boxers underneath. He tilted his hips off the bed, giving me easier access. I tugged his jeans and underwear down, pulling off his boots so I could remove his clothes completely.

He sat there, comfortable with his nakedness. And so he should be. I licked my lips, my eyes roaming his sculpted body and throbbing erection.

"I'm a lucky, lucky girl." I grinned up at him, making him smile wryly back at me.

"I'm glad you think so."

I shook my head as I stood up. "I know so." I unclipped my bra, letting it drop to the floor. Jake's eager eyes fastened on my naked breasts as my nipples tightened into hard buds.

Taking my time, I kicked off my boots, unzipped my jeans, and shimmied out of them. Wearing only my panties, I stepped closer so our legs touched.

Jake slid his hands up my outer thighs until they rested on my hips, his eyes devouring every inch of me. "I think you've got it the wrong way around."

"What?"

"I'm the lucky one."

I nodded solemnly. "Yeah, you are."

He shook his head, seeming to marvel at me, a look that turned my insides to mush. "Do you have any idea how sexy you are?"

I smiled cockily and pointedly at his hard-on. "I have an inkling."

Jake laughed, biting his lower lip as he hooked a finger into my panties. "Are these leaving us any time soon?"

Nudging his legs apart so I could step between them, I lowered myself to the floor. "Eventually. I have something more urgent on my mind, though."

"Charley," he said, breath short, his dark eyes flashing with excitement. "You don't have to."

"When have I ever not wanted to?" I reminded him.

His groan filled my ears as I took him into my mouth, sucking lightly at first at his warm, salty taste. I licked the pre-cum from his tip, teasing him mercilessly with my mouth until he begged me to stop.

I gave him what he wanted, sucking him hard as I pumped the base with my fist.

When I knew he was close, I stopped.

His chest rose and fell in pants as he stared at me in disbelief. "Why?"

I stood, only to crawl onto the bed next to him. I kissed him softly. "Now do me, but don't let me come. Let's save that."

Understanding, Jake asked, "Delayed gratification, huh?"

"Exactly."

"It fucking hurts," he smiled ruefully back at me.

"But it'll be worth it." I lay back on the bed and watched him as he pulled my panties down very slowly, torturously so. I was already turned on from going down on him and didn't think it would take much to climax. Jake had a challenge on his hands to stop before it happened.

At the touch of his tongue on my ankle, I realized clearly he was up for pushing me to breaking point. He pressed soft kisses up my legs, alternating between the two, positioning them how he wanted, bending my knee so he could lick the crease behind it. I squirmed, my whole body tingling with anticipation. My nerves sparked, begging for fire.

He pushed my legs apart, crawling between them. My hips jerked at the feel of his mouth on the inside of my thigh. He scattered soft kisses along my skin, driving me crazy.

When he proceeded to lick the crease between my thigh and my sex, I whimpered his name pleadingly. Taking pity, Jake tickled me with the stroke of his finger seconds before his mouth came down on me.

I sighed in pleasure, lost completely to the search for satisfaction as Jake's tongue circled my clit. I writhed against his mouth while he played me perfectly, his tongue moving down, sliding inside me.

I was barely aware of my cries to God, to Jake, my begging for more.

He returned to my clit, sucking it between his teeth, and I felt it coming. My body tensed, preparing for it.

And then Jake's mouth was gone.

It took me a minute to blink through the haze of lust to realize what had happened.

Delayed gratification. I pouted at him as he kneeled between my legs. "You're right. It hurts."

"You're telling me," he said quietly and my eyes dropped to his dick. It strained toward his stomach, purple-red with need.

I shivered and spread my legs a little wider. "I'm all yours if you want me."

Jake dragged his eyes over my body in a way that made my breasts swell. "Oh, I want you," he answered, his voice thick. "I want you to turn over."

"Over?"

"I want to see all of you. Now turn over."

Immediately turned on by his commanding attitude, I let my sliding hair hide my smile as I rolled over onto my stomach for him. I rested my chin on my arms. "Now wha—oh…" I melted at the soft touch of his warm lips on my lower back.

"I love these dimples," he muttered, his breath whispering over my skin. "When you wear jeans and a small tee, it shows off these sexy dimples just above your ass. Turns me on every time I see them."

I grinned. "That's good to know."

And then all thought flew swiftly from my mind as Jake pressed kisses over my butt cheeks, his tongue licking lightly at my skin as he did so.

I began to writhe again as he licked the crease between the bottom curve of my right cheek and the back of my thigh. "Jake," I groaned, deliciously surprised by the sensual assault.

Two fingers slid inside me and I clenched my hands into fists, arching my neck, raising my ass as he pumped those fingers slowly in and out. My body tensed.

"I'm going to come," I whimpered, warning him.

"Not without me, you're not."

Suddenly, he had me on my back again, his expression fierce. He pulled me under him, his chest brushing mine while he gripped my thigh in his hand, parting my legs.

He thrust inside me and we both moaned at the feel of my tight inner muscles pulsing around him. Jake held still for a moment and that something magical that was always there passed between us. Eyes connected the whole time, Jake's grip on my thigh tightened and he pulled back out only to surge back inside me so deeply, I cried out. I arched against his thrusts, meeting each one with a building urgency.

My muscles tightened, my body stiffened.

I came on a cry of his name, tears in my eyes as I stared into his, my hips shuddering against his with release as he continued to pump into me.

Jake's jaw clenched and he tensed a second before he came, jerking against me, his warm, long, wet release flooding me.

"Fuck," he panted, relaxing into me.

I wrapped my arms and legs around him, holding him close.

"Definitely worth it," he mumbled against my shoulder. "Delayed gratification."

I chuckled. "Oh, yeah."

He kissed my collarbone and pushed up, easing his weight off me. I caught the note of seriousness in his expression and waited with bated breath. "Something happened here. I'm not pressuring you into going too fast, but I need you to acknowledge when our relationship is moving forward. I know I don't deserve it, but it'll stop me going crazy." He smirked unhappily. "I've been going crazy wondering when you're going to decide this is a bad idea, and I know I'll have to live with that. But… I felt something with you tonight…"

"Hey," I curled my hand around his neck, "I felt it."

Jake studied me a moment and then whispered, "I love you."

I gave him a weak smile, pulling him down for a kiss so I didn't have to see the disappointment in his eyes.

Desperate to move past those three little words and the sudden disconnect between us, I broke the halfhearted kiss to change the subject. "I'm sorry I didn't tell you sooner about Alex."

Jake rolled off me to lie on his back. I was relieved when he curled an arm around me to pull me into his side. "It's okay. We're a work in progress."

"That we are."

Silence, not entirely uncomfortable, fell between us and I didn't know whom I was most disappointed in—myself for being emotionally stunted or Jake for ruining the moment with another "I love you."

Chapter Nine
Lanton, October 2013

In silent mutual agreement, Claudia and I didn't talk about Lowe's party. She knew it was final between me and Jake and that I wouldn't be accepting any new requests to hang out with the guys. She seemed fine with that because it meant she could hide from Beck.

I was sad to lose the guys in losing Jake. Especially Lowe, despite his move to the dark side. We'd traded a few texts over the last few weeks but it was clear that our friendship wasn't really going to go anywhere if I was hell-bent on avoiding Jake.

Senior year and studying for the LSATs were a great distraction from everything, as were Alex and Sharon who always had something planned for us on the weekend. I wanted to be distracted from Jake. He was a lost cause for me.

My parents weren't a lost cause, however, and it was becoming increasingly difficult to deal with the estrangement between my dad and me. I think the finality of losing Jake finally broke me. After talking it over with Claudia, I packed a bag the weekend before Halloween and headed to Lanton.

Dad didn't seem to care whether I tagged along with him to

work that Saturday, which hurt my feelings since he loved me tagging along when I was a kid. I was his little assistant. Andie was never interested in cars, but I was curious about anything my dad found interesting and he loved that he could share his work with me.

It was a different story altogether now.

We got to his auto shop and instead of stopping to have coffee and donuts with the two guys on his payroll like he normally would, he went straight to work. He left me in the office with Jed Stewart, a guy around Dad's age who'd worked for him for ten years, and Milo Atwater. Milo was a cute, slightly unkempt guy who'd been in Andie's class at school. He'd graduated high school with his GED and come straight to work with Dad because he loved cars more than he loved anything else.

Jed frowned at the door as Dad walked out. "I suppose I'd better get to work too, then," he grumbled, taking another sip of coffee before striding out.

I picked up a donut and looked at Milo. "You going too?"

He gave me his lopsided grin and leaned back in his chair. "Nah. We don't start for another ten minutes." He nodded toward the door. "What's up with Jim?"

I chewed on the donut and slumped against the wall. After swallowing, I replied honestly, "I'm here."

Milo raised an eyebrow. "He thinks the sun shines out of your ass. What the hell could you have done to piss him off?"

"It's complicated."

"Drugs?"

"No," I laughed and shoved the rest of the donut in my mouth.

Milo smirked at me. "Sex?"

I made a face at him.

"Gambling?"

I finished eating. "No. Like I said, it's complicated."

His eyebrows drew together. "Now I'm curious. I want to know what the Great Charley Redford could seriously have done wrong."

Now it was my turn to make a face. "The Great Charley Redford?"

He laughed. "Yeah. You have to know you're kind of a legend around here. Supergirl."

I tried not to flinch at the nickname. "I'm not perfect."

His eyes raked over me. "I don't know about that," he murmured.

"Are you actually flirting with me right now?"

Eyes filled with laughter, he shrugged. "Can't a man appreciate a pretty woman?"

"Not when she's his boss's daughter."

"See, now you're just turning me on with the whole 'forbidden fruit' thing."

"I'm going to seriously kick you in the nuts."

"There she is!" he laughed and stood up. "It's not like you to walk around town looking like a kicked puppy. I don't like it. It throws everything off."

Grimly, I stared out of the office. "Yeah, well, my dad has a way of making me feel like a badly behaved four-year-old."

"Hmm… it's not got anything to do with that guy that was here a couple of weeks ago, does it?"

My eyes snapped to his face. "What guy?"

"That kid." He gesticulated with a donut in hand. "The kid… you know… the kid you used to date. Jesus, I can't remember his name."

A wave of nausea crashed over me and I felt slightly faint as my heart rate knocked itself out of whack. "Jake? Jake Caplin?"

"Mmm-hmmm!" Milo nodded profusely as he chewed.

Jake had come to see my dad? And Dad hadn't said anything.

I hurried out of the office and across the workshop to where Dad was glowering at a computer screen. "Dad, I know you're working but we need to talk."

He didn't even look up at me. "Charley, I *am* working. I *can't* talk."

Maddened, I growled, "Jake came here and you didn't tell me?"

Dad froze for a second but only for a second because suddenly, my arm was in his tight grasp and he was marching us both through the auto shop and out back into the courtyard.

"What did Jake want?" I asked without preamble.

Dad put his hands on his hips and stared at the ground for a bit. It took every bit of patience within me not to force an answer out of him.

Finally he looked at me, squinting against the low autumn sun. "Jake is worried about you. He was looking for answers, answers I couldn't give him. He doesn't seem to know why you two broke up but thinks I might be to blame."

"Oh God," I leaned against the building. "Everything is so messed up, Dad."

"You want to know what I told him?"

Actually, I really wasn't sure I did, but I nodded anyway.

"I told him maybe you broke up with him because he's a jackass."

I narrowed my eyes. "Eloquent, Dad."

"What else was I supposed to say?"

"Not that," I replied, infuriated. "I treated Jake horribly. No matter what you think of him, I shouldn't have treated him the way I did, and he didn't deserve that from you."

Dad shook his head. "He was looking for answers in the wrong place—what did he expect? Only you can tell him why you broke up with him." It sounded like a question but I ignored it.

Now that I had my Dad talking, I guess we had a more relevant topic to discuss. "You know, I came home this weekend to spend time with you. To try to mend fences."

He cut me a look and his voice was hard when he replied, "This ain't the fence you should be trying to mend."

Shot down on my first attempt?

The unbending disappointment from him finally snapped something inside of me. "Are you perfect, Dad?" I yelled, jerking away from the auto shop wall.

"Charley, don't start—"

"No, really, are you perfect? Can you just deal with anything life throws at you? Can you answer to your mistakes?" I sagged back against the building. "Haven't you ever been so paralyzed, because you're terrified whatever move you decide to make is the wrong one and it'll just make everything worse?"

The quiet in my voice, the question, caused some of the hardness to soften in his eyes.

"You were one of my best friends," I whispered, trying to hold down the emotion. I didn't want to cry right now. I didn't want to be hysterical. I just wanted him to stop hating me. "And now it's like you can't even stand to look at me… and I don't know if I've really done anything to deserve that. I'm not perfect, Dad. I make mistakes, and sometimes I don't know how to fix them. But you shutting me out… I feel alone." And damn those fucking tears but they pushed forth, spilling down my cheeks. "I'm lonely."

I heard my dad curse under his breath and the next thing he'd closed the distance between us and I was in his warm, safe, strong arms. He held me tight until my tears reduced to sniffles and then I felt him kiss my hair before leaning back to look down into my face. "Baby girl, I never meant to make you feel that way. I guess I just hold you to a higher standard than most. I ask more from you than I do others."

I nodded and stepped back, wiping my cheeks. "I want to be the person you can hold to higher standards. I do. But I've gotten so stuck and I don't how to break free."

He brushed the hair off my face. "You start by taking control of your life, of your actions, Charley. You've got a few things to face and you need to take them one at a time. If I've been hard on you, it's because this isn't the Charley I know. You face things head on. You're only going to start feeling better about yourself if you start dealing with everything. First thing…" He rubbed my shoulder in comfort. "Andie."

I gave him a nod in agreement, sinking back against him for another hug, but in truth, my gut was churning. Facing that… I just didn't know if I'd ever be ready.

Chapter Ten

Edinburgh, March 2013

When Dad left Edinburgh, he hadn't changed his mind about Jake or my decision to become a cop. One great day of doing touristy stuff together and one seriously awkward and painful dinner with Jake later, Dad got on a plane back to the States. He told me he loved me and that he was glad I was okay. However, he also told me he would maybe take me more seriously if I were mature enough to pick up the phone and apologize to my sister.

I hated that I hadn't spoken to Andie in weeks. I hated that right now she was pissed off and that she didn't like me very much. I hated it even more that I didn't like her very much right now. More than anything, I hated that she wasn't there to talk to when I needed her the most. But I still didn't feel like I was in the wrong. Stubbornly, I refused to call her, which meant my whole family was still pretty upset with me.

And Jake…

I was hurting him. I still hadn't said *I love you* and each time he said it without a return, it looked like he was taking a bullet. Along with the hurt, I was beginning to sense his growing impatience.

Because the truth was we both knew how I felt about him. I should've just said it out loud. I didn't know why I couldn't. It seemed my stubbornness extended from my dealings with my family to how I was handling Jake.

For some reason I believed Jake would patiently wait for my head to sort itself out.

Jake had another idea in mind.

It was a Thursday, just after midnight, and I'd just finished a paper. I was stepping out of the bathroom when I heard a key turn in the apartment door.

Surprised, I watched as Jake stalked down the quiet, dark hallway toward me.

The determination in his eyes made me gape at him wordlessly as he pushed past me and stalked into my room. "We need to talk."

I hurried inside after him, shutting the door behind us as he spun around to face me. "About what?"

His answer was to close in on me quickly, his hands braced on the door on either side of my head so I was trapped. My heart accelerated, goosebumps prickling all over me at his proximity. "I'm done fucking around," he said, his words almost dancing on my lips our mouths were so close. "I've had time to think. I made a mistake." He pressed his body into mine and grinned triumphantly at the way my breath stuttered. I would've punched him for his arrogance if I weren't completely turned on. "My mistake has been my patience. Now I'm done. I should've tied you to your bed until your stubborn ass was ready to admit it." Jake brushed a kiss across my jaw and I shivered. "You love me," he whispered hoarsely in my ear, before pulling back to watch my reaction.

I was surprised. Uncertain. Maybe scared.

But I also wanted him.

I always wanted him.

"I know you love me," Jake persisted. "I need you to admit it so we can put all this shit behind us and start over."

I felt a surge of annoyance at him taking the situation out of my hands. "Bossy Jake is back, I see."

"He never left. He's just been walking on eggshells for the past few months, scared of losing you."

"You… scared? Puhlease," I teased, trying to shift onto easier ground as a last-ditch effort to pull back from the destination he was forcing me toward.

"Will you stop jerking around and tell me you love me?" he growled back.

"You can't push me to say it!"

"Why are you being such a prima donna? I know you feel it."

"You don't know that!" I yelled, pressing my hands to his chest again, trying to move him away.

Jake stood his ground. "I guess…" He rested all his weight into my hands, until they were flattened between his chest and mine. Our noses touched. "I guess I'll just have to fuck it out of you. I'm okay with that."

Holy… "Ja—" My protest was silenced by his mouth.

He groaned as I instantly melted for him. I couldn't help myself. I was exhausted fighting what I felt, and I no longer knew why I was fighting.

Giving in tasted sweeter.

His kiss was hard, punishing almost, but I gave as good as I got. I ran my fingers roughly through his hair, pressing my body close to his. He wrapped his arms around me, tightening his hold until there was no space at all between us.

He slid his hand down my back, his fingers slipping inside my panties. He gripped my bare ass in his hand, pulling me into his erection. I gasped into his mouth and followed his lead, holding onto him as I wrapped my legs around his waist. He lifted me easily, seeming to relish my heated response.

He pulled back from our kiss. "Tell me you love me," he whispered, his eyes searing.

I blinked through a haze of lust, my fingers tightening in his hair as my gaze searched his. "You don't play fair," I muttered.

"I learned from the best."

Giving him a small smile, I trembled at the sound of the blood whooshing in my ears. "I'm scared, Jake."

Jake took a few steps until he found the bed. He slowly lowered himself onto it, taking me with so I straddled him. He stroked my back in comfort. "Baby, I'm scared too. But I'm more scared of fucking this up because we can't get over the past."

He watched me struggle with my decision and I could see the mounting anxiety in his eyes. Knowing the time for stubbornness was over, I closed my eyes and leaned my forehead against his. "You have to promise you won't walk out on me again. Ever."

His hold on my hips tightened. "I promise."

Hearing the absolution of his vow, I leaned back to stare into his face. Tenderness, need, want, affection, adoration… it all moved through me. Gently, I caressed his jaw, my fingers coasting, drawing faint patterns in his skin. When my eyes met his again, everything I felt flooded out of me and I watched him suck in his breath.

"I've never stopped loving you," I told him quietly. "When I saw you at the party last semester… it hurt, Jake. I've never been so hurt."

"Baby—"

"I need you to know this because I'm deciding to trust you again."

He nodded, waiting.

"I will never love anyone the way I love you. You're part of me. You make me feel like I can be anyone, do anything... but you also have the ability to make me feel weak. You have the ability to crush me like no one else can. I don't like that part of myself, Jake, and I hate that you can do that to me."

His breathing sounded a little uneven as he whispered back, "You make me feel the same way."

Leaning close, my lips an inch from his, my eyes blazing, I uttered darkly, "Good. I need to know that we're on equal footing here."

In answer Jake caught my lips with his, drawing me into a deep, drugging kiss. He pulled back, jerking down the zipper on his jeans as he told me in a voice thick with need, "We love each other so we can hurt each other, but I'm making a promise," he tugged down my panties and I lifted myself up to help, "to do everything I can not to hurt you again. I want that promise from you."

I settled back over him, my uneven breathing seeming to spur him on, making him hotter and harder as his dick brushed between my legs. I bit back a moan, nodding. "I promise," I whimpered. "Jake, I promise. I love you."

He closed his eyes for a moment, appearing to savor it. "Say it again."

My breath whispered across his ear. "I love you, Jacob Caplin."

And just like that, his control snapped. He gripped me by the nape, holding me still for his rough, desperate kiss. With his other hand, he guided himself to my entrance. He then took hold of my hip and thrust up into my wet, tight heat. We gasped into each other's mouths, our sexual chemistry, chemistry we'd never had and would never find with anyone else, overwhelming us.

"I love you" fell freely from our mouths as we held onto one another, chasing the high of finally coming together, in every way we could.

"So this is why I woke up to an empty bed and a cryptic note?" Jake's tall figure cast a shadow over me.

I smiled up at him from the picnic blanket. "I thought we should take the day away from everything. You're not missing anything too important in class, are you?"

He shook his head, an amused grin on his lips.

"Well, sit down, then." I patted the blanket and Jake slowly lowered himself onto it. His eyes drifted over the items on the blanket and widened with recognition. I was warmed all the way through from his laughter.

"Peanut butter sandwiches, cookies, chips, and two bottles of water." His dark eyes twinkled. "Just like our first date."

"Yup. Unfortunately, we're missing Hendrix, but I thought the view more than made up for it."

We were on Arthur's Seat, the peak of a group of hills east of Edinburgh Castle. It was popular with hill walkers and such. I was hoping to find it quiet on a Friday morning, and I had. I should've been exhausted after last night.

But I wasn't.

I woke up next to Jake, excited about the future for the first time in a really long time, and I wanted the future to start today. I left a note telling him to meet me on Arthur's Seat at eleven thirty. I then put together our first-date meal and hiked up before him to prepare.

"The view definitely makes up for it," he murmured, eyes glued to my face.

I tingled all over but put it aside. Sex was always easy for us. It was time to work on the relationship. "We never talk about our past. I think we've been so scared to bring up the bad stuff that we've forgotten all the good. Like our first date."

"When you named my truck."

I laughed. "When I named your truck. And when you teased me by not kissing me good night."

It was Jake's turn to chuckle. "I was waiting for the right moment."

"And decided English class was the right moment?"

He shrugged. "I wanted it to be a moment you'd never forget, so that no matter what happened between us, you'd never forget me."

"Well, mission accomplished. It's a pretty amazing kiss for any other guy to live up to."

Jake leaned closer, his expression serious. "And after last night… there are never going to be any other guys, right?"

I shifted close enough I could rest my chin on his knee and looked up at him from under my lashes. "It's just you and me from now on. No games. No walls. I told you, I love you. I'm letting the fear go."

I closed my eyes at the feel of his fingers on my skin as he brushed my hair behind my ear.

"No games?" he asked softly.

My eyes opened. "Yes."

"Then I have a question."

I lifted my head, but only to rest my arms across the top of his knees. "Shoot."

"The nape thing," his fingers tickled under my hair, brushing gently over the back of my neck, "what's it all about?"

I grimaced but determined to be honest, I said, "It's stupid."

"It bothers me. It'll always bother me when you pull away."

"Okay. I get it." I smiled unhappily and forged ahead with the truth. "You used to hold me that way. I used to think it was something you did unconsciously, asking me for my entire focus. I loved it. I thought it was hot but sweet at the same time."

Jake frowned. "So what changed?"

"The night at Teviot… the night you chased me out of the bar, asking me to give you a chance to apologize…"

"Yeah?"

"The reason I ran out that night is because I turned around and I saw you with Melissa… your hand on her nape, holding her the way I thought you only ever held me. See? Stupid."

We were both quiet as the words danced on the air between us. Finally, Jake exhaled. "I can't fix those mistakes, Charley. Even though it kills me that I've done things to hurt you, meant or not, I can't take them away. I can't undo it. But I can promise you this… no one will ever mean to me what you do." His eyes took on a faraway look. "When I first met you at the bonfire, I was freaked out by what I was feeling. I was nearly seventeen, I could get girls, I'd been with a few, so I was cocky and arrogant and had no plans to date a girl exclusively." He chuckled and I grinned as I remembered our first meeting. "You were kind of intimidating at first, but then you were funny and unconsciously sexy. I'd never met a girl like you and I'd never met anyone who I connected with so quickly. At the end of that party, I knew that everything had changed. I couldn't give a shit about any other girl. I wanted to get to know you better." His smile was a little shy. "I wanted to *deserve* to get to know you."

I blinked back tears at the memories, reassuring Jake with a small grin when he saw the wet in my eyes. "Those six months with you were the best I've ever had in my whole life. It's like… I don't know, I'm just so relieved to be able to look back on them now and remember falling in love with you without feeling like one of us died."

Jake nodded solemnly. "That's how I felt too."

"We don't have to feel that way anymore. We've made it through."

Jake cupped my face in his hands. "I'm never letting you go," he murmured his vow. "Even if you try to make me… never again."

I nuzzled into his touch. "Right back at you, Caplin."

Jake laughed, pressed a soft kiss to my lips, and pulled back to stare down at the picnic. "Are we going to eat? I'm a little hungry after all that making up we did last night."

"Mmm, me too." I handed him a sandwich. "I should be exhausted, but I'm not."

He grinned. "I'll just need to try harder next time."

"Try any harder and I won't be able to walk afterwards."

We laughed and continued to eat in perfect, comfortable quiet. Scrunching up my sandwich wrapper, I settled on my back and stared up at the cloudy sky. "You were kind of bossy last night."

"Yeah. You didn't seem that upset, though," he pointed out.

"Nah, I wasn't. That was just you asserting your dominance in a pre-evolutionary kind of way." I rolled my head on the blanket to meet his gaze. "I just went with it, but you should know I would never have given in if I wasn't about to anyway."

"Yeah?" He caressed me gently, trailing his fingertips along the bare skin peeking out between my sweater and the waistband of my jeans.

I shivered at his touch. "Hmm… yes."

"Ah, I see how this is," he whispered, drawing invisible circles on my skin. "You think you're in charge here."

"I am in charge, mister." It would've sounded a lot more convincing if my breath hadn't hitched.

"We'll just see about that." He plucked at the top button on my jeans.

"Jake, don't." I covered his hands with mine. "Someone might come up here. They'll see us."

He smirked, brushing my hands away. "Come on, Supergirl. Be brave."

"Jake…" I lost my breath completely at the feel and sound of him tugging down my zipper. My belly flipped as his warm hand slid inside, slipping beneath my panties. "Jake…"

"Ssh." He was leaning over me now, his eyes on my face as two of his fingers found my clit. "Just feel it."

I bit my lip, everything else in the whole world disappearing but Jake and the sensations swelling through me. I arched my hips into his touch.

"Do you remember that night in my truck?" his voice rasped in my ear. "Halloween. I do. I remember every second. I'd never been so turned on in my life."

"I remember," I whimpered as I grew wet from the memories and his touch.

"Do you remember the first time I went down on you?"

"Uh-huh…" I pushed into his hand, seeking more.

"Do you remember the first time you sucked me off?"

"Mmm."

"Do you remember how hard you made me come?"

"Yes, yes, yes…" My whole body tensed and soon I was climaxing in jerky shudders around the fingers he'd slipped inside me.

As I came back to earth, Jake zipped my jeans.

Melted against the blanket, I stared into his gorgeous face in a daze. "What was that for?"

"That," he smirked, "was punishment for taking your sweet time telling me you loved me."

"Um… I hate to tell you this but that kind of punishment isn't going to deter me from pissing you off in the future."

Jake laughed. "I didn't think it would. Lucky for me, I get off on the punishment."

"You're hard," I said, feeling him against my hip.

His eyes darkened. "As a rock."

"It's your fault for talking dirty and getting me off in a public place."

"So I take it that means you're not going to take care of me?"

My eyes widened at the suggestion. "I am not doing that on Arthur's Seat. You can wait until later."

Jake brushed his lips over mine. "You're a cruel wench."

Chuckling, I pushed him off me, pressing his back to the ground. "Down, boy." I laid back. "No more sexy stuff right now."

"Okay. I'll be good." He put his hands behind his head and stared at the sky. A few moments later, he said, "You're something special to me, Charley Redford."

I felt a flutter in my chest as I remembered him saying that to me on our first date. "You're something special to me too."

"Yeah?"

"I haven't let anyone else put their hands down my jeans on top of a hill in Scotland, you know."

"Well, that's a relief. I do like to be original."

I giggled. "You are certainly that."

"The pressure is now on, though, to feel you up when you least expect it."

"I can deal with that kind of pressure."

"You say that now, but wait until I give you an orgasm in the camping section of a department store."

"You just ruined *that* location. Now I'm expecting an orgasm in the camping section of a department store. You took the spontaneity out of it."

Jake tsked. "I'll just need to come up with somewhere—"

"Sexier?" I suggested.

"What is not sexy about a tent in a department store?" he huffed. "Who have you been dating and what has he been teaching you?"

"Just some guy who was all romance and picnics."

"He sounds like a tool."

"Meh, he had his moments. We did have some pretty amazing sex in his pickup, though."

"Ah, well," Jake turned his head to smile at me, "that I can do."

As his meaning sank in, I felt a rush of giddiness. "You still have Hendrix?"

He nodded. "I stopped driving it… well… because it reminded me of you, but my dad kept it in his garage."

I turned on my side, even more excited about going back to the States now. "The first thing we're doing when we get to Chicago is taking your truck out, finding a secluded park somewhere, and rechristening that baby."

Jake grinned. "Have I told you I love how your mind works?"

"We should probably have dinner with your folks first, though, huh."

"And then you ruined it." He rolled his eyes in mock disgust.

Smiling, I leaned in close. "But you love me."

He made a face. "Who told you that?"

"Some tool I know."

Jake laughed. "You know a lot of tools."

"Nah." I shook my head. "Just the one."

Smiling into my eyes, Jake sighed, seeming more happy and relaxed than I'd seen him in a long time. "I'm looking forward to going home, but I'm also not."

"How do you mean?"

"We've got the summer and then we're back to school in different states."

I slumped at the thought but said, "We're only three hours away."

"That's long enough to kill me," he muttered, brushing the back of his hand affectionately across my cheek.

"It's just one year," I promised him. "And we'll make the most of it. I'll come see you one weekend, you come see me the next. We'll make it work."

"You're right." He pulled me into his arms so I was snuggled against him, my head on his chest. "But for now, let's just enjoy this. I thought I was happy when you decided to give me a second shot... but nothing compares to this."

"What? Talking nonsense and eating peanut butter?" I teased.

"Exactly." He kissed the top of my head. "We're Jake and Charley again. Older but no less immature."

I giggled and burrowed deeper against him. "Isn't it awesome."

Chapter Eleven

West Lafayette, November 2013

Edinburgh was laid out before me. As I looked out over the cityscape from my perch on Arthur's Seat, hugging my arms around myself against the bracing wind, I felt content. At peace.

The air was so crisp here, fresh, alive in a way I couldn't explain. I'd never felt more awake.

"Do you miss it?"

Startled, I looked over my shoulder to see Jake walking toward me. "Miss it?" I asked as he came to a stop and took my hand.

He was so warm.

"This." He nodded to the view. "And this?" He tugged on my hand.

I smiled, confused. "How can I miss it? It's right here. You're right here."

Jake looked at me with his soulful eyes, his countenance too grim for such a beautiful day, such a beautiful moment. "Am I?"

The sadness in him caused me alarm. "What are you talking about?"

He leaned into me. "Open your eyes, Charley."

"They—"

"For God's sake, open your eyes!" he yelled and I flinched, closing them instead against his attack.

When I opened them, he was gone.

Edinburgh was gone.

I stumbled, discombobulated. My eyes swept my surroundings, taking in the trees, all the green, and all... the gravestones. I tripped over one, leaning on it to right myself.

The name engraved on the gray stone froze me to the spot.

Andrea Delia Redford.

"No," I whispered, falling to my knees, my hands rubbing over the letters as if I could make them go away.

"You can't."

My head jerked up and I looked at my mother, standing over me. "Mom?" I licked the tears from my lips.

"You can't make it go away."

I shook my head. "No. This isn't real."

Mom cocked her head in thought and then pointed down the rows of the gravestones. Tears glistened in her eyes. "It feels real."

I followed her gaze.

A black gravestone with the engraving *Charlotte Julianne Redford.*

My lips felt numb. "It's not real."

The air shifted around me and Mom lowered herself beside me. She had flowers in her hand. She put a few on Andie's grave and then a few on the one next to it. My eyes flew to the headstone.

Sophia Roberta Brown.

"Grandma?"

Mom nodded. "She understands me."

"I don't... I'm so confused."

Misunderstanding me, Mom gave me a sympathetic smile. "We

couldn't lay you to rest together, sweetie. You and Andie. Not after everything. It would be hypocritical."

"What?" I gasped. "We're not dead! We're not dead!"

Her face clouded over. "I'm sick of this. You have to face up to your mistakes." She frowned. "What is that noise?"

What noise?

"Do you hear it?" She stood and stamped her foot. "This is a cemetery! What is with that incessant noise?"

"Mom?" I watched her stride away. "Mom?"

I stopped. I could hear it too now. I whirled around, looking for the source. Was that Bastille?

THIS IS THE RHYTHM OF THE NIGHT!

My eyes slammed open in the dark and I gasped for breath.

It took me a moment to come out of the dream and realize what had woken me up—the ringtone on my phone. Lunging across my bed, I whacked my hand off the corner of my bedside table before snatching the glowing phone. I squinted against the blur of sleep-fogged eyes and tensed at the caller ID.

Jake.

Why was Jake calling me at... *five in the morning?*

Too tired to fight, too unsettled to deal with whatever it was he was planning to throw at me after weeks of radio silence, I ignored his call and rolled back over.

Seconds after it stopped ringing, it started again.

Huffing, I grabbed it back up. This time it was Lowe.

Did Jake really think I was that stupid?

I slammed the phone down and closed my eyes.

It started ringing again.

"Jesus effing Christ," I hissed and snatched up the phone, ready to decline the call when I noticed the caller ID now said Denver.

Worry instantly shot through me. Denver never called.

"Hello," I answered, hastily sitting up and leaning over to switch on my lamp.

"Charley, it's me," Denver said quietly. "We're sorry to be calling so late, early, whatever, but we're looking for Beck."

Hearing the concern in his voice instantly quadrupled my own. Denver was pretty laid-back. If he was worried, then there was cause for worry. "I haven't spoken to Beck in weeks," I told him. "Not since Lowe's party. Neither has Claud."

"Are you sure? Charley... Beck's dad died. And now Beck's missing."

"Oh my God." I closed my eyes, feeling an ache deep in my chest.

From what I'd gathered from Claudia and Jake, Beck's mom and dad split along time ago. Beck lived with his mom and a stepdad he didn't get along with, and he visited his father whenever he could. His dad lived not far from where Jake's parents settled in Chicago. He was a musician who lived off the royalties of a couple of famous radio and TV jingles, but he was a raging alcoholic and not the best role model.

"We tried to call Claudia but she's not picking up."

"I'll check," I told him softly. "Just give me a second."

I put on my slippers and robe and hurried out of my room, down the hall to Claudia's. "Claudia," I knocked loudly.

The door opened a few seconds later and I was surprised to see her awake and so alert. My eyes drew past to her bed and I stilled at the sight of Beck lying sprawled out across it. He was fast asleep.

Claudia slipped out of the room, and followed me back to mine.

I picked up the phone before she could say anything. "He's here," I told Denver.

"Thank God."

I jerked, surprised to hear Jake's voice. "Jake…"

"I'm coming for him. Keep him there."

He hung up and I stared at the phone a second too long.

"That was Jake?" Claudia asked, her voice a little hoarse.

I nodded and slumped down on my bed. "When did Beck get here?"

She ran a shaky hand through her hair. "He turned up at the door about one. He was hammered and crying—" She choked on the word as she rubbed at her eyes. "Oh God, Charley. How do I handle this? He lost his dad and he needs me but—"

"There are no buts." I drew her in for a hug. "You'd hate yourself if you didn't give him the comfort he needs."

My friend clung to me. "I know you're right. But I'm scared. How selfish is that?"

"It's not selfish," I promised her. "It's natural. But Claud… the worst thing in the world just happened to him and you're the one person he sought out."

She processed this and I felt her arms tighten around me.

Although Claudia was skipping class, she insisted I go to mine. I decided not to argue with her because I thought it might be best if she spent the day alone with Beck. She'd managed to get the story out of him before he passed out in her arms the night before. His dad's death was completely unexpected—a heart attack.

What made it worse was that he'd been dead for almost twenty-four hours before a neighbor called police because his stereo was playing loudly through the night. Claudia said Beck was agonizing over the fact that if the music hadn't been playing, it could've been days before anyone found his dad.

He blamed himself for not visiting enough, for not trying to take better care of him.

Guilt. Blame. Those were things I was pretty familiar with lately, and I'd be there for him, no matter his connection to Jake or our history. Honestly, though, it was pretty clear by his presence in West Lafayette that Beck only wanted one person to see him through this.

Despite Claudia's misgivings, despite her resentment, I could see her concern for Beck overtaking everything. She found strength I didn't think I could've had to see the bigger picture... and just... be there for him.

I left her making him the homemade soup she'd finally perfected.

I had one class in the morning and I didn't register a word of it. Afterward, I hurried over to the library where I split my time working on my thesis and studying for the LSATs. My exam was only a week away but my mind wandered, and by the time I walked across campus to my law and society class, I'd processed about ten minutes of work in all.

Every five minutes I glanced at my phone in case Claudia texted but I heard nothing, so I sat through class, foot tapping impatiently, waiting for it to end. All I wanted was to hurry back to the apartment to check on my friends.

Finally, our professor dismissed us and I stuffed my notebook in my bag, preparing to run back to the apartment. However, Alex stopped me in my path.

He had attempted to hang out with me whenever he could. He asked constantly to tell him what was wrong, but I never confided in him. I knew he was frustrated but he kept at it, trying to be there for me even though I was a miserable asshat to be around.

Go figure.

"I called you this morning. You didn't call back," he said in greeting.

I winced apologetically. "Sorry. I'm not having a great day. I meant to call but…"

"Oh?" He held the door open and we walked outside into the cold November air. "I can help with a bad day."

"How?"

"Waffles and chocolate milk."

I laughed. "Not tequila?"

"Puhlease," Alex scoffed. "That shit is for pussies."

Chuckling, I nodded. "You're right, that helped."

"Charley!"

I blinked, jerking my gaze from Alex's affectionate one to across the lawn. Hurrying toward me from the sidewalk was Claudia and Jake. The breath whooshed out of me at the sight of him.

It was like I was a recovering addict and I'd just taken my first hit in years. The rush of feeling that flooded through me held me frozen.

"Charley!" Claudia yelled again, running up the stairs toward me. Her eyes flicked to Alex. "Hey, Alex. Sorry, I have to borrow her immediately." She grabbed my arm and hauled me down the steps toward Jake before Alex could even open his mouth to protest.

Her frantic behavior yanked me out of my Jake fog. "What's going on?"

Jake shoved a hand through his hair. It was really getting long now. "Beck's gone."

"Gone?" I gaped at Claudia. "How did that happen?"

She shook her head, her chest rising and falling in shallow breaths. "He was fine. I mean, not fine, but he had some soup and he was sobering up. He wasn't talking but he was sitting with me and I thought… anyway, he eventually said he needed some aspirin and we didn't have any so I ran out for some and when I got back, Jake was there and Beck was gone."

I rubbed her shoulder, trying to soothe her. "Take a breath. He can't have gotten far. In fact…"

"In fact what?" Jake asked impatiently.

I ignored his tone. "My bet? He's out somewhere getting hammered again. And since he's only been here once before, it would make sense that he'd try to find somewhere familiar."

Claudia threw her hands up in annoyance. "I'm so stupid. He's at The Brewhouse."

"I think it's worth checking out."

Some students were kicking around The Brewhouse but not a lot given that it was afternoon. The gorgeous, tragic-looking rocker certainly stuck out.

Beck sat on a barstool, head bowed, hand on his head, the other wrapped around a glass of scotch.

"He's hitting the hard stuff," I murmured.

"Wouldn't you?" Jake said.

"I'm not really into numbing my pain with self-medication."

"That's probably because you have a high pain threshold," he muttered dryly. "Some of us actually have feelings."

I blinked, feeling my cheeks heat with hurt and anger.

Claudia threw me a sympathetic look as Jake pushed past to get to Beck. I waved her off and she hurried after him. Trailing at the rear, I reached them as Beck told Jake to go fuck himself.

"Beck, you don't want to do this." Claudia pressed in on his other side, her arm sliding around him. I watched as his body instinctively moved into hers. "Drinking isn't going to help."

"Isn't it?" He shook his head and that ache in my chest hurt harder than before at the pain in his voice. "I was a shitty son. I wasn't there for him. I should've been there for him."

"Beck," Jake said, "he wasn't exactly father of the year. You can't blame yourself."

"Seriously?" Beck swung around to glare at him. "He's fucking dead, man."

This was getting us nowhere.

I gently nudged Jake out of my way. "Beck." I took hold of his glass and forcefully tugged it out of his grasp, scotch spilling over the sides. "I get it," I told him quietly. "It doesn't matter what anyone says, or the reasons why you didn't see your dad a lot. The facts are you didn't. The facts are he died and you never got a chance to fix everything between you." His eyes clung to mine, dazed and desperate. "I get it. The guilt. The blame. Believe me, I get it. You don't like yourself so much right now. You wonder if you ever will. Well, you don't know the answer to that, but I do know you're not going to find it in a glass." I leaned into him, clutching hold of his hand. "I can't promise you anything and I'm not going to give you platitudes—you've got to work out all those feelings yourself. But I can tell you that you've got three friends here who will do anything they can to help you get through this. *Anything* but watch you drink yourself under a table."

Our eyes seemed to hold for a long time, a deep understanding passing between us.

Finally, Beck nodded and made to stand up.

I felt Jake and Claudia relax a little. Claudia tucked herself into Beck's side so he could hold on to her. Jake paid Beck's tab, and we walked back to the apartment, shrouded in Beck's grief.

The mug of coffee felt soothingly warm between my hands. I curled my legs underneath me and stared out our balcony window, wishing I wasn't feeling the hush of grief fill every space in the apartment. It didn't seem so long ago I was suffocating under that feeling.

"He's sleeping," Jake said as he walked into the living room. I followed him with my eyes, somehow unable to look away after weeks of being deprived of him. "Claudia's staying with him."

I nodded, unsure what to say. An angry tension radiated off Jake and I knew I was partly to blame for that.

Jake yawned and collapsed into the nearest armchair.

The silence between us grew steadily harder to deal with.

"Listen—"

"His dad was from San Francisco," Jake cut me off, his voice brittle. "His favorite place was Baker Beach." He looked at me directly for the first time. "He wants the four of us to take his dad's ashes out there. A road trip."

I felt sick with nerves at the thought of going on a road trip with Jake.

As if he sensed my instant dislike of this plan, he smirked unhappily. "You were the one who promised him we'd do anything."

Did he think I'd break that promise just because I didn't want to be subjected to Jake's anger and my own longing? "I'll do this for him."

"So will I."

I looked away. A road trip with Jake.

Beautiful… just beautiful.

"What you said to him," Jake said, his tone a little softer, "is that what you're going through right now?"

I didn't know what was worse, his anger or the concern in his voice. More than anything I wanted to confide in Jake, and only Jake. Funny, how he was actually the last person that I *could* confide in.

"I'm hungry. I'll order pizza." I got up and walked past him, my face perfectly blank. "Pepperoni, right?"

Chapter Twelve

Barcelona, April 2013

Our hotel was in the center of Barcelona on Plaça de Catalunya. As promised, Claudia's mother had hooked us up with first-class plane tickets and the hotel was cool and modern with French windows that offered amazing views over the plaza and the city. I shared a room with Claudia while the guys shared a room next door.

We were all excited and ready to explore the city that night. Before we'd gotten on the plane, Claudia had asked me to sit with her so she didn't have to sit with Beck. I couldn't understand why she wanted him there if she planned to avoid him, but I was going with it for her sake. Beck *wasn't* going with it. He'd insisted on sitting with her and when I'd glanced across the aisle, I saw he was listening quietly to her as she talked about her parents. She was a wreck about meeting her real dad and no matter what her head was telling her, I knew her heart was telling her she needed Beck.

I guessed when it counted, he was there for her, which made it difficult to be mad at him for being a part-time ass.

Jake and I sat together, discussing all the places we wanted to visit—Le Sagrada Família, Park Güell, Mount Tibidabo, Barcelona

Cathedral, Casa Calvet, Gaudí House Museum…

There was so much to see, we knew we couldn't cram it all in. But we'd certainly try.

"Tomorrow's the big day." I smiled reassuringly at Claudia as I shimmied into my best skinny jeans for dinner that evening. The next day we were going to be taking Claudia to meet Dustin at his apartment. From the few emails they'd exchanged, Claud had discovered Dustin lived in an area of the city called El Raval. Apparently it was popular with artists and musicians and creative types. He'd given us his address, warning us that his "quirky" apartment building didn't have an elevator and he lived on the top floor.

Claudia seemed to ignore my comment as she zipped her dress.

"Claud?"

She smiled at me. "You and Jake are so good together. It's amazing to see you this happy. Has your dad spoken to you yet about possibly giving in?"

I frowned at the subject change. "We're in Barcelona… for you. I'd really rather talk about that."

"And I really rather wouldn't. I feel like I'm going to upchuck. I spent the whole time on the plane talking to Beck about meeting Dustin and now I just want to try to forget about tomorrow's life-changing moment and enjoy this beautiful city tonight with my good friends." Her chin jutted stubbornly, almost daring me to defy her.

"Fine. If that's what you want." I pulled on a light cardigan over my thin tee, not knowing how chilly it might get. "Things are still bad. And Andie and I still haven't spoken. We've never been this angry at each other or for so long." I rubbed a hand over my chest unconsciously, right over the spot where I ached every time I thought of the discord between my sister and me.

"And the cop thing?"

I grimaced. "We're still butting heads. I told them I'm not taking the LSATs."

"That's pretty much taking a stand." Claudia grinned. "I'm proud of you for going for what you want."

"It's like this huge weight off my shoulders, I can't even explain. I mean, can you imagine? In the end I would've made a terrible lawyer."

"Actually, I can imagine you as a litigator. It's all about championing someone. Or prosecuting a bad guy. That's you through and through. Why am *I* taking the LSATs again?"

I made a face. I had no idea why Claudia was taking the LSATs but that was a conversation for another time. "Being a lawyer is stuffy suits and papers, and I'm more of a polyester-uniform-and-action girl."

Claudia snorted. "Okay, true."

The knock at our hotel door made me grin. Claudia smirked. "What?" I asked as I strode toward the door.

"Nothing." She laughed lightly. "I've just never seen you like this."

"Like what?"

"All giddy and loved up. It's cute."

I know she said it to annoy me so I didn't give her the satisfaction. Instead I opened the door to reveal my gorgeous boyfriend and his sexy best friend, and I grinned, refusing to give up the giddy. "Hey, handsome."

"Hey, yourself." Beck flashed me a wicked smile before brushing past into the room. His low-lidded eyes swept over Claudia. "Lookin' good, babe. How you feeling?"

"Like I don't want to talk about my father tonight." She grabbed her purse and looped her arm through Beck's. "Let's just have fun."

Jake wrapped his arm around my waist, and I leaned into him as he gave me a smoldering look. "I can do fun."

"Mmm," I agreed, standing up on tiptoes to press a soft kiss to his lips.

"And of course we have to put up with these two," Claudia remarked behind us. "We may need vomit breaks."

"Oh yeah," Beck said dryly.

Jake and I ignored them.

"I can't believe we're in Spain and we're eating at the Hard Rock," Claudia said loudly over the music, making a face.

I laughed, not at all put out. Frankly, I was looking forward to my cheeseburger and fries.

We'd stepped out of the hotel and started walking east, only to discover the Hard Rock Café on the plaza.

Claudia had shaken her head at our pleading eyes. "No, I want to explore."

"We'll explore once we're fed." I'd grabbed her wrist and pulled her inside the café.

"Could we be any more American right now?" she said before taking a feisty bite out of an onion ring.

"I like it." I leaned back against the diner-style seat and Jake draped his arm across my shoulders. "I'm starting to get a little homesick."

"Me too," Beck said as he watched Claudia chew petulantly. It was so clear from the soft look on his face that he thought everything she did was adorable.

Stubborn ass.

"Well, only seven weeks until we're back home," Jake reminded us.

"And then we have all summer." I grinned. "I wonder what we could get up to."

"If I'm going on tour with these creeps," Claudia gestured to Beck, "you're coming too."

"Uh-uh, no way." And I meant it. "I'm spending time with my family and Jake this summer, not parading from state to state as a roadie. Close quarters with Matt? I don't think so."

Jake snorted. "I don't blame you."

Claud glowered at me. "But you said *I* should go."

"And so you should." I laughed at the horrified look on her face. "You'll have Beck and Lowe. And Denver's not entirely terrible."

"I don't think that makes up for close quarters with Matt."

Beck laughed. "She may have a point."

I chuckled at the way Claudia's eyes bugged out.

"All right, I'm definitely not going now." She pinched her lips tight and shook her head.

"I think you're all underestimating Matt," I said, trying not to laugh and ruin my defense of him. "I think underneath the frat-boy attitude is a nice, misunderstood young man with awkward social skills. Who knows, Claudia… maybe *the one* has been under your nose the whole time."

"Matt? *The one?* He once asked me if I was shaved."

"He did what?" Beck looked at her sharply, his tone not at all happy.

Jake and I exchanged a knowing look.

Claudia shifted uncomfortably under Beck's direct stare. "He was really drunk and being more of an idiot than usual. He did apologize later…" Her voice trailed off at the gathering thunderclouds in Beck's eyes.

He finally lifted his angry gaze to look at Jake across the table. "Can you believe that dick? What's the matter with him?"

"You know Matt," Jake treaded carefully. "He says shit without thinking."

"Yeah, well, I think he and I need to have a talk."

"Beck, don't." Claudia scowled at him. "It's no big deal. I shouldn't have mentioned it."

"He crossed the line."

"Yes, and he apologized," I reiterated for Claud. "And don't pretend you haven't done assholey things when you've been drunk."

Beck grunted.

It was time for a subject change. "I was just telling Claudia I told my parents that I'm not taking the LSATs." I glanced at Jake for his reaction.

His eyes lit up with affection. "Proud of you, baby."

"Did they hit the roof?" Beck asked.

"They're not happy, but I think they realize they're not going to win this one."

"Well, then…" Beck grinned and lifted his Coke in the air. "To Charley, our future sexy cop."

We raised our glasses, clinking as Claudia and Jake cheered, "To Charley."

We had a fun night even though we got a little lost, walking down one narrow cobblestone street and the next and somehow ending up on the one we'd started out on. Eventually, we ended up grabbing a cab and the driver in his broken English recommended a club called Moog. All wood, iron, and smoke, the place was packed. It wasn't really our scene, but Claudia wanted to dance her troubles away.

I danced with her while the guys skirted the edges of the room, beers in hand, but we were pretty soon pressed in upon by other guys and girls and before we knew it, Jake and Beck were on the dance floor with us, keeping the wolves at bay. They didn't dance, just kept their eyes on us and shooed off any guys who attempted to get near us. Claudia didn't seem to mind. In fact, I think she enjoyed tormenting Beck with the gorgeousness that was a dancing Claudia.

And Beck definitely looked tormented.

I'd feel sorry for him if it weren't self-inflicted.

We got back to the hotel pretty late, buzzed and full of energy. It was disappointing to be that buzzed and not be able to unravel it all with Jake in private, but I wanted to be there for my friend.

So we went into our separate rooms, and lying in bed, I talked with Claudia about everything and nothing until she fell asleep.

Collectively we'd kept her calm and taken her mind off meeting Dustin for as long as we could. But now, the morning after, as the four of us walked the twenty-minute journey to Dustin's apartment, Claudia was so quiet. Jake and I were more than competent with a map, so we got there without any wrong turns. But while Jake, Beck, and I soaked in the fact that we were in Barcelona, staring up at the apartments with their wrought iron balconies, on their quaint narrow streets, small boutiques beneath them, Claudia was too lost inside her own head to take notice.

As we stepped onto Dustin's street, I strode forward and grabbed Claud's hand. "We're right here with you," I reminded her.

Her breathing had grown shallow and by the time we walked up the cramped, dark stairwell to the top floor, she was completely out of breath.

I held her hand a little tighter as we stood outside the door. "Just breathe."

Her frightened eyes met mine and she nodded slowly, pulling air in through her nose and exhaling. Jake gave her shoulder a squeeze and Beck stepped close behind her, leaning down to press a kiss to her temple.

"You'll be fine," he murmured reassuringly.

Claudia stared at the door, a trembling smile on her lips. "Thanks, guys."

She knocked.

A few seconds later, the door swung open. Staring out at us was an attractive forty-something guy with a dark, graying beard and piercing green eyes. Claudia's eyes. He wore light slacks and a loose linen shirt rolled up at the sleeves. His feet were bare.

His eyes swept over us before coming to a stop on Claudia. He took a deep breath and gave her a soft smile. "Claudia?" he asked with an English accent.

Wide-eyed and more nervous than I'd ever seen my vibrant, confident friend, Claudia nodded. "Dustin?"

He swept an arm out gesturing us to enter as he stepped back from the door. "Please, come in."

We ushered her inside and Dustin came forward to give her an awkward hug. "You look so much like your mother."

"But I have your eyes."

"That you do." His smile was a little uncomfortable. He broke eye contact with her to stare at us. "And these are your friends?"

"Yeah. This is my best friend, Charley, and her boyfriend Jake, and this is my friend Beck."

"Well, nice to meet you all. You must all be such good friends to be here for Claudia today."

"We are." I nodded, sizing him up.

Even more uncomfortable under my scrutiny, Dustin laughed nervously and walked farther into his apartment.

He had the whole top floor to himself, the space like a loft apartment. Lots of light streamed in through the windows and I could see in the far corner was his studio. Whatever he was working on was covered up, but paint smattered the floor and walls. A kitchen ran half the length of the adjacent wall and in the center of the room was a massive corner sofa and coffee table.

My eyes stopped abruptly on the sofa.

There was a woman on it.

"Uh, I hope you don't mind, but I invited my girlfriend Pedra to join us," Dustin said, hurrying toward the woman. She stood up and eyed Claudia grimly. Pedra was younger than Dustin. A lot younger. Tall, olive-skinned, pretty, with dark eyes and hair, she looked like a model.

"I brought my friends, so I understand," Claudia said. She stepped forward, holding her hand out to Pedra. "It's nice to meet you."

Pedra looked at her hand and I thought for a minute she wasn't going to take it. She eventually did but her grip was loose and the action reluctant. "You have his eyes," she said, somehow managing to sound flat in her musical Spanish accent.

"Yup." Claudia threw me a look that clearly screamed, "Help!"

"Why don't we sit?" I stepped forward, gesturing to the sofa.

"Right, right, of course." Dustin watched us take a seat. "Can I get you all anything? I have water, herbal tea, and a few beers."

"I'll take a beer." Beck nodded congenially and I noticed Pedra's eyes swing to him and stick. Typical.

"I'll have a beer as well, thanks." Jake leaned back against the couch, his arm around my waist, resting on my hip. His grip tightened, telling me to relax, but I couldn't.

This situation was too important.

"Water, please," I said.

"Me too." Claudia gave a long, shaky sigh that Dustin didn't even seem to notice. I was guessing he was too nervous.

When we were finally settled with our drinks, the conversation continued to be stilted and awkward. However, slowly, as smiles became less tremulous and laughter less forced, Claudia and Dustin touched on more serious issues—such as her parentage and the fact that her parents had asked Dustin to stay away.

Pedra sat tense throughout the entire thing, her lips pinched into a sour, disapproving look. I wondered if it was because she didn't want to give up the spotlight to a daughter.

It was clear that despite both needing people there for backup, neither Claudia nor Dustin were comfortable discussing the whole situation with us in the room. We talked about college instead and Dustin told us about his artwork and his upcoming show. It was clear that art was his life, his passion; it totally consumed him, turning him from this nervous guy into a pretty intense one. He insisted we should go to Plaça St. Josep Oriol, a square in the Gothic Quarter not far from our hotel where we could view amazing artwork from some of the best local artists.

After a few hours, Claudia said quietly, "Well, I know you're busy so we'll go, but I thought maybe we could have dinner, just the two of us, while I'm here."

"Of course." His seemed genuinely happy and I felt a spark of hope for Claudia. "I'd love that. Tomorrow? I'll make reservations at

El Pintor and email you the details."

"I have my phone. Do you want my number instead?"

"Yes. Let me..." He stood, looking around the space with a furrow between his brows. "Let me just find my phone..."

"I saw it on the bathroom sink," Pedra muttered, scowling at Claudia.

Usually Claudia would scowl back but I knew she was playing nice, so I scowled for her. As if sensing my stare, Pedra looked at me, and whatever she saw on my face made her look quickly away.

I probably looked murderous. It was the momma bear in me.

Dustin returned with his phone and took Claudia's number, promising to text her soon with the details of their date. He gave her another awkward hug and we left.

As soon as we stepped outside the building, Claudia sagged into Beck's side and he wrapped his arm around her waist. "You okay?" he asked, concerned.

She shrugged. "It wasn't so bad, right? He seems nice?"

"He seems really nice," Jake assured her.

"Dinner will be better." I smiled. "Just the two of you. It'll be less uncomfortable without listening ears and Bitter Pill Pedra."

Claud laughed shakily. "Yeah, what was that?"

"Ignore her. You didn't come here for her. You came for Dustin and he seems really happy to meet you."

She grinned, finally relaxing. "He did, didn't he? Ahh," she exhaled. "Let's go explore and get something to eat. I'm starving."

The guys knocked on our door half an hour ago to tell us they were ready to face the day, but Claudia and I had just woken up. We promised to meet them for breakfast at a café across the plaza and then rushed around the hotel room to get ready.

As we did so, Claudia chatted about Dustin.

Something niggled at me about how well things were going for her with her real father. Perhaps it was the cynic in me, or maybe I was terrified of my friend getting her heart broken, but it took everything within me to not warn her to be careful. I didn't want to ruin this for her.

We dressed in shorts and tank tops since we'd woken up to a particularly hot day and headed along the plaza to meet Jake and Beck.

"So, Dustin says he wants to paint me." Claudia smiled. Though her eyes were covered with oversized sunglasses, I could hear excitement in her voice.

"Would you do that?"

"Sit for him? Yeah. He wants to do a portrait."

"Well, you're beautiful and he's an artist, of course he does."

"Yeah, but also, I'm his daughter," she added, a little indignantly.

"Of course. I just meant… of course he'd want to draw you, daughter or not."

She grimaced. "I think he might have painted my mother nude. I asked if he painted her and he got all shifty and uncomfortable."

I laughed. "Oh, he definitely painted her nude."

Claud shuddered. "My mother. The disloyal muse."

We crossed the plaza toward the café. "Have you spoken to your mom since you got here?"

"No," she snorted. "My parents are pretending this isn't happening."

Typical.

"Well, my folks emailed last night asking about you. They hope everything's going great with Dustin and said that they love you."

"I adore your parents. Do you think *they* would adopt me?"

I would've answered but I was too busy staring across the street at the café. Sitting at a table on the sidewalk was my boyfriend and Beck. They weren't alone. Two girls were sitting in my and Claudia's seats and Jake and Beck were laughing.

Something unpleasant pinched my chest.

I felt a nudge at my shoulder and turned to look at Claudia.

She lifted her sunglasses off to meet my eyes. "Hey. You okay?"

I sighed, glancing back at the flirting girls and our flirting idiot male counterparts. "Jake and I are in a great place, but I thought the whole jealousy thing was behind me. But I see that girl, laughing into his face, and he's not doing much to put her off and I want to kill him. He was like this in high school." I wrinkled in my nose in annoyance. "And he used to accuse *me* of being a flirt."

"You are a flirt."

I frowned. "I am not."

"Oh, please. You can't even help it."

"Well, what about you?" I waved a hand in the direction of the café. "Doesn't it bother you anymore to see Beck flirt?"

It was Claudia's turn to scowl. "We're friends. And girls flirt with him. If we were anything more than friends, I'd have to get used to that fact. Just like you have to get used to the fact that your boyfriend is hot and I hate to say it, babe, but since you two got back together, there's this light around him... it's totally attractive." She patted me on the shoulder. "I guess you've only got yourself to blame for the hot señorita flirting with him right now."

I groaned. "Okay. So how should we play this? Cool, unaffected... or pissed off?"

"Let's be grown-ups and play it cool and unaffected. You know Jake's gone for you. You don't need to be jealous. Ever."

I shoved the horrible feeling away and let rationale take over. "You're right," I agreed, studying her carefully. "When did you get all wise and mature?"

Claudia tilted her chin up in thought. "Hmm… I think it's a fairly recent development."

"I like it."

"We'll see how long it lasts."

Laughing at her, I followed as she crossed the street toward the café. Jake caught sight of us and when our eyes met, I felt our connection zing through me as always. I raised an eyebrow, nodding my head toward the girl next to him, but I wore a smile so he'd know I wasn't mad. *Anymore.*

He shrugged and then tapped Beck on the arm. Beck looked over, his eyes instantly moving to Claudia. He straightened in his chair. Jake turned to the girls and said something. Whatever it was, it had them looking over at us walking toward them. The girls gave us curious looks but got out of our seats, waving flirty goodbyes to our boys.

A few seconds later, we rounded the table and as soon as my ass was in the chair, Jake wrapped his hand around my neck and pulled me in for a slow, sweet kiss. I smiled softly as I pulled back. "Good morning to you too."

"Soooo…" Claudia drawled, relaxing back in her chair. "This is what you guys do with your time when we're not around. Flirt with gorgeous Spanish girls? It's a little unfair. If we'd known, we would've taken up with those two hot guys on mopeds who asked us if we wanted a private tour of the city."

I looked at her with both eyebrows raised.

She smirked. "Guess it didn't last long," she said, referring to her wisdom and maturity.

I laughed, shaking my head. When I looked at Jake, he had an annoyed furrow between his brows. "Guys? Mopeds?"

I shoved him playfully. "Claudia's lying."

I thought his expression would clear but now Jake looked worried. "The girls just came over. We didn't invite them to sit."

"You are so whipped," Beck muttered, reaching for a glass of cold orange juice.

Unamused, I glared at him. "Jake's dating me. I'm freaking awesome. I love him and he's getting it regularly and *it is mind-blowing*. Even if he *is* whipped, he's sitting a lot prettier than you right now."

Jake and Claudia burst out laughing and Beck smirked, his eyes filled with mirth as they met Jake's. Jake pulled my chair closer and I turned to find his face inches from mine. His eyes danced happily. "You're wrong. You're not freaking awesome. You're freaking phenomenal." He brushed his nose alongside mine. "About that getting-it-regularly thing," he whispered against my mouth, "I miss you."

I missed him too. We hadn't slept together since we'd gotten to Barcelona. Three nights might not sound like a lot but they were a lot after having slept with each other every single night in the past few weeks.

"You know what I'm thinking," Claudia said loudly, bringing our attention back to her. She was smiling at Beck. "I'm thinking you and I should spend the day together. Leave these two to be all icky and in love. I could do with a breather. It's nauseating."

I knew she was teasing but that sounded like an amazing idea.

Beck grinned back at her. "You're on."

"I'm good with that," Jake murmured in my ear.

A shiver rippled down my spine and I felt my body respond to the promise in his voice.

Suffice it to say, we shoveled down a light breakfast with Claudia and Beck and said a hasty goodbye. Jake practically dragged me by the hand all the way back to the hotel. When the elevator doors shut, he was on me, pressing me against the wall, kissing me voraciously, like he couldn't get enough.

I panted as he hurried out of the elevator and along the corridor to my room. We got the door clicked open and shut and Jake yanked off my tank top and quickly pulled his own shirt off. I unbuttoned my shorts and shimmied out of them as Jake divested his jeans and then I was in his arms again, sprawling over him as he took us to the nearest bed.

Jake groaned as my searching hands found him hot and hard. He kissed me as I touched him, sliding his hands around to unclip my bra. He pulled back as it fell away from my chest and he whispered, smirking, "We have such good friends."

I laughed in agreement, the sound soon swallowed up in his hot, deep kiss.

"I told you, I'm not going." I shook my head stubbornly and stared at the posters and street art lining the sidewalk.

Jake laughed. "It's not in use. They don't do that anymore."

"I'm not going to La Monumental and that's that." I shot him a warning look and he gave a huff of incredulous laughter but shut up.

It was day five. Claudia had left us an hour ago to go see Dustin again and Beck had decided to give Jake and I some alone time.

Honestly, I think he was just sick of our honeymoon phase. While Beck was happily wandering the streets of Barcelona by himself—or not by himself, as I knew how easy it was for him to pick up random girls on his travels—Jake and I wandered the streets of Barcelona in the opposite direction.

We'd wandered about half an hour northeast of the hotel and were closing in on the famous bullring, La Monumental. Jake was right. The bullring hadn't been used as such since 2011 after Catalonia banned bullfighting, but still, I hated the idea of it all and wasn't interested in seeing the place.

"You are so obstinate," Jake said, throwing me a small smile so I'd know he wasn't irritated.

"You bet your ass I am." I flashed him a cheeky grin. "Good luck with that, by the way."

"You're lucky I like my women stubborn."

"Your women?" I snorted. "Am I part of your harem?"

He pulled a face. "What? You thought you were the only one who appreciates all my fineness?"

"Are you taking lessons from Matt on how to talk to women now?" I chuckled, taking a hold of his hand to move him away from the touristy stuff for sale on the sidewalks.

"I think his technique is flawless," Jake replied deadpan. "Every day my man crush grows stronger."

Remembering Beck's reaction to Matt's "technique" with Claudia, I winced. "I think he might be in trouble with Beck when we get back to Edinburgh. That guy is… I have no words. He's so overprotective and possessive. Such an oblivious tool."

Jake cleared his throat. "Actually…"

I stopped in the middle of the street, tugging on his hand so he'd stop avoiding eye contact. "Actually?"

He shrugged. "Nothing. I just… I think Beck is more aware of how he feels for Claudia than you realize. He's got his demons. But he cares about her and I think he's maybe coming around."

My eyes narrowed. "Do you know something, Jacob Caplin?"

"Charley, I love you, but there are some things I can't tell you."

Nosy and curious and desperate to give my friend what she wanted, it didn't sit well with me that Jake may be holding the answers and the key to Claudia's future happiness. However, I understood. "Girl code," I grumbled, "but for boys."

"Exactly."

"Ah, I get it." I snuggled into his side. "Maybe, just in case, though, we should set them up for dinner alone tonight? I know Claudia had a fantastic day with him yesterday."

"Why don't we just let them sort themselves out? They did that favor for us."

I frowned. "Stop being right. It's throwing me off balance."

He laughed, pulling me close, and we walked back to the hotel in perfect contentment.

We were waiting for the elevator when I caught sight of a familiar figure out of the corner of my eye. I turned to see Claudia striding into reception and my breath was knocked out of me by her appearance.

Her eyes were bloodshot. She had no color in her cheeks. Worse… There was something so desolate in her expression that I felt panicked. "Claudia!" I called out, my voice trembling.

She glanced over at me in surprise, her feet abruptly stopping their momentum.

And then suddenly, she rushed toward me, her face crumpling as she impacted with me. I wrapped my arms around her as she sobbed into my neck. My arms tightened as I looked over her head at Jake.

We exchanged worried looks and a silent message that we needed to get Claudia somewhere private.

I got her into the elevator, Jake shadowing us protectively. I tried to ask what was wrong but she just kept crying these deep, shuddering, heartbreaking sobs.

Jake let us into our room and I settled her on a chair, crouching in front of her.

"Claudia, please talk to me," I begged.

She hiccupped as she tried to control the tears. I waited patiently for her to pull herself together enough to look at me. Jake handed her tissues and she blotted at her face, fingers shaking.

"Dustin…" her voice cracked, "after being so cool and excited about us… he told me today he can't do it." Her tears fell silently now. "He doesn't want the responsibility of being a dad and he thinks anything else is just confusing. He thinks it's best we don't see each other again."

SON OF A BITCH!

Fury shot into my blood and it took a huge amount of self-control not to march out of that room and go and hunt down the weak piece of shit.

Another man. Another parent… rejecting her. I hated them so much for doing this to her.

"Claud," I whispered, reaching for her hand, "I am so sorry."

She shook her head. "Don't be. I should've known. I got my hopes up and I should have known." She started crying again and I reached forward, pulling her into my arms.

"Ssh," I attempted to soothe her. "It's okay. It's going to be okay. We love you, babe. You don't need them."

Her arms tightened around me. "I don't want to be here anymore," she sobbed.

Jake's expression looked as murderous as I was sure mine was. He stepped forward and I read his body language. I gently eased Claudia out of my arms and Jake took my place. Claudia clung even harder to him, soaking his T-shirt with her tears.

He stroked her hair in comfort. "We'll get you out of here," he promised.

Chapter Thirteen

Iowa, November 2013

My parents were surprisingly okay with my announcement that I'd be missing out a few days of school to drive across six states with Jake, Beck, and Claudia. It helped that the LSATs had passed. I wasn't sure how it went. One minute I was sure I'd done okay, the next I was filled with doubt.

That was kind of a theme for my life right now.

Anyway, I'd have accompanied Beck on this quest to find peace over his father's death even if my mom and dad had been against it. A promise was a promise and my friend needed me. My parents... they actually understood, however, and even if they had reservations over Jake's presence, they didn't bring it up.

That's how, almost two weeks after Beck arrived on our doorstep, I found myself in Jake's dad's borrowed SUV with the aforementioned. I was nervous. Beyond nervous, especially after Jake's cold attitude toward me last time I'd seen him. However, I was determined to mask my nerves with cool silence and the occasional smart-ass remark.

Claudia and I had gotten the shuttle from Purdue to O'Hare and

Jake had picked us up from there. Beck had gotten out and helped us with our bags and then promptly sat in the back with Claudia, leaving me to haul my ass up into the passenger seat beside Jake.

Awkward didn't even cover it. I said hello and was surprised to get a perfectly nice greeting back. However, silence fell almost immediately between us. Claudia and Beck spoke quietly in the back and every time I looked in the rearview mirror, they were sitting close, heads together. Beck seemed better than he had before. Claudia had been chatting to him almost every day and now that he had focus, something to do, he was coping with his father's death better than any of us could've expected.

It helped that Claudia was in his life now. I knew it did.

I had to wonder about that—about Claudia's intentions. It was such a delicate subject I hadn't wanted to bring it up in case we started arguing about it. Yet, I was curious to know what their behavior with one another meant. Had Claudia decided to give him a shot?

I mused over this in silence as Jake drove us down the I-80W. We'd driven through Illinois. Much of the snow that had fallen a few days ago had been cleared and was disappearing, so we made good time. We'd been driving for about three hours when we hit Davenport, Iowa.

"Pee break?" Jake asked.

"Yes, please," Claudia said. "I didn't want to be a total girl and ask but my bladder has been ready to burst for the last half hour."

I glanced back at her. "That's because you drank almost two bottles of water."

"It's warm in here." She shrugged.

I eyed Beck and the fact that his left side was glued to her right. Of course she was warm back there.

"I was thinking we could stop for something to eat in Des Moines and then stop somewhere near Lincoln for a motel," Jake suggested.

I nodded. "You're driving so you should decide. That's a while to be behind the wheel."

He shrugged now. "About eight and a half, nine hours in total."

"We can stop before then."

"Well, we left Chicago at eight o'clock. It's just coming up for eleven now. We'll get to Des Moines about one thirty. Break for an hour. We should get to Lincoln by five. I'm cool with that."

"Sounds like a plan," Beck agreed.

I was concerned Jake was going to be exhausted constantly on this trip. "I can take over driving if you want."

He surprised me by shooting me a small smile before turning his attention back to the road. Where had the moody, snappy version of Jake gone? "No worries. Beck's on my dad's insurance. He and I will alternate days."

Jake pulled over at a gas station in Davenport and we got out to see to our needs. Afterwards, as Claudia and I were washing our hands in perhaps the world's nicest gas station bathroom, she said, "You need to start talking to Jake or this road trip is going to be beyond awkward."

I grinned at her. "I thought you were too busy cozying up with Beck to notice what was going on in the front seat."

She made a face. "No. You and Jake are acting like there's a plate of soundproof glass between you. I was hoping you could at least try to get along."

"We've been perfectly pleasant with one another. We're not going to whisper in each other's ears and brush one another's hands and press up against each other like you and Beck—all of which is questionable behavior and note that I am keeping my nose out of it."

Claudia snorted. "That's you keeping your nose out of it?"

I rounded my eyes in mock innocence. "What? I didn't ask one question about you and Beck and whether this means you're going to start seeing each other…"

Her answer was to punch me in the arm like a five-year-old and prance out on a huff. I think I struck a nerve.

Smirking, I followed her out and into the gas station where we bought some snacks to tide us over until we hit Des Moines.

Keeping Claudia's comment in mind, I attempted to make small talk with my ex-boyfriend as we got the show back on the road.

"It was good of your dad to let you borrow his car."

"It's safer than most vehicles we could've afforded to rent. Dad's borrowing mom's while we've got this."

I opened a bag of potato chips and offered them to him. He took some, eating one-handed. "How are they? Your family?"

He finished munching and shot me a quizzical look. "They're fine but isn't that the question I should be asking you?"

"I believe you've already asked that question."

"I did. Two months ago."

I shot him a droll look. "Let's just say not much has changed."

"I wouldn't know. You never told me how things were to begin with."

I sighed. Apparently Jake and I couldn't do small talk. Hoping a little music might quell the tense silence, I reached over to turn on the radio. Unfortunately, Jake had the exact same idea. Our fingers brushed and a frisson of electricity sparked between us. We snapped our arms back at the contact, and I hurriedly glanced out the window, willing the heat coursing through me to cool.

Just like that, my whole body was aware of him. I was aware of every time his hands shifted on the wheel, every little sound he made, or when he'd look into the rearview mirror to answer a question from Claudia or Beck. That awareness had me stealing glances at him. Little glances, little stolen snapshots of his enviously long eyelashes, of the two little freckles on his left earlobe, of his large, masculine hands, of the slightly fuller lower lip that had fascinated me since we were sixteen…

I was flooded by memories.

Those memories hurt all over.

Clenching my hands into fists in case they reached out to involuntarily touch him, I tried to remember a time when Jake wasn't a part of me, but the memories of when he was were just too overwhelming.

They won and I lost. But I'd gotten really good at pretending that wasn't true.

There were no words to describe how happy I was to get out of the car when we reached Des Moines. Beck was in the mood for lunch at IHOP, so Jake used his dad's GPS to find us the nearest one. It took us off our main route, but as soon as Beck mentioned it, I couldn't stop picturing pancakes, waffles, scrambled egg, bacon, and maple syrup.

But mostly, I was just glad to be leaving the world of awkward silence, stifling tension, and unspoken words.

The four of us slid into a booth and, after we ordered, I remembered the last time the four of us dined out on a trip together.

Things had been so different back then. Hard to believe it was only a little over seven months ago.

"Okay, let's play a game." Claudia grinned at Beck and Jake across the table. I noted the mischievous twinkle in her green eyes.

"Do we have to?" I asked.

"Yes, Grumpy Betsy, we do."

I snorted. "Grumpy Betsy?"

Claudia waved off my teasing. "Never mind. Anyway, Beck and I play this game all the time."

"Maybe IHOP isn't an appropriate place for a game you and Beck play," Jake offered slyly.

I laughed because he'd beaten me to it.

Our eyes met, his smiling into mine like he knew exactly what I was thinking.

"Get your minds out of the gutter," Claudia scolded. "It's not like that. The game is you choose a couple, or two friends or whatever, who are eating out together and you have a conversation for them. We'll show you." She glanced around the room and then surreptitiously pointed. "There." She gestured to a young couple who sat with their elbows on the table, leaning a little across the distance so they could speak in lowered voices. "Beck."

He looked at the couple and smiled. "Baby, you smell better than apple pie and taste better than maple syrup."

I groaned but grinned.

Claudia gave an exaggerated sigh of happiness as the girl tilted her head to the side, causing her hair to fall away from her neck. "It's my new perfume. It's called Eau de IHOP."

We laughed and Claudia nudged me. "Your turn. You and Jake."

And that's when I understood her plan with this stupid game. "I don't know."

"Ah, c'mon, it'll pass the time," Jake encouraged. He pointed across the restaurant to an elderly couple. Although it was cold outside, it wasn't freezing, but both were wearing layer upon layer. The woman, wearing an ugly multicolored hat, was eating quietly, while her husband ate and tried to read the newspaper. His face was bent low over the paper as he chewed.

The woman looked at him over her spectacles and started to speak.

I smiled. "Could you get any closer to that paper? Are there naked women in it or something?" I filled in for her.

As the man replied, Jake said, "If there were, I wouldn't know it. Last time I saw a naked woman, I'd just helped oust the Nazis from Holland."

I could hear Claudia and Beck laughing but I managed to stay in the game as the woman apparently snapped something at her partner. "Don't remind me. I had to get a cream for the itch you brought back."

The older man peered up from his newspaper and Jake said in his stead, "I'd treasure that memory. It's the most daring thing that ever happened to you."

I choked on a chuckle and replied as the woman tapped a hand on the newspaper. "That's it. You better start looking in the classifieds for your own place."

The man didn't say anything, but he took a bite of omelet as he looked at the woman. He started to speak and Jake answered with, "I think you'll find it's my name on the deed to the house."

The woman leaned over the table to him and I said, "If I left, you wouldn't know what hit you. Do you think just anybody would wash out your skid marks and deal with the glasses of false teeth you leave lying around?"

"Ugh," Claudia giggled.

"Me? You think I'm hard to live with?" Jake replied. "What about all those ceramic owls you got lying around the whole house? I can't move an inch without walking into a damn ceramic owl. And don't get me started on the pot pourri."

I shot a look at Jake and mouthed, "Pot pourri?"

He grinned.

Looking back at the couple, I watched as the woman dug into her breakfast but continued to speak to the man. "If I didn't have pot pourri everywhere, the house would smell of cigars and feet."

"Don't start in on me about my cigars, woman," Jake snapped as the man waved his fork at his wife. It really did look like they were arguing about something. "My cigars mask the smell of that damn pot pourri and chicken. Don't you know how to cook anything else?"

"How about arsenic and apple pie?" I answered in mock anger.

The two didn't say anything for a few seconds and then the man patted his wife's hand and she gave him a small smile.

"I can deal with the pot pourri and chicken if you can deal with my cigars and teeth," Jake said quietly.

As the woman nodded and replied, I said, "Sure. And tonight... I'll let you leave the light on."

"Aw, sweetheart, that's real nice of you but I think we'd both get on better with the light off."

Our eyes met at that, Jake's twinkling with laughter, and I found myself giving into that laughter, feeling it for the first time in as long as I could remember. By the time the food arrived, the tension between us had eased and we dug into our food, our foursome joking and chatting about meaningless things and enjoying the peace of the momentary distraction from all the *meaningful* things.

I tried not to meet Claudia's smug, satisfied gaze.

The drive from Des Moines to Lincoln, Nebraska, was about three hours, give or take. The light chitchat from the restaurant carried over and the hours seemed to pass faster now that Jake and I could talk without stumbling over the big stuff.

We found a cheap motel in Lincoln just off the I-80. We got two rooms and Jake said he was taking a nap before dinner. Claudia and I had just dumped our things in the room when she turned to me.

"I'd like some time alone with Beck. Will you be okay on your own?"

I studied her a moment, trying to understand what was going on. Finally, I said, "Of course I'll be fine. But I've got to ask—"

"I don't know," she cut me off abruptly, throwing her hands up in the air. Her beautiful eyes shimmered with emotion. "I really don't know. All I know is that I'm the one person who can lift Beck's mood. I'm the one person he can talk to about anything… and these last few weeks…" Her expression seemed to plead with me. "Charley, he's letting me in. For the first time I really feel like he's letting me all the way in. And life's too short, right? We both know that."

It wasn't that I wasn't happy for her. I truly believed she and Beck were meant for one another. But I also believed that there was a time for everything and I wanted to make sure she was doing this for the right reasons, and that she was ready for it. "And everything from before… the reason you decided to walk away from him for good. You've worked all that out?"

Claudia blew air out between her lips, looking a little lost. "If I'm honest, no. But I'm starting to wonder if I go on the way I am, I'll always find an excuse not to trust someone. If I don't see where this is leading, if I don't try, I'll regret it."

"And Will?" I said, reminding her of the TA.

She looked a little ashamed as she said, "I broke that off a few days after Beck's dad passed."

I raised an eyebrow. "You kept that quiet."

"I knew if I told you, you'd make assumptions about what's going on between me and Beck."

"Assumptions that would turn out to be right."

"Charley, you wanted me to see Beck in this light for a long time. I need you to support me in whatever happens here."

"I do." I pulled her in for a hug. "I always will. But Beck is going through this huge emotional upset right now and I just don't want you to get chewed up in it."

Claudia held me tight. "He wanted to try something serious with me before his dad died, remember?"

"Yes. It's the only thing stopping me from grabbing your hand and running a million miles away from him while he's going through what he's going through." I stepped back and gave her a small smile. "I'm here no matter what. Why don't I go check out the bar while you guys talk?"

She smiled gratefully. "You wouldn't mind?"

"Not at all."

I left my friend to it and made my way across the lot to the on-site restaurant and bar, my mind on Claudia and Beck. I did want it to work out for them, but that didn't mean I wasn't terrified for Claudia. She'd been disappointed by so many people who were supposed to love her. I didn't know if she could take any more disappointment, and I was only ninety percent sure that Beck would remember everything she'd gone through and treat her carefully while he dealt with his own demons.

Totally lost in thought, I'd only taken two steps inside the almost empty bar when my feet faltered. A blond woman sat in profile at the bar.

"Andie?" I whispered in disbelief.

My heart slammed so hard I thought it was going to launch itself out of my chest. Sweat slickened my palms as my body froze to the spot.

Then just like that, the blond turned to smile at the bartender.

It wasn't Andie.

Of course it wasn't.

How could it be?

Tears pricked my eyes and I stubbornly shoved them back as I marched up to the bar and slid into a stool.

"I'm going to need to see some ID." The middle-aged bartender smiled kindly at me. He was tall, broad-shouldered, and he looked like he could handle himself. He also looked like he wasn't born yesterday. Thank God I was twenty-one now.

I gave him my ID and he slid it back to me. "What can I get you?"

I glanced down the bar at the woman I'd mistaken for my sister. "I'll have a scotch on the rocks."

He seemed bemused by my choice but didn't question it. "Any brand in particular?"

"Surprise me," I muttered.

He grinned and set about making my drink.

After a half hour of nursing it, the bartender approached. Sensing him hovering, I looked up.

He shrugged. "Sorry, I've got to ask."

"Ask what?" I sipped at the last of my drink.

"Why a pretty twenty-one-year-old is drinking scotch in my bar while looking like the world just ended."

I stared at this curious stranger, this person who had no ties to me, no previous dealings with me, and thus no understanding or expectations of me, either. And I found myself replying, "I miss my sister."

His eyes softened and he leaned on the bar. "That's rough."

"Have you got family?"

"Two brothers in Colorado. They got wives and a whole bunch of kids. I don't see them much."

"Do you miss them?"

"Sure, I do."

"You should really visit them while you can," I offered sagely.

His grin was sad. "We had a falling-out a couple of years back. Things haven't been the same since."

Emotion clogged my throat. I took my time choking it down. "You'd think that would be all the more reason, but sometimes it's like you get frozen, like you can't move or make a decision either way. Is that how you feel?"

He nodded, eyes filled with understanding. "Yeah, that's how I feel."

"Do you think you'll ever get past it?"

"I expect I might. One day."

"What do you think will make you do it? Make you go see them?" I desperately wanted to know.

"I don't know." He stood up, contemplating me. "Maybe a sad, pretty girl telling me I should do it while I still can might do the trick."

I finished my drink and offered him a wry, melancholic smile. "Maybe."

Chapter Fourteen

Edinburgh, April 2013

After Claudia had broken down over Dustin's callous rejection, Jake called Beck to let him know what had occurred and he'd hurried back to the hotel.

Something happened, though. When Beck got there, he tried to hug Claudia but she didn't embrace him in return and wriggled out of his hold like she didn't want him to touch her. He attempted to talk to her, but she cut him off, barely acknowledging his presence while they booked tickets out of Barcelona.

The entire way to the airport, Claud gave Beck the coldest shoulder, even snapping at him when he tried to help with her luggage. She'd been adamant that I sit next to her on the plane.

Beck was stunned and clearly hurt.

I gave it twenty minutes before I plucked up the nerve to ask. "What was that all about?"

"What?" she asked flatly.

"Beck."

Claudia shot me a sharp look. "I'm done, Charley. I'm done being made a fool of by men who pretend to care. Dustin doesn't want me in his life, fine. Guess what? I don't want Beck in mine. I've spent the last six months trying to convince myself that he didn't break my heart. But he did. He hurts me all the time and doesn't even care. He's selfish and cruel and I hate him."

I knew my friend, and I knew that what she'd said wasn't her. I was convinced she was projecting what she felt about Dustin onto Beck. "You don't mean that."

The coldness in her eyes shocked me. "Yes. I do."

"Claudia…" I reached for her hand. "What exactly did Dustin say?"

Pain etched itself into her features. "When I got to his apartment, I knew something wasn't right. He was nervous and jumpy and wouldn't meet my gaze. Then Pedra showed up."

Renewed anger flooded me. "He said it in front of her?"

She nodded unhappily. "He told me we needed to talk and I sat down across from them and he told me that his life is his art and that he didn't have time for distractions. He said he'd never had to be responsible for anyone other than himself and at almost fifty years old, he knew it was too late to change that. And then he said that he thought I was a lovely young woman, but he'd rather not keep in contact because he felt it would be too confusing for both of us."

"He's a dick," I said.

Claudia looked at me with a renewal of unshed tears in her eyes. "Why was he so excited and cool to begin with, Charley? He made plans with me for the future and then he just… why did he do that? I wish he'd never emailed me back. It would've hurt less. It's like… he got to know me and decided he wanted nothing to do with me."

"No." I grasped her hand tighter in mine. "No, that's not why." I leaned closer so I had all her focus. "Dustin Tweedie is a mercurial, selfish, self-absorbed artist, Claudia. You were something new to play with for a while, like a new muse… and it suddenly occurred to him that you weren't just any muse. You were a person who would demand more from him… and unfortunately, I get the feeling he's limited. He didn't have anything more to give you. And that's about *him*. Not *you*."

The tears slipped silently down her cheeks as she nodded. "I love you," she whispered.

I leaned my forehead against hers, fighting my own tears. "I love you too. You're my family."

After a while, Claudia settled her head on my shoulder and the emotional exhaustion of the day pulled her into unconsciousness.

I'd known as I sat there beside her that I would have to work hard over the coming weeks to remind her that she had family, a family she'd made. I didn't want to lose Claudia to bitterness and rejection.

I wouldn't let that happen.

When we landed, unfortunately, Claudia wasn't lying when she said she was done with Beck. Her attitude toward him didn't sway from ice queen, and a dejected Beck was silent all the way back to our apartments.

Once we got out of the cabs, Jake helped Claudia up the stairs with our luggage and Beck held me back a minute. He had a panicked look in his eyes that unsettled me. "I fucked up, waiting around too long. She's pissed off at the men in her life and I happen to be one of them." He pleaded with me with his eyes. "She'll come around, though, right?" he asked softly.

"Right." I nodded, hoping my reassurances meant something. "She just needs time."

He looked up at the apartment. "Maybe she shouldn't be alone tonight. You know, she'll just dwell. Bring her to Milk. Everyone will be there."

"I don't know."

"Try."

"Okay," I agreed and patted him on the shoulder, pretty sure Claudia and I weren't going anywhere tonight.

I was only half right. Although Claudia stubbornly refused to remove herself from her bed, she practically screamed at me to go out. I finally cottoned on that she genuinely wanted to be left alone and I ventured out to Milk.

I felt bad leaving her behind, but I knew that if I were in her shoes, I'd probably want to be left alone too. Eventually as the days wore on, Claudia rejoined the world of the living. Jake and I spent a lot of time cajoling her into hanging out with us—even if it meant dodging the studying we were supposed to be doing for our upcoming exams and instead taking day trips to Glasgow or St. Andrews.

And then we convinced her to come hang out with everyone the night before the first of our exams.

"All right." Denver turned to Rowena with a cocky smile. "What, or should I say whom, are you going to miss most?"

Music played softly in the background of the restaurant on Nicholson Street. We gathered around a large corner table, chatting and drinking after a great meal. Merriment mingled with melancholy. We seemed to have collectively agreed that this might be one of the last nights we all hung out together.

Rowena pretended to muse over the question.

"Oh, come on." Matt winked at her. "We all know the answer, and it's in my lap."

"Whit?" Rowena raised an eyebrow at him. "Chlamydia?"

We laughed and Matt heaved an exasperated sigh, his eyes begging us not to mock him tonight.

"You walked into that one. You'll find no sympathy here," Claudia teased.

"Seriously, seriously," Rowena drew our focus back to her, "I honestly think ah will miss Matt's atrocious social skills."

"Thank you!" he said, raising his pint like he'd just been validated.

She snorted and then looked at Jake and me sitting together. "Ah'll miss the Jake-and-Charley saga. Better than any romance novel." She lifted her glass to us. "Cheers for the angst, guys."

I laughed, only somewhat embarrassed that our relationship ups and downs had played out for our friends over the year.

"And," she smiled, a genuine, almost sad smile now, "ah will miss ma favorite band, The Stolen. Ah wish ye loads eh success, guys. Ye so deserve it."

"Oh man," Denver pulled her into his side, "she had to go get all mushy on me. I think I might cry."

"Shut up." She pushed at him playfully but stopped struggling when he tugged her close for a long hug.

I felt a little weepy and when I looked over at Claudia, she was wiping tears from the corner of her eyes. She saw me looking and grimaced. "What?" she huffed. "I'm a girl. Sue me."

"Well, I would say no one would have a chance at suing you with your upcoming fancy law degree," Lowe nudged her arm with his, smirking, "but it's not final until you take the LSATs."

Claudia rolled her eyes. "Don't remind me. Just let me get through these exams first." She grinned at me and I was relieved to see the smile was genuine.

This past year had changed my best friend perhaps even more than it had changed me. Although I watched her go through heartbreak, I also watched her come out the other side stronger than before. Claudia started college with me not knowing who she was or what she wanted out of life. I guess… she still wasn't sure about that. She was still looking. But… she definitely knew what she *didn't* want. She didn't want to be second best and she didn't know if she wanted to be a lawyer, but she was going to try her hand at it until she found her answer.

Beck was a different story.

While my relationship with Jake had only grown stronger over the last few weeks, my trust in him deepening now that I knew we were facing things together, Claudia and Beck's friendship disintegrated. I knew from speaking to Jake that Beck tried to be patient and wait out Claudia's mourning period over the loss of yet another parental figure, but as the days passed and her bitchiness toward him did not soften, Beck's hurt turned into anger.

Since Claudia's friendship with Lowe hadn't changed, it was impossible for Beck and Claud to avoid one another. So now their interactions were antagonistic and a far cry from where they'd started out. Claudia had agreed to go on tour with The Stolen this summer as their manager, so I had no idea how that would work out for them. I had my fingers and toes crossed that somehow, a miracle would happen and they'd both pull their obstinate heads out of their asses.

As for Dustin, Claudia hadn't heard from him since our departure from Barcelona. It was hard at first, but once I told my parents what happened, they rallied around Claudia. They Skyped

Claudia just as much as they did me. The only one who didn't was Andie. Claudia missed Andie almost as much as I did. But I wasn't ready to let go of my anger.

My sister hadn't spoken to me in months. She'd stopped supporting me. I didn't know how we were going to get over the rift, or if we ever would with Jake in my life. I had no intention of letting go of Jake, and since Andie was the one with the problem with him, I couldn't see how it would do me any good to take the first step toward mending that fence. It was up to Andie to take the first step. I just hoped I wouldn't have a long wait on my hands. Or that Claudia would, either. Andie had given Claudia that older sister wisdom, support, and advice she'd always craved. Our argument wasn't fair to Claud. But she never once complained. Plus, I think Mom, Dad, Jake, and I did a pretty good job helping her out.

The dark in the back of her eyes wasn't completely gone, and the bitterness she felt still existed through her interactions with Beck, but I knew that Team Redford and Jake helped her mourn and try to move on.

We were obnoxiously persistent that way.

"All right, Rowena told us what she's going to miss about us, but what are we going to miss about Scotland? Rowena and Maggie, obviously, but what or who else?" Claudia smiled around, her eyes jumping over Beck like he didn't exist.

I resisted the urge to throw my napkin at her.

"I'm going to miss the accents," Denver said.

"Ooh, good one." Claudia nodded. "I'm going to miss Digestive biscuits."

"Irn Bru," Lowe named the Scottish soda drink that was surprisingly addictive.

"Milk." Beck referred to the bar they played all the time.

"Scottish girls with purple hair." Matt grinned at Rowena.

"Aw, that was kind of sweet." Claudia looked as surprised as the rest of us.

He shrugged. "I can do sweet. I do know how to tone down all this raw animal magnetism."

Claudia groaned. "Annnnnddd... he's back."

Laughing, Jake relaxed against his seat, his arm across the back of mine. "I'm going to miss," he shot me a mischievous look, "Arthur's Seat."

Chuckling, I nodded. "Yeah, I'm going to miss that too."

"Well," Lowe scratched his chin, "I just learned more about Jake and Charley than I wanted to know."

As everyone laughed, I leaned forward, looking at my friends, memorizing their faces. "I'm going to miss this. Right here."

We were silent a moment, soaking it in, knowing that there would probably never come a time when we'd all be together again. Making great friends and saying goodbye—it was a bittersweet certainty of college.

My phone blasted in my purse and everyone groaned.

"Way to ruin the moment, Charley," Lowe grinned, teasing.

I rolled my eyes at them as I pulled out my phone. "It's my dad, I'll be a sec." I answered his call, laughter in my voice, "Hey, Dad, can I call you back, I'm—"

"Charley, something's happened," he interrupted, his words so grave, unease rolled up from my stomach.

I stuck my finger in my other ear to block out the noise around me. "What? What happened?"

"You need to come home, Charley. It's Andie."

The world narrowed, black shadows creeping in at the edges of my vision and my chest... my chest felt so tight. "Dad?"

"She's been in an accident. She's in a coma. You have to come home, Charley. You have to come home."

"Oh Go—" The black swarmed my vision and I couldn't breathe.

"Charley?"

"Oh my God, what's happening?"

"Charley? Charley!"

"Jim, it's Claudia. What's going on?"

"Charley, are you okay?"

"Oh God… no… we'll get her home."

"Charley?"

"It's going to be okay. We're here."

"Charley…"

Chapter Fifteen

Laramie, November 2013

After almost nine hours on the road, we pulled into a motel in Laramie, Wyoming. Beck had driven this time, while Jake and I nursed hangovers in the backseat. The three of them had joined me in the bar last night but only Jake and I had alcohol. We got a little wasted at dinner and I could only put it down to strained nerves on both our parts.

Waking up early to get on the road was not fun but our pale faces and self-pity seemed to amuse Beck, and I was okay with anything that kept him in marginally good spirits.

For the most part Jake and I were quiet in the back of the car because we were feeling ill. Even when we stopped at Ogallala, Nebraska, for lunch, we were monosyllabic. Food seemed to help though and as Beck got us back on the road, Jake attempted conversation. He updated me on his little brother Luke who'd gone from total player to devoted boyfriend when he met his match in his first year of college. Apparently the she-player he was dating didn't give up playing like he did, however, and they broke it off when they started sophomore year.

"He's dating a library assistant now. Really quiet, shy. Luke's a different person around her."

"Good different?"

Jake grinned. "Yeah, definitely. I think my little brother might be growing up. How scary is that?"

"What's scary is the part where we're growing up," I said dryly. "Do you feel it? Grown up, I mean? Because I don't."

He gave me a consoling smile. "No. I've been applying to different grad schools—molecular engineering. Every time I take a minute to process that that's where I am right now, I feel like I've been punched in the gut."

Suddenly concerned by the anxious tone underlying his words, I turned toward him. "You're happy, though, right? It's what you want to do with your life? This is the next step that you want?"

He thought a moment before answering. "Yeah. It's what I want. It just sometimes feels like it's come at me all too soon. Before I'm ready for it. But I guess we all feel that way. We just have to suck it up and get on with it."

"You don't sound so sure."

Jake's eyes reassured me. "I'm sure. There's just a huge part of me that wishes I could go back a year or two—pause the inevitability of responsibility and adulthood. I've fucked up the big stuff before. I don't want to do it again."

It was my turn to be reassuring. "You won't. You won't because first time around, you weren't even considering whether you'd fuck anything up. Your head wasn't anywhere but in the moment you were in. Now you think about consequences, how everything we do affects our future. It's called the learning curve, Jake." I grabbed his hand and squeezed it without even thinking. "You won't repeat the same mistakes. You're not that guy."

I felt his fingers slide through mine and just like that, the handholding went from friendly and comforting to something more. It was the whisper of skin sliding against skin. An innocent touch somehow turned sensual between us.

Jake rubbed his thumb lightly over mine and I felt that barely there touch between my legs.

Biting back a gasp, I wrenched my hand from his and rolled my head on the cushioned headrest to stare determinedly out at the passing scenery.

We'd passed into Wyoming, a state I'd never been in before. We were on the Lincoln highway and after passing through Cheyenne, there wasn't much to see except plains, mountains, and trees. It was beautiful. Peaceful.

"Charley?"

Jake said my name so quietly and with such depth, I froze. I looked up front to see Claudia and Beck deep in conversation about which motel to stay in. She was busy looking it up on her iPhone.

Sure they weren't paying attention, I looked at Jake feeling a rapid flutter in my chest. "Yeah?"

"I'm sorry," he said. "For the way I acted last time I saw you. It was childish and unfair."

I turned away again, unable to meet his eyes when I replied, "Apology accepted. You're allowed to be angry with me." I was angry with myself. With everyone and everything.

I felt resentful. Trapped.

I missed him.

"I just wish I knew the whole story."

I glanced sharply up front, noting Claudia and Beck had grown quiet, alert. I shot Jake a look of admonishment out of the corner of my eye. Understanding I didn't want to discuss this and definitely not here where we had no privacy, he turned away and watched the passing scenery too.

In the early evening we arrived in Laramie and decided to pull in for the night. We found a motel, took a nap, and then went for a walk. The main part of town was pretty and old-fashioned-looking with streetlights that looked like gas lamps. Some of the buildings dated back to the 1800s, all the storefronts were well kept, and the streets were clean in a way that reminded me of home.

"Bar and grill." Claudia pointed to a place just across from the train tracks.

"Let's do it." Beck threw his arm around her shoulders and they started walking across the street to the bar.

Feeling Jake's eyes on me, I turned to him. "What?"

He nodded at Claudia and Beck. "Do you think that's a good idea right now?"

"I think we're on a road trip to scatter Beck's dad's ashes and that it's a small miracle I've heard him laugh and seen him smile as many times as I have. Claudia helps him. As much as I'm worried for them both, I won't be the one to take away the balm that she is for him."

Without waiting to hear Jake's reply, I hurried across the street to catch up with our friends.

The place was pretty packed but we managed to get a table in the back. After we ate, I felt much better, my hangover finally dissipating.

Beck and Claudia took their turn to have beers while Jake and I stuck to soda. We'd been drinking for a couple of hours when Beck and Jake managed to grab one of the pool tables. Claudia and I played against them but we lost, and then I lost in a one-on-one against Beck. I hadn't spent much time around a pool table and neither had Claudia, so we decided it would probably be more interesting to watch Jake and Beck go head to head.

During one of their games, I headed over to the bar to get more drinks. The bar was busy, so I waited while a group of ladies in tutus, jeans, and glittery pink cowboy hats—a bachelorette party?—ordered another round. After a few minutes I glanced back across the bar at my friends.

I felt unease shift through me at the sight of the young woman leaning against the pool table. Claudia was talking to Beck while this girl, who had come out of nowhere, flirted with Jake.

Jake didn't seem to be flirting back but I knew him well enough to know that his eyes were definitely taking in everything about her. I could understand why.

She was gorgeous.

Tall with long, wavy dark hair, a golden tan, and pretty, fresh features that weren't caked in makeup like so many of the other women in the bar. She wore a casual but short T-shirt that showed off her curvy bosom and toned midriff. Her blue jeans showcased her lean legs. She was wearing very cute worn brown cowboy boots.

Everything about her screamed, "I am Jake Caplin's type!"

I felt sick.

Physically sick.

I studied Jake for a reaction as she reached out and touched the iron fist logo on his Pearl Jam shirt. He'd been holding himself aloof from her but whatever she said, it brought forth that smile that could floor a woman.

And it floored her. I could tell in the way her smile widened and her body relaxed, as if she were melting under his attention.

I turned away, feeling a little breathless.

And then the berating commenced. Jealousy was something I wasn't allowed to feel where Jake was concerned. I gave him up, and giving him up entailed having to watch other women flirt with him.

Shit.

What if he spent the night with her?

The thought froze me to the spot.

You're being crazy, Charley! He's not going to hook up with a random stranger on a road trip to scatter his best friend's dad's ashes.

I looked back over at him and my eyes narrowed. The girl was standing even closer and they seemed to be having an actual conversation.

"Blondie, what can I get you?"

I whipped around at the voice and was confronted by a cute bartender. He was a couple of years older than me with dirty-blond hair, sexy stubble, and twinkling bright blue eyes. He grinned as I blinked at him, coming out of my panic over Jake and the girl.

What could he get me?

For one: a stool. I did not want to go back over there until the girl was gone.

I glanced at the filled stools in front of me, frowning.

As if the bartender read my mind, he tapped the bar in front of a big beefy guy and said, "Jay, you mind moving down the bar."

"Sure thing, Ty," Jay said and I watched in amusement as he pushed the guy beside him, and like a set of dominoes they forced everyone down a spot until the stool in front of me was open.

I slid on it and smiled gratefully at Ty the bartender. "Thanks."

Ty grinned and I had to admit, I took some comfort and pleasure in the appreciative look in his eyes. "No need. I wanted something prettier to look at than Jay."

I laughed. "Well, thanks anyway."

"So what can I get you?"

I tilted my head in thought, the blood rushing in my ears at the thought of what was going on behind me. "A time machine?"

Ty chuckled. "You think I had one of those, I'd be working here?"

"Oh? What would you use it for?"

"Ah, well, that would be telling. What would *you* use it for?"

I shrugged. "Lots of things."

He leaned across the bar, his eyes drinking in my every feature. "You're telling me someone like you has regrets?"

"Someone like me? What do you know about someone like me?"

His response was a slow, wicked grin that I had to admit penetrated my sadness and jealousy just a little. "I'll be right back." He strode down the bar to help his colleague and I checked him out from the back. Very nice.

True to his word, Ty came back after a minute or so, opened a beer, and planted it in front of me. "On the house."

I picked it up with a smirk. "And what does a filly have to do for that around here?"

He threw his head back and laughed. "A filly? Really?"

I grinned back at him.

Mirth still bright in his eyes, he shook his head. "Nothing. I promise. Except maybe stop looking so sad. You are far too pretty to be so sad."

I tipped the bottle head in his direction and avoided his compliment with a casual, "Thanks for the beer."

"What's your name?"

"Charley."

He leaned on the bar again. "It suits you. Charley, I'm Ty."

"You have a nice city here, Ty."

"Thank you." His expression turned curious. "What brings you to us, Charley?"

I shook my head. "Uh-uh. Too depressing."

"Okay." His brow wrinkled in thought. "Where are you from?"

I shook my head again. "You could be a serial killer. The less information I give you, the less chance of you finding me to serial kill me."

Ty chuckled and as our eyes locked, I didn't feel the sizzle I should have. I was too busy wondering if Jake had noticed I was talking to this guy or if he was too busy getting his flirt on with the beautiful brunette to give a shit what I was up to.

"Ah, suspicious and overly cautious. Let me guess—law student."

Wow, impressive. "You've really honed those people-reading skills bartenders are known for, huh."

"That or I'm psychic." He glanced behind me. "For instance, you were or are in a relationship with the tall guy in the Pearl Jam T-shirt over by the pool table."

My muscles tensed. "Is he looking over?"

"Mmm-hmm. And attempting to fry my ass with his eyes."

"Where's the gorgeous girl in the cowboy boots?"

"Leanne?" he smirked. "Your friend stopped talking to her the minute he saw me talking to you."

I sat on that a moment and then sighed. "Ex-boyfriend. Awkward road trip."

Ty met my eyes again. "He looks pretty furious. But I'm up for pissing him off even more if you like." His eyes lowered to my lips.

With a dry chuckle, I said, "As much as I love the idea of kissing a random bartender, especially a cute one, *I'm* the one who broke *his* heart so I don't think I'll be doing anything to hurt him any more than I already have."

Ty gave me a good-natured smile as he straightened up away

from the counter. "Well, if you change your mind, I get off at one."

My expression said we both knew I wasn't going to be there when he got off work and then I slipped from the stool and braced myself to return to my friends.

As soon as I saw Jake's face, I knew Ty was right.

He was furious.

And hurt.

I suddenly felt sick again.

My eyes flew to Claudia and Beck and I flinched at the uneasiness pouring off them. Thankfully, there was no recrimination in their faces—it wouldn't be fair for them to be angry at me for talking with the bartender when Jake had been flirting with cowboy-boots girl.

Speaking of... I glanced around the bar until I found the brunette over by the jukebox with a few friends. Her gaze was locked on Jake. I only just managed not to curl my lip into a growl of territorialism.

"Who's winning?" I attempted to ask nonchalantly as I stopped beside Jake at the pool table.

"Seriously?" he snapped.

When I wouldn't look at him, Jake crowded me against the table so I had no choice but to acknowledge him. I stared up at him, my face perfectly blank so he wouldn't realize how off balance he was making me.

"What are you trying to do to me?" he said, anguished.

"Jake, man," I heard Beck say softly. "Maybe this should wait."

"I'm sick and tired of waiting," he said. He gently took hold of my arm and started to pull me away from the table. "We need to talk."

"Jake." I tugged out of his hold, drawing us to a standstill. He glowered back at me and I returned the look. "Don't you dare try to haul me out of here."

"We're going to hash this shit out once and for all and if I have to throw you over my shoulders, I will."

"Is there a problem here?"

Oh shit.

Ty had come out from behind the bar and now we had an audience.

Jake stood in front of me, blocking Ty's view. "This is none of your business. *She* is none of your business."

"Jake." I tugged on his shirt, outraged by this behavior. "Stop acting like a Neanderthal."

"I'm pissed off," he snarled, looking over his shoulder at me with fire in his eyes.

"Well, I'm pissed off too!" I yelled back.

"Maybe you could take being pissed off outside," Ty suggested.

"No problem," Jake said as he grabbed my hand and dragged me toward the exit.

I let him because by now, I was uncomfortable with the audience and I also didn't want witnesses when I murdered him. "What the hell are you doing?" I said as soon as we were out the door. I vaguely noted that Claudia and Beck didn't follow.

"What am I doing?" Jake drew to a sudden stop, turning around on me. "What the hell are *you* doing?"

Before I could answer he started walking again, refusing to let me go. We both seethed as we marched the five-minute walk back to the motel. Jake let us into his and Beck's room and I wrenched my hand away.

"This is ridiculous," I huffed. "We're acting like five-year-olds."

Jake slammed the door shut. "I'm not the one flirting with a freaking bartender."

"Hah! No, you're just the one," I stabbed a finger at him, "flirting with boots with all her hair and tan skin."

Jake looked confused for a moment and then his expression turned grim. "That's what this is about? I was talking to that girl? She was flirting with me. I didn't encourage it. But you saw what you wanted to see, didn't you, Charley. So you decided to flirt with the bartender to get back at me. Very mature."

"Mature? We're talking about maturity? You just blew up at me in a bar for talking to another guy."

"I'm not the one who broke things off!" he yelled, his chest heaving as he grew breathless with anger. "I get to flirt with other girls. But I haven't! I haven't touched a single girl since you left me because I can't let you go! And I fucking hate you for it, Charley!"

I flinched, unbearable pain radiating from my chest—it was like he'd punched his fist through it.

"But do you know what I hate more?" he said quietly now, his voice hoarse.

I shook my head, battling the tears that were fighting to fill my eyes.

"I hate how much I still need you," he whispered.

I didn't know which one of us moved first.

One minute I was standing by the door and the next I was in Jake's arms as he crushed his mouth down over mine.

I also don't know what happened to me in that moment. For months I felt like my life had been suspended—I wasn't moving in any direction. Moreover, I was struggling with the constant confusion and my mixed-up heart and emotions over the choices I'd made. Giving into Jake may have been wrong but just then, it was a choice I understood, it was a choice that felt good, simple…

More than that, I felt alive again.

We undressed one another, frantic, desperate… our movements hurried with frustration and longing. We didn't take our time at all. We were naked and then we were on the bed and then Jake was inside me.

Together we came hard and fast.

And I didn't have time to regret it because Jake pulled me back under the spell I'd let us cast over ourselves. He kissed me slow, leisurely, tasting me as if he'd never get the chance again. I kissed him back just as deeply, holding onto him for dear life, my fingers curled in his thick, dark hair that was longer now since the last time I'd touched it.

Jake kissed his way from my lips, across my jaw, down my neck…

I sighed, feeling the heat build inside me again as his lips touched me everywhere. When his lips wrapped around my nipple, I gasped, arching into him. He licked my nipple, coaxing it into a tight bud while he stroked his thumb over my other one.

Delicious pressure was building between my legs.

"Jake," I gasped, my breathing shallow as the heat flooded my entire body.

He took his time—butterfly kisses down my stomach, fingertips gently stroking my breasts, across my ribs, as he moved down.

Jake looked up at me from under his lashes and I felt another insistent tug at my core. "Do you want my mouth?"

My breath hitched and I moved my legs apart. "Always," I whispered before the insistent voice in the back of my head could stop me—could stop any of this.

At the first touch of his tongue, I nearly came off the bed. It felt like years since we'd last had this. I parted my legs even wider, my pants increasing in volume as Jake licked me, played me, until the pressure inside me was close to exploding.

And then he sucked on my clit and I split apart.

I shuddered through my orgasm as Jake crawled back over me, his hands braced on either side of my head, his eyes searing into mine… He pushed inside me and I cried out at the sensation. He groaned deep in his throat as my inner muscles tightened around him and he began to thrust, slow, deep, and I felt the tension inside me start to build again. My fingers dug into his biceps as he strained over me and I arched under him, moving in rhythm against this new seduction.

He wanted me to come again before he did.

Sweat slickened both our bodies and Jake's muscles strained with his effort to stay his own orgasm.

Unconsciously, I dragged my nails down his arms as my climax approached. I stiffened and felt Jake's thrusts speed up, his grunts of pleasure echoing in my ears and finally piercing through the tension.

I cried out, my eyes rolling in a flutter as the intensity of this washed over me.

"Jesus… *fuck*…" Jake's words were guttural as I felt him stiffen. And then his hips jerked against mine as he came inside me.

His weight pinned me to the bed as he collapsed. I stroked his hair with one hand while the other stroked his sweat-dampened skin.

Slowly the power of our longing diminished enough for reality to sink in.

My hands stilled.

Jake tensed and then slowly lifted his head to look down into my eyes. "You're going to tell me this was a mistake, aren't you?" he said grimly.

Chapter Sixteen

Chicago, April 2013

I don't really remember how Jake and my friends got me out of the restaurant. Or how I got packed. Or how I ended up on a plane sandwiched between Jake and Claudia. It was like the world around me faded out, just a blur of color. There was no room inside me to concentrate on anything but getting to my sister and hoping I'd get to her in time.

Claudia would tell me later when I asked for him that Jake went home to his parents rather than come to the hospital because he didn't want to upset my family any more than they already were. I didn't remember that. All I remembered was rushing into Northwestern Memorial, exhausted but somehow wired at the same time. It was a weird feeling. My body didn't feel like mine. I felt like I was floating.

My parents and Rick greeted me, hugged me. I remembered it because their expressions were the first thing since hearing the news that brought me into the real world, into the reality of what we were dealing with. The bleakness in my parents' eyes, the desperation in Rick's... it had me pushing past them into the hospital room.

I'd stumbled, disbelieving the sight before me.

Andie lay there. She seemed frozen beneath the tubes and the ventilator. It was almost like it wasn't her. It was just her body.

"What happened?" Claudia said.

Sick with fear, I stepped tentatively toward my sister.

"A taxi driver," Rick said grimly. "Downtown. He had a heart attack at the wheel and crashed into the sidewalk. When he hit An—"

I grabbed for my sister's hand. It was cool, limp.

"The impact threw her against a building," Dad finished hoarsely when Rick couldn't continue.

I could hear Claudia's gasp and the choked sounds of crying.

The tears welled in my eyes as I stroked my sister's hand and leaned over to whisper, "I'm sorry."

"The doctors said we can only wait for her to come out of the coma but there's a chance..." My mom's tear-soaked words trailed off.

"There's a chance she won't wake up," Dad bit out.

The pain and guilt poured out of me and I pressed my forehead against Andie's. "I should have been there," I whispered. *I should have saved you.* "I'm sorry. I'm so sorry I haven't been here."

A buzzing sound infiltrated the darkness and I jerked awake. I blinked a few times against the harsh lighting, the blur across my vision fading to reveal my unconscious sister in her hospital bed and Rick on the other side of it, opposite me.

"Your phone," he said quietly.

I yawned and followed the buzzing sound—my phone vibrating

on the bedside table. I tried to focus on the screen. "It's Jake," I whispered.

"Yeah, he's called a few times. You should call him back."

I frowned at Rick. "How long have I been out?"

He shrugged. "You were out when I got here. That was a few hours ago." His brows drew together in concern. "Charley, you should go back to our place with your parents. Get some real sleep."

I was never going to get a real sleep until Andie woke up.

Seven days.

Seven long days she's laid in that bed, breathing through a ventilator.

"Charley."

I looked up from my sister's face to Rick's haggard one.

"Go get some sleep."

"I just slept." I shook my head.

"Then call Jake back."

Wondering if perhaps Rick really just wanted some time alone with my sister, I nodded and grabbed my phone. "Do you want a Starbucks?" I noted his cheekbones looked a little sharper. I wasn't the only one losing weight. "Something to eat?"

"A coffee and a sandwich would be great." He eyed me. "Get yourself something to eat too, before you fade away to nothing."

I reluctantly agreed and strode out of my sister's hospital room. For a little while, I found myself wandering aimlessly as I clutched my phone. After the first long few days following Andie's accident, when she showed no signs of waking up, somehow I managed to convince Claudia and Jake to return to Edinburgh to finish up their exams. It was difficult to bring them around, but since Jake didn't want to cause trouble by appearing at the hospital, there wasn't a whole heck of a lot he could do. And Claudia... well, I just... my focus was on Andie and

I wasn't able to give any other part of myself to anyone, which included reassurances to Claud that I was okay.

I was far from okay, and I needed to be that way. I didn't want to spend half my time lying to people about how I was coping when in all honesty, I was barely hanging on, but barely coping on my own was easier because I could do that without the pressure from other people to do better than barely hang on.

Once a day Claudia would FaceTime to check in. That was beyond harrowing—to have to keep using the phrase, "There's no change."

With Jake, though, it was even harder.

My insides churned with guilt that Andie was lying in a hospital bed and I hadn't spoken to her in months. The thought... the thought that she might die, that I might never have a chance to say another word to her after having spent the last few months choosing Jake over her and avoiding her...

I leaned against the nearest wall to catch my breath.

This was my fault. Andie's accident. I knew that deep in my bones. Although there was some part of me that knew it wasn't rational, I worried that somehow I'd interrupted fate all those years ago when I'd knocked Andie out of the way of Mr. Finnegan's SUV. Was this fate's way of punishing me?

I didn't know if that was true or not.

What I did know was that I was definitely being punished for treating her so badly.

And the reason for my falling-out with her... well, it was Jake. I couldn't get that out of my head.

Looking down at my phone, I fought the urge to smash it underfoot. I had to call Jake back or he would only keep trying.

After making my way outside, I found a quiet spot.

His face appeared on my phone screen and I felt a painful grip in my chest. Just looking at him made me feel a horrible mix of relief and shame.

"Baby," he said in greeting, his dark eyes filled with concern and love. "How's it going?"

I shook my head, looking away from the screen for a moment. "Same."

"She'll come out of this, Charley. Andie's strong. She's a Redford."

Biting my lip to stem the tears, I shrugged loosely. "We'll see."

"You've got to stay positive."

"I know."

"Charley? Charley, look at me."

I did as he asked, turning my head back to the screen.

His expression was tender. "I can come back. If you need me, I can come home."

"No," I said adamantly, my pulse racing just at the thought. "You have to finish up there. I... I'm better on my own," I said honestly. "I feel like I don't have to worry so much about worrying everyone else when I'm on my own."

"I get it," he said and I knew that he did. "You're not completely alone, though, right? Your mom and dad and Rick are there."

"Yeah, but... I guess we're all dealing with it differently." I didn't even want to think about how much this had broken my parents. My parents had always been larger-than-life characters who could deal with anything life threw their way. But this... they seemed older, more fragile, and every time they looked upon Andie in that hospital bed, I could see another crack form in the armor they'd worn their whole lives.

That scared me just as much as the sight of my sister in a coma.

"I better get back," I whispered, my throat constricting.

"Okay, baby," he said softly. "I love you."

"I love you too."

I hung up and stuffed the phone in my pocket.

Okay, baby. I love you.

I love you too.

But I hate you too. I hate me too.

Trembling, I sucked in a huge gulp of air and tried to calm myself. After a minute or so, I felt a little more together and walked back into the hospital.

I'd barely left my sister's side. The only time I did leave the hospital was to go back to Rick and Andie's for a shower. My parents tried to get some sleep there, but I just couldn't sit in that house. It was filled with Andie. Her pictures, her perfume, her things, her work, her clothes, and the funny refrigerator magnets she collected.

I'd gone into the kitchen to get some orange juice and I'd stopped at the sight of the magnets. In the middle was the black and white one I'd found during my sophomore year at Purdue. When we were younger, my sister was obsessed with pirates. I'd never forgotten the many times I found myself sitting on a sofa cushion in the middle of my parents' living room floor with my hands bound behind my back while my sister stood triumphant on the arm of the sofa, a patch over her eye. With that, she'd command her invisible crew to haul anchor and her ship (the sofa) would sail off, leaving me to die on deserted island (the cushion) for betraying her to the navy.

The black and white fridge magnet had the words "To Err is Human, to Arr is Pirate" printed over a skull and crossbones. When I'd given it to Andie, she'd laughed so hard, she cried.

At the sight of the magnet, I collapsed.

My mom found me and held me while I let it all out.

I'd refused to stay in that house for any longer than the length of a shower since.

Returning to the hospital room with coffee and sandwiches for both me and Rick, I found him sitting close to Andie, holding her hand in both of his. When he heard me come in, he ducked his head and swiped at the tears I knew he hoped I hadn't seen.

Placing the coffee and sandwich down beside him, I didn't offer him comfort or bring up his grief, because I think he needed to feel strong in all this. Rick wasn't a stupid guy—he could see my parents were barely holding it together and I knew he felt some obligation to be strong for us all. It was no use attempting to convince him otherwise. It was just the person he was.

I sat back in my chair and sipped at my coffee.

"You better open that sandwich," Rick said softly.

He started to eat his slowly and I felt a pang in my stomach.

I guess I was a little hungry.

Nibbling at it, I listened to the sounds of the monitors around my sister.

"She was mad at herself too, you know," Rick suddenly said.

I almost choked on the bite of sandwich as I sucked in air. After a sip of coffee, I asked, voice hoarse, "What do you mean?"

"You're not to blame for the argument, Charley. It happened. The two of you are stubborn."

"I should've called," I said flatly. "I should've been here."

"'Should haves' only hurt you, kiddo. Don't do that to yourself."

"Why? Aren't you doing that to yourself?"

We stared at each other a moment until Rick finally sighed and looked back at Andie. "I should've married her sooner. She wanted to get married right away. I should've done it."

After a moment of silence, I whispered, "I should have put her first."

"What?"

I glanced up at Rick. "Nothing."

His phone rang and he excused himself. I took the opportunity to shimmy forward in my chair and clutch my sister's hand. "I'm sorry I chose Jake over you, Andie. I'm so sorry."

I kissed her hand and screwed my eyes shut and for the first time in a long time, I prayed. I prayed that God could hear me… I prayed that if He could, I'd be repentant. My penance—*If you save her, I'll give him up. If Andie wakes up, I'll let Jake go. I'll choose her over him.*

I hurried into the hospital, my hair damp, eyes heavy with lack of sleep. I always hurried back after a quick shower. I didn't want to miss anything.

We were on day fourteen.

I felt hope sliding through my fingers, the tips grasping for purchase.

"Charley!" My mom's eyes were bright, brighter than I'd seen them in fourteen days, as she strode down the corridor from my sister's room.

"What? What is it? What's happened?"

"Andie started choking," Mom said, her words rushed and excited. "She's breathing on her own. She's awake, Charley. She's awake."

I burst out crying. "Awake?" I sobbed, overwhelmed by the relief flooding me.

"She's in and out." Mom tugged on my arm, pulling me toward the room. "The doctor says it might take a day or two for her to come fully around. But she's out of the coma."

I froze in the doorway of my sister's hospital room, suddenly paralyzed with fear.

I watched as Mom, Dad, and Rick hovered over her while the doctor spoke. The ventilator was gone and although her eyes where shut, Andie's lids fluttered. She moved her head and emitted a small groan.

I pressed back against the door, fighting the urge to flee.

Andie was awake. She was going to make it.

In amongst the relief I felt a wave of nausea, and I ducked outside the door to press my forehead against the cool wall.

My bargain with God.

I had to let Jake go somehow.

Trembling, I took out my phone and called him. This time I didn't use FaceTime.

I told him Andie was awake. I ignored his relief. I ignored his love. I had to in order to say what I needed to say. I told him not to call me anymore. I told him it was over. And then I hung up and switched my phone off.

I dashed into the nearest bathroom and made the toilet right as I threw up. After a while, I was just dry heaving.

I gave Jake up for Andie and I didn't even know if she forgave me. What if she hated me? What could I say?

And worse... how could I face her when there was a darkness deep inside me that resented her and the choice I'd just made?

I never did go into the hospital room again.

During the first twenty-four hours, I hovered outside, looking in through the windows, ignoring my parents' and Rick's pleas to come inside and speak to Andie while she slept.

The next day when Andie became cognizant, I did the same—hiding and peeking in when I was sure she wasn't aware. The doctors said she had a recovery period ahead. She was a little dazed, confused, and although she recognized everyone, she couldn't remember much before the accident.

I hid out at Starbucks a lot and on the third day, Dad hunted me down to bring me to Andie.

"I told her you were here," he said, disappointment and annoyance in his eyes. He didn't like the way I was behaving. Hiding from her. He didn't understand.

"Did she ask for me?" If she asked for me, I'd have to go to her.

Dad frowned. "No."

"Does she remember the argument?"

Dad scratched his unshaven cheek and looked away uncomfortably. "I think so."

"Then I'm staying right where I am."

A week later I returned home to Lanton with my parents without having spoken to my sister. I'd spied on her a lot as she sat talking to friends and family, but she'd had no idea I was there.

Andie was recovering fast—she had some physical and mental therapy to go through, but the doctors were impressed with how well she was doing and Rick insisted he could take care of her.

Mom and Dad had to get back to work, but they told Rick they'd come to Chicago every weekend until Andie was fully recovered. They seemed stronger back in Chicago. They seemed like themselves again.

But when we returned to Lanton, I realized it was all a mask for Andie's benefit. That fragility that had scared me so much reappeared. Mom started disappearing to the cemetery almost every day—it pissed me off. I thought it was morbid. I was helping Mom out in the florist a lot because she was so distracted all the time. She was constantly calling Rick or Dad for reassurances. I realized that she and Dad were both afraid that someone was going to tell them that Andie's recovery was a sick joke—that any minute now, she'd close her eyes and never open them again. As for Dad, he didn't talk to me much in those first few months.

As far as he was concerned, I'd abandoned Andie as soon as she woke up.

I hadn't abandoned her.

I just didn't know how to face her, or deal with my conflicting emotions.

I missed my sister. I missed Jake. So much, it hurt. Especially at night, when I'd lay my head on my pillow and I couldn't think of anything else but how much I wanted my life to go back to the way it used to be.

I argued with myself over and over that what I'd promised God... it wasn't rational, I couldn't be held to it. But what if...

What if I accepted Jake back into my life, what if I made my family accept him into their lives, and suddenly, Andie's eyes closed and they never opened again?

It was a little better when Claudia finished up in Edinburgh and flew to Indiana to live with us. She eased my parents, lit them up in a way I couldn't right now. She eased me too. I felt like I was forever on the brink of an argument with my folks, and Claudia always reminded me that they didn't need to deal with my issues right now. So we suffered in stilted silence.

The only time it broke was when I yelled at Mom for visiting the cemetery. I told her it was morbid and it creeped me out—like she was just waiting for something bad to happen to Andie.

Mom told me calmly but with tears in her eyes that she was visiting her mom's grave. "She's the only one who would understand what I'm going through right now. I talk to her and I know she can hear and it gives me comfort."

At that, she'd walked out of the house and my dad said more than two sentences to me for the first time in weeks. He shouted at me for being self-involved and told me to apologize.

I did. I tucked my tail between my legs and apologized.

And then I promptly went online and found out what I needed to do to sit the LSATs in the fall. I'd upset my parents enough this year. It was time to do something for them—something selfless.

Throughout the months Jake called, he texted, and part of me wished he'd move on, while the other half—the half that was utterly heartbroken—was selfishly relieved that he still loved me as much as I loved him.

Chapter Seventeen

Elko, November 2013

We were losing layers of clothing the farther west we traveled. It wasn't too hot, but we'd driven from melting snow to clear skies and sunshine in a matter of days. Eleven hours after we left Laramie, Jake pulled into a motel in Elko, Nevada.

It had been another quiet car journey. Jake was full of silent questions and I was...

I was searching for me. The me who just said what was on her mind. Told it like it was.

I wanted that me back, because maybe then I could be brave enough to give Jake the answers he was looking for, even if he thought I was crazy once I did.

Beck got out to get us rooms and the three of us sat in the car in silence. Memories from last night had been replaying over and over in my head.

"You're going to tell me this was a mistake, aren't you?"

I stared into Jake's eyes, brushing his hair back from his forehead. "Yes," I answered honestly.

We didn't say anything for a few seconds and then Jake said, "Will you stay with me tonight at least?"

Too selfish to say no, I'd stayed.

A few hours later while I was sleeping in his arms, I was awoken by voices. Jake asked Beck to stay in Claudia's room. I didn't register it at the time because I fell right back to sleep, feeling warm and safe tucked into Jake's side.

The next morning, after dealing with the awkwardness of waking up next to Jake, I had to deal with even more awkwardness upon knocking on Claudia's motel door to get my clothes. Beck opened the door, eyes bright as he threw me a pleased grin before hurrying out. I noted the bed that should've been mine wasn't slept in.

My questioning gaze had flown to Claudia who lay in rumpled sheets, the covers pulled up to her chest, showing off bare shoulders. She looked flushed and flustered, just like I felt.

I guessed I wasn't the only one who'd thrown caution to the wind last night.

"It finally happened, huh?" I said, a small smile playing on my lips.

Claudia stared at me warily and nodded.

I thought of Jake and the pain in his eyes when I left him this morning, compared to the happiness in Beck's. I reassured my friend. "Don't question it."

Claudia gave me a tremulous smile in return. "Thanks, Charley." She glanced at the door. "So last night you and Jake—"

"It shouldn't have happened," I cut her off as I grabbed my stuff and strode into the shower.

That day on the road was a difficult one. Claudia and Beck were loved up in the backseat while Jake and I were... I didn't know what we were.

Beck came back with room keys but as soon as we pulled up to the motel, Jake turned to him and held out his hand. "I'll take one of those keys."

"I've got ours, man." Beck waved him off.

"No. Charley and I are sharing tonight."

I gaped at my ex-boyfriend a little stupidly.

"Uh…" From my peripheral I could see Beck turn to me, but I didn't look back at him because I was still gaping at Jake in confusion. "Are you sure—"

"Key, Beck," Jake insisted.

"I want to make sure Charley's okay with that first," Beck returned impatiently.

Jake looked at me. "Well?"

As we looked at one another, I dug deep for my courage. I knew why Jake wanted us to share a room. He wanted privacy because he wanted answers. He was done pretending he didn't deserve them. Maybe before I could justify shutting him out, but last night I'd made a choice that had confused and hurt him even more. Jake deserved better than that. He deserved the truth, even if I was scared to share it.

I suddenly heard his voice in my head, words he'd said not too long ago but now felt forever ago. *"Come on, Supergirl. Be brave."*

"It's fine," I told Beck quietly. "As long as Claudia's okay rooming with you."

"Oh, I'm cool with that," Claudia shrugged with fake nonchalance and I rolled my eyes at her. I could tell she was more than happy with this new arrangement.

It was clear to me that Jake was beyond impatient to talk when he suggested we go to a McDonald's drive-through and eat back at our room. By now I'd lost whatever appetite I had, but I was so used to pretending none of this affected me that I ordered a double cheeseburger.

Just before Jake closed the door, I heard Claudia giggling happily as Beck let them into their room next door. Despite my own messy life, I was glad for her. I was relieved the experiences with her parents and biological father hadn't scarred her permanently, hadn't stifled her generous heart. She was giving Beck a chance, and I believed that chance might just save him from himself.

They deserved the joy they'd found. I had to find time to tell Claud that because every time she looked at me, I saw guilt in her eyes, like she felt bad for being happy when I was more miserable than I'd ever been in my life.

It was time to remind her that that wasn't how real friendship worked.

I chewed on a pickle as I watched Jake sit on the bed opposite me. He unwrapped his burger but he didn't lift it to his mouth right away. Instead, he sighed.

"What's going on with you, Charley?" His dark eyes pierced through me. "And not just why you broke up with me… Everything. Because right now—this person you've become, it isn't you. You know it isn't you because your light has gone out. You're somewhere dark right now and I'm worried sick about you."

Your light has gone out. It sounded so permanent. Like my light wasn't switched off, but broken.

Tears stung the back of my eyes and I took another bite of my burger to have something to concentrate on, something that would focus the tears away.

Finally when I felt in control, I met his gaze. "I haven't seen or spoken to Andie since before she woke up out of the coma."

That surprised him. "How? What... I'm confused."

And so I tried to explain.

"You remember I was there every day while she was in the coma?"

"Of course."

"Something... something happened to me when she woke up." I shook my head, feeling the bottled emotion in me well up. "I tried to take a step into the hospital room but I just couldn't. I felt paralyzed." I dashed away a tear that slipped down my cheek. "And somehow I haven't stopped feeling that way."

Jake leaned forward, his brows drawn together in concern. "Baby, paralyzed? Why?"

"You're not going to like that answer."

"Give it to me anyway."

I pushed my half-eaten food away and drew my knees up to my chest. "The whole time Andie lay in that hospital bed, breathing through a ventilator, I couldn't shake the guilt. I couldn't shake the fact that I hadn't spoken to my sister—one of my best friends—in weeks... because of you." Forcing myself to be brave, I looked at him. He'd grown pale with realization. "I didn't blame you directly, Jake. I blamed me. I resented myself for making that choice, for putting you before my family. I didn't know how to talk to you or be around you during it all because you reminded me of all the bad decisions I'd made regarding Andie and my parents."

Jake blew air out between his lips and whispered, "Fuck," as he dragged a shaky hand through his hair. "You have no idea how much I get that, Charley. I wish you'd told me that was how you were feeling."

197

Surprise shot through me. "I don't understand."

"After Brett died, I was filled with this irrational guilt," he explained, the steadiness of his words testament to how far he'd come emotionally since Brett's death. "At the time it didn't feel irrational. I truly believed that there was something I could've done to avoid that outcome. And there was a huge part of me that couldn't separate you from Brett's death. I couldn't be around you because of it."

As I processed this, the love I felt for Jake seemed to grow too big, too much, and I ducked my head to break our eye contact. There was so much relief that he understood me, but more than that, I was in awe of his understanding and compassion.

"I should've told you," I said softly. "I'm sorry I didn't give you that chance."

"I forgive you."

"Why?" I laughed unhappily.

"Because," he said, his countenance solemn, "*you* forgave *me*."

I started to smile but it wobbled as the tears spilled down my cheeks without control. "I'm such a mess, Jake. I look in the mirror and I don't recognize myself."

Suddenly he was there beside me, holding me as I sobbed into his shoulder.

Once I'd soaked his shirt through, he got up and strode into the bathroom, returning with toilet tissue so I could wipe my tears and blow my nose.

"I'm sorry," I told him, still shaking.

"You don't have to be." He tucked my hair behind my ear and smiled kindly. "So why don't you recognize yourself?"

Bunching the used tissue in my hand, I shrugged. "I used to be able to put my fear aside in most situations. But when it comes to the people I love, I seem to fall apart. When you left when I was sixteen, it took me a long time to stop moping around and start living again, and now with Andie... it's happening all over again except it's worse this time—more complicated."

"Explain it to me," he encouraged.

I studied his gorgeous face, his patient, soulful eyes. "You'll think I'm crazy. Or worse... you'll hate me."

Jake frowned. "You know when I said I hated you... I didn't mean it. I was just pissed off."

"I know," I said. "But now you might really hate me."

"Try me. I might surprise you."

Taking a sip of my drink, I stalled a moment, gathering the remnants of my courage. "When Andie was lying there in that hospital bed, I watched Rick fall apart, but worse I watched my parents fall apart. It scared the hell out of me, Jake. Jim and Delia Redford do not fall apart. They're the strongest people I know. But as one day crept into the next, I watched them age, I watched them crumble, and there was nothing I could do to help them. I'd failed Andie and now I was failing them. I felt like her accident was punishment. That I was to blame for it. Which made the fact that I couldn't do anything to fix it or my parents even worse."

"How was it your fault?"

"Because of the way I treated her before it happened. Because we hadn't spoken since I'd told her to fuck off... because," my voice lowered, "I wasn't there this time to shove her out of the way, to save her."

"Charley, somewhere deep down you know that's not true."

I shook my head. "But that doesn't mean I don't feel that way, that I don't feel to blame, ashamed and guilty as hell."

"And this is why you haven't spoken to Andie? Because you feel like her accident was your fault to begin with?"

"That," I drew in a deep breath, bracing myself to tell him the whole crazy truth, "and because there's this sick, dark little part of me that resents her."

Jake frowned. "Resents her? For what? For the way you feel?"

"No." This time when our eyes met, I let all the love I felt for him shine out for the first time since before it all happened. I knew the instant he felt it because he froze and his eyes grew round with surprise and confusion. "I made a promise to God, Jake. I'm so sorry." Tears started falling again.

"Charley, I don't understand." He reached for me, his thumbs swiping at the salty escapees.

"I promised God that if he saved Andie... I would give you up."

Realization struck him and he looked like it had punched a mighty blow. "And then Andie woke up."

I nodded. "I know it's crazy. I know that it was probably a coincidence but I can't get rid of this fear that if I let myself be with you, something bad will happen to Andie. And now I can't be with you and I resent my sister for it. Which is outrageous and wrong. So I haven't faced her. I haven't faced the way I treated her or the way I'm still treating her. That's not me, Jake." I punched at the mattress below me in anger. "I'm not this coward. But that's who I've become. A coward. I'm a coward, I can't have you, and I can't be a cop because my parents don't want to go through what they just went through again. Where does that leave me? Who am I without my ability to act despite my fears, or be with you, or be the person I'm meant to be?"

Jake looked shaken. "Christ, Charley." He shifted closer to me and put his arm around me, drawing me into his side. "I can't believe you've been carrying this shit around for months without telling me. Without telling anyone."

I hugged him close. "I love you," I told him softly. "I love you so much. But I can't be with you."

San Francisco, December 2013

The wind whipped my hair forward around my face as I stood on the bluffs by Baker Beach holding Jake's hand.

Beck stood lower down on the rocks from us, Claudia at his side, as he stared out at the Pacific Ocean. He spoke, his words muffled by the wind. That was okay. Those words were for his dad's ears alone.

After a little while, Beck let go of Claudia's hand and removed the lid from the small lacquered box. Without a moment's hesitation, he released the ashes and they caught in the wind as it blew out toward the ocean.

He wiped a tear from his cheek and Claudia wrapped her arm around his waist and drew him closer. He accepted her comfort, sliding his own arm around her shoulders and kissing her head in thanks.

Jake stroked my hand, drawing my attention from my friends to his face. He looked grim. Sad. Wary.

After my confession he didn't tell me I was crazy for feeling the way I felt, but I sensed a new desperation in him and I feared that it was borne of him letting go of the hope that I would come around—that eventually we'd find our way back together again.

That I had given up hope was bad enough. Selfishly, I didn't want Jake to.

I spent the night with him again, positive now that he understood there wasn't more to it than me grasping at a last chance to soak in the temporary pleasure of being with him.

Jake leaned down to be heard over the wind. "Let's leave them for a moment."

I nodded and followed him back over the bluffs to where we'd parked the car up on Lincoln Boulevard. It was much warmer in San Francisco but it was windy off the water and I was glad to return to the car.

We were silent for a while, taking in the magnitude of what Beck was going through. I never wanted to be in a position to understand what he was dealing with. It was bad enough being distant with my father these last few months. I couldn't imagine losing him completely.

"It all comes back to me walking away when I was seventeen," Jake suddenly said, jolting me out of my thoughts.

Confused, I said, "What does?"

"Everything that's happened to us. Brett's death. Me breaking up with you. The shit we went through to find each other again only for your parents and sister not to forgive me like you did. You stopped talking to Andie because of it, Andie got in an accident, you blamed yourself, you made a pact with God and now have this irrational fear, irrational but real nonetheless, which means you're afraid we can't be together." Jake shook his head. "I don't believe that. I don't believe that we have to keep being punished for what happened when we were kids. I don't believe that the choices we both made to walk away from each other define us. I don't believe that we can't trust one another, and I don't believe that we wouldn't make it work a third time around. If you and Andie, if you and your parents, hadn't fallen out before the accident, I'm one hundred percent sure you would have had me by your side during Andie's coma. You would have let me in. I really believe that fate just got in the way of this one." He grabbed my hand, his eyes imploring. "But really, we're still kids, Charley. We've got so much to work out about ourselves and about life. Who says then that this is all we get? We've got a whole lifetime that we could use to make up for our past."

Although my heart was pounding from his optimism, I found myself attempting to remind him of one glaring fact. "But Jake—"

"I know, I know. Your fear." He sighed and sat back in his seat. "We can't be together until you work it out, Charley. We can't be together until you work it all out. Your sister, your parents, your career—*you*. Go home and face your sister, Supergirl." He brought my hand to his mouth and pressed a gentle kiss upon my knuckles. "Go home and find yourself. Take all the time you need. And when you're done and if you still want me," he gave me a sad, crooked, boyish smile, "come and find me."

Chapter Eighteen

Chicago, December 2013

There was a possibility I was going to upchuck all over my sister and Rick's front stoop. It felt like one minute I'd been in San Francisco and the next I was in Beverly ready to face the firing squad.

It wasn't a minute but it *was* only eight hours.

What Jake had said to me in the SUV was absolutely right. I'd known it was right for over five months but after my first semester in Edinburgh, I thought I finally had a grasp on who I was and where I was going. So to suddenly find myself lost was overwhelming. I hadn't handled the uncertainty of what lay ahead for me. I'd let myself be changed by the cracks in what had always been a strong family bond and rather than face those changes, I'd run from them and all the reasons for their existence.

Perhaps if I'd confided in Jake sooner, I would've ended up on Andie's doorstep months ago. Or perhaps I needed the time and distance from all the players in my story to find my way back to them. I guess I'd never know. And I knew I'd never know if Andie and I could find our way back if I didn't knock on her door.

Claudia and Beck had been really understanding. Beck was

coping with his own issues and I didn't want to take anything away from that. The road trip was about him and I needed to let the three of them go so they could help him work that out. I was going to call my parents and ask them to book me a flight to Chicago from San Francisco, but Claudia insisted on using her parents' credit card. I tried to say no. Our road trip had been funded by that credit card and I didn't want to take advantage. Claudia said it was the only thing her parents were good for, so in the end, that—and my desire to hold onto my courage while I still had it—was the reason I accepted her help.

I got a taxi to the airport, leaving the three of them at the beach.

I couldn't bear to say to goodbye to Jake in the airport… I didn't know when or if I'd ever say hello to him again. We shared a look before I got in the taxi, his so hopeful and mine filled with regret. I'd treated him terribly these last few months and yet it hadn't stopped him from trying to save me.

Suddenly my sister's door flew open and there she was.

Beautiful and fresh-faced, Andie was standing upright and she looked healthy. Her expression, however, was blank. "Were you planning on knocking or are you holding out for a career as a porch ornament?"

Feeling breathless, I whispered, "Funny."

Andie stood back from the doorway and made a gesture for me to come inside. "You're only seven months late."

I flinched but somehow managed to meet her eyes as I stepped inside her home for the first time since her accident. She shut the door and I waited for her to make the next move. The fact that I felt like a complete stranger in her house made me even more nauseated than before. Panic held me to the spot.

Andie eyed me for a second. Whatever she saw made the flatness in her eyes disappear. Concern shone through. "Don't look at me like that," she said. "It doesn't suit you."

"I'm sorry," I blurted out.

After a moment of intense scrutiny, Andie nodded. "I know. Come on." She walked through her spacious entry hall and into the living room. "Rick's at work."

"Probably a good thing," I muttered.

"Why's that?" She flopped down into the armchair and I realized my parents' reports on her recovery were true, and I'd missed all her hard work.

I shrugged as I lowered myself onto her couch. "I'm guessing he's not too happy with me right now."

Instead of yay or naying my suspicions, Andie just stared at me.

Forcing the nausea aside and trying to find the me who wouldn't be intimidated, I kept my gaze steady on hers. "How have you been? How has the recovery been?"

"My recovery has been fine. I missed my own graduation and I was worried for a while that the job I had waiting for me was in jeopardy, but it all worked out." She shrugged, barely giving me any emotion.

I narrowed my eyes. "Are you just telling me what you've been telling everyone else?"

"Well, what do you want to hear, Charley?" She narrowed her eyes right back at me. "That waking up from a fourteen-day coma was petrifying? That I had nightmares for months? That my fiancé worries every time I step outside the door? That I've developed a fear of yellow cabs? That I had to be emotionally and mentally evaluated and cleared before they'd let me start work? That all of this pales in comparison to the fact that nine months ago, my little sister stopped talking to me and I feel like I've been missing an arm ever since?"

I held her stare and let her anger and hurt flood into me like a tsunami. She deserved the chance to let me have it and I believed I deserved to take it.

"So are you going to say anything ever again?" Andie asked patiently. She glanced at the clock on the mantel above her fireplace. "It's been ten minutes."

I eased back against her sofa. "I'm trying to put the right words together to apologize but I can't. There are no right words. I'm sorry we argued. I'm sorry I chose Jake over you. I'm sorry I didn't talk to you for weeks. And I am beyond sorry that I couldn't get unstuck from the quagmire I've found myself in since Jake... and everything... I'm sorry I didn't get unstuck and brave and face you. I'm sorry I didn't help you get through this."

Andie placed coffee on the table in front of me before sitting back down on the armchair, her own mug clasped in her hands. She curled her feet underneath her and took a sip.

I waited for her to say something.

I'd been waiting for twenty minutes.

"Are you going to say anything now?"

She cocked her head to the side to study me. "What would you like me to say?"

"I don't know. Anything."

"You're lying."

I almost rolled my eyes. She was using her therapist voice. I refrained and nodded. "Okay, I admit it. I want you to forgive me."

Time seemed to move slowly as I waited for Andie's reply. She made me wait while she sipped her coffee until there was nothing left to sip. I waited while she leaned forward to place her empty mug on the table before slowly sitting back.

"Does this lengthy silence mean it's irreparable?"

Andie's expression turned curious at the question. "What's irreparable?"

"The damage I've done to this family."

She was silent so long, I feared we were about to sit through another twenty minutes of torturous quiet, but then her expression turned pained. "I knew it. I hoped I was wrong, but I knew it."

"Knew what?"

"That the reason it's taken you this long to turn up on my doorstep is because you've taken on the blame for this whole thing."

Shocked, I said, "Don't you blame me for this whole thing?"

Instead of answering my question, Andie leaned forward. "Is it true you took the LSATs? That you're going to law school?"

I wasn't there to discuss my future career. I was there to mend our relationship. "Andie—"

She held up a hand, cutting me off. "Law school?"

I sighed and reluctantly nodded. "Yes. Law school."

"Last time we spoke, you'd decided to pursue the police academy. I want to know what changed."

"Why are we talking about this?"

Andie raised an eyebrow at me. "Because it's important."

"An answer any time now would be good."

I didn't want to talk about my career or anything that wasn't about Andie and repairing our relationship. This time was supposed to be about her. But I'd been sitting there for ten minutes trying to dodge the question.

I heaved another sigh. "I would think it was obvious." When she made no reply, I continued, "Andie, you didn't see what your accident did to Mom and Dad. They held it together but barely. They nearly lost you and it took its toll. It made them... fragile, vulnerable in a way I didn't expect, in a way that scared me. I don't ever want to put them through something like that again. You don't know how relieved they were when I told them I wouldn't pursue a career as a cop."

I could tell by the look in her eyes that my sister understood, but there was something else there too. "And what about you? What about what you want? What about your happiness?"

"I'm not doing this out of martyrdom. I don't want them to have to go through that again. I wanted to be a cop. But I need my family to be okay more. I'm compromising." I leaned forward, hoping she could see the sincerity in my eyes. "It was hard to make that decision. And yes, I feel a little lost right now, but I don't regret giving Mom and Dad peace of mind. Careers... they come and go, right? It's the people in our lives who are important. So I'm okay with this decision."

After a few moments, Andie nodded. "Okay."

"I felt lost for a while after the accident," Andie spoke up, breaking the silence.

I waited for her to elaborate.

"You said you feel lost." She explained, "I'm just saying, I get it. Everything felt different after the accident. Mom and Dad were different. Even Rick. And you… you weren't there at all. Was part of that because you feel lost?"

I nodded. "You're a part of me. Like a limb. Like lungs. To be me, truly me, I need you in my life. It's always going to be hard for me to find myself if you're not in my life." Emotion clawed at my chest. "I couldn't move past the guilt and it changed me. I'm sorry I wasn't stronger."

"I was mad at you," she said. "Like I mentioned before, when I was in recovery, I was pretty scared. I've never been scared like that and that's partly because I've always had this brave little sister in my life who somehow managed to make me feel safe." She glanced away and I caught the shimmer in her eyes. "I was lost too and I was mad at you."

I looked at my hands, trying to find the right words. "I don't know how to make sense of why. I can try to explain…"

"I'm listening," she prompted.

My stomach flipped as it all rushed me, all the reasons my life had spiraled out of control these last few months. It all tumbled out of my mouth, just like it had done with Jake. "I felt like I was being punished. Your accident, I felt like it was punishment for the way I treated you, for putting Jake before you. The guilt was just…" I sucked it up and for the next twenty minutes, I told her everything I'd confessed to Jake. My terror that Andie would die. My guilt, my bargain with God, the resentment, and then the paralysis when she woke up.

Andie was quiet for a while, scrutinizing me in that inner psychiatrist way of hers. She was so quiet, I was afraid I'd mucked up the explanation.

But then she said, "I stopped being mad at you pretty quickly during my recovery. I went back to worrying like I had been for the months we didn't talk. Especially after Rick and Mom and Dad told me you were by my side more than anyone when I was in the coma. It hurt that you didn't come around for my recovery or after, but I forgive you for that, Charley. I forgave you months ago."

Once the little niggle of resentment I'd been feeling over Andie's confession was swamped by the relief that she'd forgiven me, I asked calmly, "If you forgave me, why didn't *you* come to see *me*?"

Andie gave me her *I'm smarter than you* look that always drove me crazy. "Because of who you are. Everything you just told me, with the exception of your pact with God, I already guessed. Mom and Dad told me about law school and I knew that this whole thing had to be impacted by that. I know you better than anyone, maybe even better than you know yourself. And I knew that if I made the first move, you'd hold on to your guilt until your fingers bled. You needed to be the one to push past it, to be brave like always, and come to me first. It was the only way you'd feel okay about yourself."

I shook my head. "You say you forgive me, but we both know I still should've been here."

"How could you have been? You were in another country."

"I wasn't even here emotionally, though," I insisted, a part of me needing her to be mad at me to substantiate my own self-reproach.

"Charley, why do you always need to save people? Who you are is going to crush you unless you learn to ease up on yourself. You can't control fate. You can't save everyone."

"But I shouldn't have put Jake before you. I shouldn't have treated you like that. Surely you agree I'm to blame for that?"

"No, I don't." Andie shook her head stubbornly. "About two weeks after that telephone conversation, Rick and I got into a big argument about it. I'd been snapping at him for every little thing because I was pissed at you. Finally he'd had enough and told me that I was partly to blame for my argument with you." She laughed softly. "And you know that pissed me off even more because I knew he was right." Andie leaned forward, her expression sincere. "Charley, I should never have put you in that position. I was living in the past. I was scared Jake was going to hurt you like he did before. When he left last time, I came back to this kid who wasn't my sister and it scared me shitless. And not just for you but selfishly for me, too. I've always needed you to be strong and brave, and when Jake left you, I suddenly realized you were mortal, just like the rest of us."

Stunned, my voice was husky with emotion. "I never knew you felt that way."

"Because it sounds silly. I'm a grown-up. We're supposed to stop hero-worshipping and putting people up on pedestals after the age of ten. But you bounced back from Jake, and yeah, you were different, but you were strong still and you were my sister again. I just didn't want to lose that. So I pushed my opinion on you and I let Dad's overprotectiveness about the whole thing fuel my opinion and somewhere along the line, I forgot to trust you. Our argument was my fault. You shouldn't have handled it the way you did but I shouldn't have tried to make you choose between the people you love. It put you in an impossible position, Charley. I told Dad that too." She smiled. "I think he may even have listened. So if Jake is the guy for you, I promise I'll support you on it. I promise I'll trust you."

I blinked rapidly against the tears. "It doesn't matter now."

"Of course it matters. You just told me how you treated the guy these last few months and still he was there for you—he helped get you here. For that alone, I'm willing to give this kid another shot."

"Didn't you hear me earlier? I promised God I wouldn't be with Jake if He saved you."

Andie reached for my hand and I squeezed hers in return, so grateful for her forgiveness. "This irrational fear of yours that if you break your pact with God something bad will happen to me, it's not uncommon. I read about these kinds of fears in my research. Men who lose their fathers at a young age often have a crippling belief that they themselves won't live past the age their fathers were when they died. People who offer to sacrifice something to God if He'll save a loved one is a common occurrence. When the loved one lives, the person often believes that God held up His side of the bargain. They then sacrifice what they promised for fear of reprisal. These kinds of beliefs and fears seem beyond irrational to other people, but they can take such a strong foothold that people make choices around it that they shouldn't." Her grip on me tightened. "You stopped going to church when you were old enough to decide whether you had faith in God or faith in the people around you. You told me that for now, you'd stick with people because they had proven themselves to you and so far God hadn't. Listen to me when I tell you that I woke up from that coma because *I* wasn't finished here." Her eyes shone bright with tears. "I need you to have faith in *that*, and not in some deal you made with a deity I'm not even sure you really believe in."

I brushed at the tears falling beyond my control. "I don't know if it's that easy. These last few months without you have been the hardest of my life, and now I'm just terrified of losing you."

"Getting through that fear… it's not going to happen overnight, Supergirl. This is the first time we've talked in months. It's going to take time. But we're going to make time." She moved and wrapped her arms around me. I hugged my sister tight. "You'll find yourself."

"What if I can't get back to who I was?" I whispered.

"You won't because it's not about going back. It was never about going back. It was about doing something, anything, but standing still. You did that. You came to me even though you were petrified of the outcome. So now… it's about moving forward and growing up." She kissed my forehead. "It sucks at first, but it gets better."

Chapter Nineteen

Chicago, February 2014

"So I talked with my Mom and Dad about careers."

Dr. Bremner gave me a nod of encouragement. "And?"

"It went well, actually. We compromised. I study law next fall. When I graduate, we'll talk about the police academy again and whether they're comfortable with the idea."

After finally getting up the nerve to face my sister, I went home to Lanton with Andie for the weekend. I swear to God the distance between my dad and me melted as soon as I walked in the door with my sister at my side. He hugged us tight, relief and pride back in his eyes. Mom was much the same. As a family we sat down and talked everything through with honesty and as much calm as we could muster.

It wasn't all tied up neatly in a bow. Andie had forgiven me but she was still mad it had taken me so long to come check on her. And she had every right to be angry. I was still a little pissed at my dad for the way he'd treated me and after I explained everything I'd been going through, he and Mom had guilty looks on their faces. Especially when Andie told them it was Jake who'd helped me work it out. I'd tried to tell my dad at his auto shop that day, and although it made him ease up on me, he hadn't gone out of his way to help me work it out. He expected me to do it alone because that's who he thought I was. That's who I thought I was too.

But over the last few months, Andie and Dr. Bremner, her colleague, had shown me that it didn't make me weak to ask for help from friends and family. It didn't make me any less of a person.

Andie had talked me into seeing a psychiatrist because she thought it would help me organize my thoughts and realize what it was I wanted out of life. Dr. Bremner and I were taking it step by step and had spent time talking about my career. She didn't just take my word at face value—she wanted me to dig deep so I'd know for sure if giving up the academy was something I could live with in the long run. I was willing to do what it took to give my family peace of mind, but I also wanted a career that would make me feel less powerless. Because Andie was right in the end. I had a crazy savior complex and it needed an outlet.

I passed the LSATs with flying colors and was accepted into law school at the University of Chicago. A few weeks ago Andie invited me to stay with her and Rick for the weekend and they had Rick's friend over for dinner. He was a public defender. He didn't make the kind of money I'm sure my parents would want me to make after paying for such an expensive education, but this guy was so passionate about his job, that aspect of it didn't bother me. He said it came with good and bad. It was hard to defend people who were guilty of heinous crimes no matter if you were a public defender or working for a private law firm, but it was balanced by the fact that he got to help people in impossible situations and maybe give them a second chance.

It was another viewpoint I hadn't considered.

And that's when I really started to think. The smart plan for me was to get a law degree, do the internships, and then decide what I wanted to do with my life. It was three years away, and anything could happen in three years. However, I was also not quite ready to give up on the idea of the academy.

So Andie had accompanied me for moral support last weekend while I discussed the possibility with my parents. They still felt uneasy about it but agreed that they wouldn't know how they'd feel about it in three years' time, either, and we could talk about it then.

"How do you feel about that?" Dr. Bremner said. "Does the uncertainty make you uneasy?"

"Not anymore. I'm learning patience."

She smiled. "Good." Her eyes flicked to the clock. "That's time."

I stood up. "I'll see you in a few weeks?"

"In a few weeks," she agreed. "Perhaps we can finally talk about Jake."

My breath whooshed out of me at the thought. "Okay," I said quietly.

I felt a little off balance as I wandered down the hall to my sister's office. The light outside her door wasn't on, which meant she didn't have a patient.

She sat behind her desk in the corner of the room, her back to the floor-to-ceiling windows that looked out over the Streeterville area of Chicago. Her office was cozy and comfortable compared to Dr. Bremner's clinical one. Andie had a fat, comfy fabric sofa for her clients while Bremner had a black leather chaise that squeaked with the slightest movement.

My eyes strayed to the framed quote behind Andie's desk.

It sucks at first. But it gets better.

I thought the words she'd said to me all those weeks ago were so fitting for her job that I'd had them printed on thick white paper in embossed dark gold and framed for her office. I wasn't sure if she'd actually hang it, but it went up right away. She said it was the first thing her clients saw upon entering, and most thought it funny.

"That time already?" Andie said, looking up from her laptop.

"Yup. You ready?"

"Give me two minutes."

I visited Chicago every three weeks to talk to Bremner and afterwards, Andie drove us to Lanton to spend the weekend with our parents. It wasn't a permanent thing but I think we both felt we needed to do it to return our family to some kind of normality.

We arrived in Lanton a few hours later and walked into our parents' house, greeted by the magical aroma of brisket and steamed veggies.

Sitting at dinner, I noted that the grim quality in my father's eyes was gone now. There was still something weighty in his expression and I don't think that would ever go away. He'd come close to losing a kid and I think he and Mom would carry that with them always. But they were both doing so much better, and Mom no longer visited the cemetery to find understanding from her dead mother. I saw that as a plus.

"I'm sorry Claudia had to cancel this weekend," Mom said after passing around the broccoli.

I almost sniggered at the thought of my love-struck friend. "Well, Beck's band is playing a popular bar in Evanston and she likes to be at his gigs to keep the groupies away. They're starting to really make a name for themselves in Chicago."

Dad frowned. "If they hit it big, she'll have to learn to deal with that. She better think on it carefully—I don't want her to get hurt."

I felt warmth in my chest over my dad's concern for my best friend. Her parents were never going to provide that for her, but I was glad she had a good substitute. "She has. It makes her uncomfortable, but she's willing to deal with it for Beck." I snorted. "He told her she had nothing to worry about. He convinced her with his usual hard-to-say-no-to charm."

Dad shook his head, smirking. "He should teach that stuff."

My dad liked Beck. He'd gotten to know him a little when they joined my family for Christmas. Dad liked the way he was with Claudia and was just as susceptible to his easy charm as everybody else was. But it was more than that. The death of his father had made Beck a little grave. He seemed to have an understanding of what was important and how little time we have to appreciate it. An air of maturity floated around Beck that hadn't been there before, and my dad liked it.

I chuckled. "He's only speaking the truth. It's hard to compete with someone like Claudia."

"Yeah, but if they get famous, they'll get the crazy girls who don't care how beautiful a rocker's girlfriend is or how much in love with her he is. They'll do anything to get in his pants," Andie warned.

"I know. And Claudia knows that. But she trusts Beck and so do I."

And that was a good thing now that he and Claud were a package deal. They alternated weekends at each other's apartment, so I saw quite a bit of him. When Claudia was in Chicago for the weekend, I hung out with Alex and friends from college.

I didn't hang out with the rest of The Stolen. For obvious reasons.

I talked to Lowe on the phone occasionally and caught up with the guys' antics through him and Beck. And also through Jake.

Jake and I emailed one another now. We hadn't spoken on the phone and we hadn't seen each other since San Francisco, but we hadn't completely let go of one another yet, either.

It started with me. I knew I wasn't ready to deal with our relationship or lack thereof, but I also didn't want us to be strangers. So I sent him an email, telling him about my reconciliation with Andie and asking him about the rest of the road trip.

And so we became pen pals. I received and sent an email once a week, and I looked forward to Jake's email like I was waiting on a million-dollar check to arrive. I even sent him a birthday present last month. It was an imported seven-inch red vinyl of Pearl Jam's "Daughter." I thought it would look cool on his wall, and Jake seemed to agree when he emailed to thank me.

I wish I could've seen his face when he opened it.

"Your mom and I were thinking it might be nice to rent a place in Grand Haven this summer. Thought the five of us could spend a long weekend up there."

Andie grinned. "Sounds good, Dad. Just let me know what dates so I can schedule it, and so Rick can get time off."

Dad turned to me. "Charley?"

"I'm there, definitely."

Pleased, he nodded and returned to his brisket.

I felt Mom's eyes on me and I looked up to meet her gaze. She gave me a small smile that I wasn't quite sure I understood. It didn't matter what it meant. There was peace in it and comfort in the air around us—not an ounce of brittle tension to be found.

I was finally getting my family back.

My phone had vibrated in my pocket over an hour ago, but I hadn't wanted to be rude and bail on my family to check my email. I waited impatiently until Andie called it a night and I quickly did the same. Once in my old room, I shut the door and hurried to my laptop.

The email from Jake was waiting in my inbox.

I felt a flutter of nerves in my belly as I sank into my desk chair and clicked the mail open.

Charley,

My mom asked me home for dinner tonight. Sounds innocent enough, huh? Well, let me tell you it wasn't. I expected a home-cooked meal and watching sports with my dad. Instead I walked in on my little brother having sex with his shy little librarian.

I'm scarred for life.

Let's just say shy librarian has a kinky side and I now know more about my brother's sex life than anyone should ever know, let alone a blood relative. I went back to my apartment as quickly as possible to try to rid myself of the image. I think if I return to therapy sessions, I'll somehow get back on track with my life.

Speaking of, I got accepted into the University of Chicago graduate school for molecular engineering. The parents are very proud. I'm crapping myself. The guys are finished with school after graduation, and I'm going to continue to be a student for the next however many years. I still feel like I'm deliberately prolonging the inevitability of adulthood. Knowing you'll be going to law school makes me feel better about it, though.

On that subject... are you ever going to tell me which schools you got accepted into? Are you deserting the Midwest for Stanford like you said you probably would?

Inquiring minds would like to know.

It's going to be weird next year without the guys. I know they'll be there, but they'll be doing their band stuff and whatever manual labor they can find until the day they hopefully get signed. Our worlds are going to be different. All of our worlds are, I guess. I didn't realize how much I depended on them. Don't tell them that, though. Matt gets clingy when you show him too much affection.

Claudia is here at the apartment. She said you're home with your parents this weekend. That's good. I take it that's good, right? You, Andie, and your folks are finally back to normal? Claudia seems a whole lot less worried about you and you sound better in your emails, so I'm guessing things are starting to pull together for you. I'm glad to hear it. I know what it's like to be where you are and it's not great. But you're strong, Charley. I knew you'd get through it.

As for Claudia, it's cool to see how much she's changed since Barcelona. I thought we'd fucked up majorly taking her to meet that dick, but it's all turned out okay. Beck's crazy about her. It's a little unsettling but I'm learning to live with it since Claud's happy and deserves to be. Although I would like it if she'd stop making soup. Our apartment reeks. Maybe you could casually mention it to her for me?

I gotta go now. Denver's yelling at me to get my ass out the door to some party. Have a nice weekend with your folks.

Talk soon.

Jake

I stared at the screen, feeling a whole bunch of emotions I wasn't sure I had any right to feel. Jake's emails always made me laugh and this time was no exception. Yet there was panic upon hearing we'd both be at U of C next fall. There was the stupid jealousy I felt over the fact that Claudia got to spend time with him when I didn't. There was anxiety over him going to a party and possibly meeting someone. That question plagued me all the time. I didn't know if he was seeing anybody. I didn't know if he'd meant it when he told me that he'd wait for me. All I knew was that as much as I loved reading his emails, they also kind of devastated me. He never flirted. He never alluded to his feelings, our broken relationship, or if there was a future for us. So I didn't, either.

That emotional distance was crippling.

Yet I couldn't give up those emails. While I floated in limbo over Jake, those emails kept me tethered to him.

West Lafayette, March 2014

The Brewhouse was packed, bodies crammed together at the bar, around tables, but mostly around the stage. And most of those bodies were girls.

A friend of Denver's worked at WCCR, the college radio station here at Purdue, and he'd gotten The Stolen some serious air play over the last few weeks running up to their gig at The Brewhouse. Claudia and I pinned posters of the band everywhere. All the marketing seemed to have paid off.

I smirked as a girl tried to grab Lowe's leg and he somehow managed to avoid contact while wearing a wickedly sweet smile that placated her. I shot a look at Claudia and was surprised to see she looked calm about the girls panting over the band and over her boyfriend.

It might have had something to do with the fact that Beck didn't look at any of those girls. He either watched Claudia or was too lost in the music to be focused on anyone else.

Alex, Sharon, and Claudia were trying to talk—shout—over the music, but I'd given up on conversation. I wasn't in a chatty mood anyway and hadn't been since receiving Jake's email two days ago.

Charley,

I know the guys are playing Purdue this weekend but I wanted to let you know I won't make it. It's my mom's birthday that weekend and Dad's got this whole big dinner thing planned.

Have a great time.

Jake

Up until the email, I'd been worried sick about Jake appearing because I wasn't sure how I would cope. I knew that I loved him, but I still wasn't sure we were in the right place to start our relationship up again, so I didn't want to see him. I knew seeing him would rip open the longing inside me and maybe cause me to act rashly.

Now that he wasn't coming, I was worried. His emails were

getting shorter and if possible, even more emotionally distant.

I was losing him.

Honestly, I wasn't surprised. He'd been more than patient and I had been more than confusing.

Claudia nudged my side and I glanced at her. "You okay?" she shouted over the music.

"I'm fine," I mouthed and turned back to look at the stage, feeling her concerned stare burning into the side of my face.

When the guys finished their set, I was relieved—not because I didn't love listening to them play, I did, but because hanging out with them usually took my mind off other things. Such as Jake's absence.

The guys managed to magically finagle a table once they'd gotten past most of the flushed, bothered girls trying to cram their numbers in the guys' pockets. Even when we all sat down, girls hovered nearby, watching them all. Beck pulled Claudia down onto his lap and she willingly sat there for him because she was his human shield against obnoxious girls.

Lowe smirked at the maneuver before he quirked a questioning eyebrow in my direction.

I shook my head. "Don't even think about."

"I have a very nice lap." He pouted and his lip ring stuck out comically.

With laughter in my voice, I said, "Tempting, but I'll pass."

"Will you at least help me get the drinks?" He nodded his head toward the bar and I stood in answer.

We weaved our way through the crowd, getting stopped by guys and girls who wanted to congratulate Lowe and tell him how much they enjoyed the show.

"Wow," I said as we moved into the crowd around the bar. "You're, like, famous."

He gave me a droll look. "Just catching on."

I punched him playfully. "I'm serious. You guys are doing well. Paid gigs, airplay…"

Lowe gave me a shy grin. "Yeah, things are starting to get serious. People actually know us back in Chicago. It's surreal but it's good. We've got a meeting with a small label next week. I don't think we're going to take an offer, but we want to talk, get experience with that stuff, show our interest in moving forward with the band."

My eyes rounded at the news. "Lowe, that's amazing. You guys deserve it."

I felt his arm slide around my waist and he gave me a friendly half hug. "Thank you." He ducked his head, bringing it close to mine. "It's good to see you, Redford. We've all missed you."

"I've missed you guys too." I smiled a little sadly and he caught it and gave me another squeeze.

Unable to stop myself, I said, "How's Jake?"

Lowe's eyebrows drew together. "I thought you guys were emailing."

"We are." I shrugged. "But we don't really talk about anything real anymore. I just…" My heart pounded so hard in my chest, I felt it in my throat. The nausea quickly followed. "Is he seeing someone?"

Lowe instantly stiffened with discomfort.

"Oh my God." I looked away, feeling panic claw at my insides.

"No, not oh my God." Lowe tugged on my waist to draw my eyes back to his. Sincerity shone through them as he said, "He's not seeing anyone. I just don't think it's my place to talk about this stuff."

"I know. It's just Beck and Claudia refuse to talk about it, and I wanted to know if he's moved on. If he's sleeping with other girls."

Studying me for a moment, taking in my pleading eyes with a huff of annoyance, Lowe replied, "I can't not give in to you." He shook his head in consternation. "This is how Jake must feel all the time."

"Well?"

"Truth? Jake has girls come on to him. Does he go home with any of them? No."

Relief whooshed through me. "Really?"

His expression suddenly turned disapproving. "He knows what it's like to have *you* in his bed. Nothing else measures up right now because he still loves you. I feel bad for the guy. I'm also confused as fuck because I look at you and I know how crushed you'd be if you found out he was with some other girl. I look at you and I know you love Jake. What I can't understand is why you're not with him."

"Because," I tried to explain, "if we do this a third time, we both better be sure. Right now, I'm still trying to figure other stuff out."

Lowe rolled his eyes. "Not to be a shit, Charley, but you're twenty-one. We're all trying to figure stuff out at twenty-one. You think you're the only one who has a crisis of identity in college? You're not. And it doesn't mean you should put the important stuff on hold."

Feeling a little stung, I moved out of his embrace. "You're right. You're a shit."

"Yeah, well…" He curled his hands around my upper arms and turned me to face him. "I have a little bit of a blind spot when it comes to you and I've found myself making excuses for the way you've acted this last year. But I can't justify the way you've played Jake. Last January I was the one telling you to watch your back with Jake. I was pissed for what you had to go through watching him be with Melissa while he dangled you on a string. Now *you're* doing the same thing to *him*."

I glowered at him. "It's not like that. *Jake* knows it's not like that."

Lowe was immune to my glower. "Jake's been a fucking mess since he got back from San Francisco, but I get the feeling he's not going to keep putting himself through this, whatever this is, so yeah… maybe you should get used to the idea of Jake moving on with his life."

Feeling angry tears prick my eyes, I asked through gritted teeth, "Why are you trying to hurt me?"

His eyes washed over my face and whatever they saw made his expression soften. "I'm not trying to hurt you, Charley. I'm just trying to prepare you."

"You're mad at me."

"I don't know if I could ever really be mad at you," he confessed, sounding almost sad. "But right now, I don't get you."

Angry, but this time at myself, I glanced away and pretended to watch the bar staff as they tried to cull the crowd around the bar.

Lowe's warm hand slipped into mine and clasped it tight. I didn't look at him—I couldn't for fear I'd fall apart. Instead I just squeezed his hand back and took comfort from the fact that I had such good friends who would stick by me and try to understand, even if they never really could.

It was an understatement to say I was in an even lousier mood after Lowe gave me a talking-to. I had a drink and pretended that everything was okay for a while, until the room started to feel like it was closing in on me.

I excused myself and pushed through the socializing students toward the exit. I practically lunged outside, gulping the air as I flopped against the building.

The noise from the bar gradually became a hum as I stared up at the sky, remembering a time before when life was simpler. It would be easy to blame Jake— to pinpoint the time and say it was the day before I met him when I was sixteen. Except that wasn't the truth. The truth was life was simpler the day before I left to spend the summer in Miami with my aunt, uncle, and cousins. It was the summer I felt the impact of my cousin Ethan's death. The hole he left behind, the tear his death caused in my family's hearts, and all the answers his mom and dad never got. The justice they never found.

Life wasn't simple after that. For the first time in my life, I felt powerless, and I hated it. I wanted it not to be that way, and that's when the idea of becoming a cop lodged in my head. There was a naïveté in that, I knew that now. Being a cop wouldn't make me feel less powerless in bad situations. There was no remedy for that.

"You look deep in thought."

I jumped, turning wide-eyed to find Beck leaning against the wall beside me. I hadn't even heard him come outside. "Yeah," I said dryly. "And I think I was on to something before you interrupted."

He gave me an apologetic half smile. "Sorry. I needed some air."

My gaze sharpened, processing the hint of melancholy in the back of my friend's eyes. "You okay?"

He nodded, swallowing a pull of his beer.

Taking a stab in the dark, I said, "You thinking about your dad?"

Beck's eyebrows drew together. "He's been on my mind a little lately. Did Lowe tell you we have a small label interested in us?"

"Yeah."

"Did I ever tell you my dad was in a band?"

"You told me he was a musician, but I thought he wrote jingles and stuff."

He shot me an unhappy smile. "Yeah, but that's not how he started out." He exhaled, turning so his back was flat to the wall. He stared up at the sky like I had only moments before. "Dad was in a rock band in his early twenties. For a while it was the most important thing in his life—until he met my mom. But then the band got signed to a small label in San Francisco and they started touring." He stopped talking, his eyes meeting mine, something heavy and grim in their depths. "He loved my mom but the tour killed her love for him. This was a guy who moved us to Chicago when the band was on break because Mom got a teaching opportunity he didn't want her to pass up. And he loved San Francisco. It was like losing an arm to leave that place. He loved her, though, simple as that. But then the band starting touring again and Mom couldn't take it." I suddenly realized that look in Beck's eyes was desperation. "They argued whenever he was home. She accused him of cheating but my dad was adamant up until the end that he never screwed around on her. She didn't believe him, and she hated the rock-star lifestyle. So she left him." His voice cracked. "She left him and even when he left the band for her, she wouldn't take him back. He stayed in Chicago to be close to us, started working for advertisers and stuff like that. And he turned to alcohol."

I didn't know what to say, it was so heartbreaking. "Beck…"

His eyes burned into me suddenly. "I don't want that to happen with Claudia. My music means a lot to me, but I don't want to lose her because of it."

I was stunned. Shocked even. I had no idea Beck had these thoughts running through his head. "It won't. Claudia loves you."

"Yeah, and my mom loved my dad. But all the girls… I've not been a saint, so Claud will have that in the back of her mind all the time. And you see what it's like." He gestured toward the bar. "If by some miracle The Stolen actually got signed, touring would change everything. I'd have crazy girls trying to get into my pants all the time, and I have a smart girlfriend who knows exactly what goes on in these tours. How much of that do you think Claudia could take? I would never cheat on her, *ever*, but it would drive me crazy thinking of just one guy who wanted her and kept coming on to her, never mind hundreds. You're not telling me she wouldn't feel that way too eventually." He leaned in to me, his voice low with emotion. "Somehow the most miraculous person I ever met in my life has spent most of her life feeling unloved and neglected. She deserves to feel like no girl in the world could ever come close to her. I want her to feel that way every fucking day, and I can't do that if I'm on tour."

"Beck, what are you saying?" I gasped. "Are you thinking about quitting the band?"

He shrugged. "I don't know. I applied to grad school at the same time as Jake and I got in. He's the only one who knows."

I pushed off the wall to face him. "Beck, you have to talk to Claudia before you make a decision. She knows how much The Stolen means to you and if she thought for one second you were thinking about throwing your dream away because of her, she'd—"

"Have a shit fit," he interrupted dryly. "I know."

"You have to give her a chance to prove that she can do this for you. Look at her in there." I pointed to the bar. "She handles those girls fine. Somehow, out of all the craziness and all your conquests and dragging your feet about the two of you, she's actually pretty secure about you. Beck, she knows that you love her. Give her a chance. She might surprise you." I grinned. "She's been surprising me since the day we met."

Beck gave me a small smile but that darkness in his eyes hadn't dissipated. "We could try it, and it could all work out. But there's a fifty percent chance that it won't, and she means too much to me to risk losing her."

"Beck, we're not talking about a small thing here—we're talking about you giving up your career," I reminded him, feeling more than a little overwhelmed for him.

He raised his eyebrows. "Right," he agreed. "It's called sacrifice or compromise or whatever you want to name it. It boils down to one thing—what we're willing to give up for the people we love. I thought you of all people would understand, Charley. You gave up the academy for your parents. And I get it, I do. *They* are what matters. What's the point in the memories I'll have of touring if at the end of my life, Claudia isn't by my side? What's the point if the person I love the most never made enough memories with me to make me feel okay about my life coming to an end? My dad had no one in the end. I don't want that to be my story too. You understand that, right?"

"You've put the academy on the back burner because you know that you being a cop could potentially make your parents' lives worse. And you love them so if they're not happy, you're not happy. Other people can say whatever the fuck they want. They can say there has to be a line, that you have to chase your dreams, other people be damned." He slumped against the wall. "But I get it."

"You do?" I whispered.

"Yeah. The people we love are one of our dreams too. Sometimes you just can't chase them all. So you've got to choose." He shot me a sad smile. "A guitar won't keep me warm at night, so something's got to give."

I slumped against the wall too. I was confused for Beck, worried for him, but at the same time, I got him and he got me. I suddenly didn't feel so bad about putting a halt to the whole police academy thing. "They never told us it would be like this," I grumbled.

"What?"

"Adulthood."

Beck sighed. "Nope. They certainly did not."

Chapter Twenty
West Lafayette, April 2014

"Do you still believe that something awful will happen to your sister if you were to resume a relationship with Jake?" Dr. Bremner asked.

I shook my head firmly. "No. I think you were right to begin with. I think that the anxiety I was feeling over the breakdown of my relationship with Andie and my parents' disapproval amplified that fear that if I broke my grief-stricken pact, Andie would pay for it. It's taken me a while but the stifling weight is gone."

"But you still have moments where it affects you?"

"When I think about my future and whether Jake is a part of that future, I won't lie. The thought flits across my mind, but I squash it with rationality. It's like a little mantra. I give myself a talking-to."

Dr. Bremner nodded. "That's excellent progress." She shut her notepad. "So what about Jake? Do you think you're ready to face him and make a decision about your relationship?"

My uncertainty took hold as it always did when thinking about that. "Jake told me that he thought we needed a chance to start over without our past clinging to us. I'm still not sure that's true. We failed to trust one another in times when we really needed each other most. I'm not sure what that says about us as a couple."

"So you don't agree with Jake that circumstances interfered? You don't think he's right when he said that if your parents and Andie hadn't been so disapproving of your relationship, he would've been by your side through your sister's accident and through all the issues you've been dealing with these last few months?"

"I think he would've wanted to be."

"The question is would you have wanted him to be?"

"Well, yeah, he was my boyfriend."

Dr. Bremner smiled softly. "Then wouldn't that make Jake right?"

"Okay, now you're just confusing me."

I'd been thinking about Jake constantly, now that everything else seemed to be falling into place. It was time to work out the best thing to do. My conversations with Dr. Bremner would probably be moving along a lot faster if my true feelings weren't so inhibited by the memory of both Jake and my actions since we'd met at Alex's party all those years ago.

I had to decide whether I could forgive the folly of our youth and bet all my money on the wisdom of our experiences in the hopes that third time around, we'd do it right.

But all my hedging was brought to a halt by Jake's last email.

Charley,

I can't write you anymore. One way or another, we have to move on. I thought these emails were the best way to keep you in my life, but they started to feel empty weeks ago.

I just want us both to be happy, and we're not going to find that in these emails.

I miss you. I miss you so much, it kills me.

But I can't go on that way forever. There will never be a

day that passes that I won't miss you, but I know that I have to get back to the days where the pain is dulled enough I can live with it.

I told you to find yourself and when you were done to come find me.

Well, you found yourself and I'm guessing I'm no longer a part of that equation, and that's okay. All right, it's not okay, but I understand.

I guess I'll see you at Claudia and Beck's wedding in a few years. By then I think we might be able to share a smile, maybe even a drink, without it hurting like fuck.

Don't write back.

Just be happy.

Jake

There was no way to get that email out of my head. I had the words memorized.

They broke my heart.

"What's with the sad face?" Beck said as he walked in, Claudia on his heels. I looked up from the kitchen counter where I'd been standing, staring off as I replayed Jake's email over and over in my mind.

Seeing Beck was a constant reminder of his best friend.

"Uh, this?" I pointed to my face as I threw him a fake grin. "You've got your emoticons upside down, mister."

Beck smirked at Claudia. "Do you think we could make money off her smart-assery? Put her in a sideshow?"

Claudia frowned at me in concern. "Are you still killing yourself over Jake's email?"

Beck's face immediately closed down at the mention of his best friend. Although we were friends, and our talk outside The Brewhouse had definitely strengthened that friendship, it didn't mean Beck was any happier with me regarding Jake. However, it was something he didn't push me on, just like I didn't push him to talk to Claudia about his future with the band. He was still musing over what he would do.

Still, I didn't want Beck to think I was a total bitch, and I didn't want Jake to, either. I got the impression from his email that he might be starting to hate me for real. It occurred to me—if I was honest with Beck, then perhaps that honesty might find its way back to Jake.

"Yes," I said. "It was just so final."

"Maybe that's for the best," Beck said tightly.

Claudia punched the top of his arm. "No, it's not," she argued.

"It is for Jake." Beck refused to be cowed. He shot me a look. "I'm sorry, Charley, but he's been waiting around for you for a whole fucking year now. He needs to let go and you need to let him go."

"She loves him, you jackass."

"Babe," Beck tried to placate her, "I think *you* need to let go of this particular hope."

"I do love him," I cut off whatever scathing reply Claudia was about to shoot back. "But I finally feel like I can breathe for the first time in a year and I'm scared that everything will get crazy again if Jake and I got back together."

That shut them both up.

Beck's gaze softened and he leaned across the counter. "It's always going to be a little crazy. You can't control this shit." He shot Claudia a sardonic look and said, "Believe me."

She rolled her eyes at him before turning back to me. "Charley... you're going to lose him for real if you don't make a move.

And what happens if you bump into each other at U of C next fall? What if you have to endure watching him with another Melissa? Can you handle that?"

"Wait." Beck shot up from the counter in surprise. "You're going to Chicago for law?"

I nodded, feeling a little sheepish that I hadn't told Jake or the guys.

"And you knew?" Beck asked Claudia. "This will kill Jake. You can't go to the same school unless you're together. It'll majorly fuck with his head." He slumped down onto a nearby stool looking suddenly exhausted. "Okay, we have to fix this."

"How?" I said, feeling a little frantic.

Beck studied me a moment. "Do you really love him?"

"Yes."

"Are you willing to lose him?"

I bit my lip, knowing that despite the fear inside me, there really was only one answer to that question. "No."

Beck grinned. "You got any money?"

"For what?"

"As we speak, Jake is on a plane to Europe for spring break with Luke and a couple of Luke's friends. Luke thought he needed to get away for a bit."

Immediately catching on, I felt adrenaline shoot through me. I felt jittery, impatient, anxious, and scared shitless. "Europe." It couldn't be Las Vegas, huh? Then again, flying clear across an ocean was a pretty big statement. "Do you have his itinerary?"

I had to make a decision and I didn't have the luxury of time. Jake's heart couldn't take much more, and mine needed to learn how to cope with all the craziness that came with loving someone as much as I loved Jacob Caplin.

I was fearful. But I was also excited and ready to do this, no matter if I was walking into a lifetime of drama, or a moment of rejection that would live with me forever.

I was going to do this, unknown be damned.

Chapter Twenty-One
Amsterdam, April 2014

The hotel reception was clean and tidy but basic. The polished beech floor shone beneath my feet, the walls brightly finished in an off-white paint. However, it looked somewhat sterile with so few paintings. I sat in an uncomfortable lobby chair beside three other empty lobby chairs, avoiding the smiling receptionist whose grin seemed to wilt with more and more concern every time our eyes met. I'd been waiting in the hotel since nine o'clock in the morning. I told the receptionist I was waiting on a friend who was staying here, but it'd been a couple of hours and I was still sitting there.

I began to worry that Beck had gotten the itinerary wrong.

Until the elevator doors pinged open.

My eyes flew to it and my heart leapt into my throat at the sight of Jake. He'd cut his hair short again but his cheeks and jaw were scruffy with sexy stubble. He looked a little tired and his mouth was turned down in that unhappy way I hated seeing on him.

My eyes hungrily took in his broad-shouldered, tall frame. He was wearing a T-shirt and jeans and he had a small backpack thrown over his shoulder, but to me, he looked amazing.

Being so close to him for the first time in so long... Man, my whole body felt alive. I'd told Beck I was breathing again for the first time in a long time, and I was. But I'd forgotten there was so much more to living than breathing. The evidence was standing only a few feet from me, making my every nerve spark and every sense open up as if they hadn't been used at full capacity since last December.

Realizing Jake was going to walk out of the hotel, I called out, "You're from Chicago. I can tell."

His head jerked at my voice and as soon as his eyes lit upon me, he froze. His gaze roamed over me, taking in every inch of me as if he were trying to process if I was real.

Finally, I guess he decided I was because he walked slowly over to me, stopping to tower above me. I craned my neck to keep my eyes on his gorgeous face.

I love you so much.

His eyes flared at the unspoken sentiment. "What are you doing here?" he asked breathlessly.

I shrugged, a small smile playing on my lips as I used nonchalance to cover my nerves. "Looking for a boy."

Jake's mouth twitched at that and I felt hope bubble inside me. "That so?"

"Yes. Chased him clear across an ocean. Luckily, I sleep like a baby on a plane."

Jake scratched his chin in thought. "That's a long way to come for a guy."

I shrugged again. "He's worth the air miles."

This time Jake gave a huff of laughter before his expression turned searing with gravity. "I guess this means you came to find me?"

"Yes," I answered, remembering his words from months before.

"Go home and find yourself. Take all the time you need. And when you're done and if you still want me, come and find me."

Tears filled my eyes.

He saw. "What are you going to do now that you found me?"

"Keep you."

He sucked in his breath, like I'd knocked the wind out of him. After a moment of staring at me with his chocolaty-brown, soulful eyes, Jake looked over his shoulder at the elevator. When he turned back to me, I saw all the love in the world on his face. "I was on my way out, but now I'm thinking I really need to take you up to my room."

My pulse raced so hard. "That sounds great."

"I take you up there, though, you've got to promise me it's forever. And mean it this time."

I crossed my heart. "Forever."

We stared at each other a long moment. The blood whooshed in my ears as everything stopped....

Until Jake held his hand out for mine.

Epilogue

Chicago, September 2014

The Tent was packed with people who'd come out to hear The Stolen. I glanced curiously at all those faces, knowing somewhere in the crowd was an A & R executive from a major record label.

The Tent was a rock club in Chicago's South Side and to just be playing it was a huge deal for the guys. To have a talent scout in the audience, an even bigger deal.

A rumble of husky laughter met my ears before warm lips brushed my neck and a strong arm slid around my waist. I turned to look up into Jake's handsome face.

"Claudia's a wreck," he said loudly. "I left her with Beck backstage."

"She wants this for him." I hugged him close. "And you know how concerned he is."

Jake didn't look concerned at all. "I told him if the band gets signed and it starts taking its toll on his and Claudia's relationship, he walks away from the band. Easy solution."

I frowned. "And you're sure the guys are all okay with that?"

He shrugged. "They're his boys."

I gave a little huff of laughter. "It's that simple?"

"With these guys, yeah."

"Wow. I'm impressed. It's all very mature." I made a face. "Are you sure Matt was involved in that decision-making?"

Jake smirked. "Yes. But with Matt, it's more a case of being laid-back rather than mature and understanding."

I grinned. "Yeah, that makes more sense."

Before Jake could respond, the lights dimmed and the guys doing the sound check on stage quickly shuffled off. The crowd grew quiet.

The Stolen walked onstage and the noise exploded, people clapping, yelling, and whistling. I'd watched the guys perform more times than I could count, but the atmosphere was different tonight. There were at least a couple hundred people here—their biggest crowd yet. Along with that was the air of electricity, anticipation, and expectation.

This could be the beginning of everything for The Stolen.

Lowe stepped up to the mic and gave the trademark smirk that was sure to cause millions of women all over the world to fall in love with him if/when the band hit the big time.

Denver started the rhythm on the drums and the guys soon followed as Lowe sang in his deep, husky melodious voice. The crowd surged forward around the stage and the electricity in the room went full power.

Throughout the set, I'd shoot looks at Jake as he stood singing along to his best friends' songs. He was proud of them. We both were.

An hour later they finished out the set with my favorite, "Lonely Boy."

The crowds cheered and whistled and catcalled at the guys as soon as the song ended. I watched Beck and Lowe share a grin, shaking their heads in disbelief at the atmosphere they'd created tonight. Lowe turned back to the mic and gave a small salute to the crowd. "You've been listening to The Stolen. Thanks and have a good night."

They began to make their way off stage to the chants for more. Jake grabbed my hand and tugged. "Backstage," he mouthed. I nodded and held on tight as he maneuvered us through the crowd so we could congratulate the guys. I put a hand behind my back, fingers crossed, hoping that when we got there, the A & R executive would've beaten us to it.

I gasped into Jake's mouth as he rocked inside me.

"You there?" he panted, the muscles in his arms flexing.

He had my hands pinned at the sides of my head as a deterrent to my impatience. Jake liked making lazy love to me in the mornings, and I had a tendency to turn things a little wild. He'd taken to holding me down, which was seriously hot.

I gripped his hips with my thighs, lifting my hips into his slow thrust. "Almost," I said breathlessly. "Harder, Jake."

He gritted his teeth and shook his head as he continued on his determined torture. It was worth it. The drawn-out building of tension toward orgasm only made my climax that much sweeter and longer.

I shattered, and my inner muscles clenched around Jake, expelling his own orgasm from him. He gave a muffled yell, his grip on my hands momentarily tightening.

And then he collapsed over me, his warm breath puffing against my neck as his hands loosened their hold. Free, I wrapped my arms around his sweat-slickened back and gripped his waist with my thighs. "Good morning to you too," I laughed, my voice a little husky from having yelled and clapped for the band last night. Not to mention the yelling and celebrating we did afterward when the A & R exec told the guys he was impressed and he'd be in touch to set up a time to chat.

Jake pressed a kiss against my shoulder. "Morning," he mumbled and nuzzled his head back against my neck.

I stroked his back with one hand and ran my fingers through his hair with the other. This was my favorite time with Jake. Don't get me wrong—the sex was awesome and the closer we grew again, the better it got—but these moments, holding him with my whole body while he lay replete and happy, was the best feeling in the world.

We'd done a lot of talking in Europe during spring break. Okay, yes, there was a lot of sex as well, but mostly we let it all out—our apologies, our hurts, our resentments, our hopes for the future. We had a lot to work out and it hadn't been easy. We'd argued at lot in those first few weeks. However, I felt like we were finally where we wanted to be.

I'd been apprehensive about admitting to Jake we'd both be at U of C as grad students but I shouldn't have been. He was relieved that we wouldn't have to contend with long distance on top of everything else. School had started, and we worked our butts off during the week so we could spend the weekends together. Jake was still living with the guys but since they could live anywhere, they'd opted for an apartment on the South Side so Jake could be close to school and me, and Beck could be close to Claudia. Claudia and I had gotten an apartment together, only a block away.

Reluctant to get up, I sighed and patted Jake's delicious ass. "We've got to go."

He groaned and pushed back so he was leaning over me again. His lids sat low over his beautiful dark eyes. "I want to stay inside you."

I smiled and reached up to caress his cheek. "I want you to stay inside me too, but it's that time again."

Gently pulling out of me, Jake's eyes burned into mine as he stroked my hip. "We could just fuck each other's brains out all day."

My breath stuttered at the suggestion but I somehow managed a semi-nonchalant response. "Another time maybe."

He flashed me a grin, not buying it. "You know you want to."

I smirked at him as he rolled off me and onto his back. "Sometimes we can't always get what we want."

"But to endure torture? Every month? It doesn't seem right."

I slid out of bed and strode across the room to my bathroom. "You're going to endure this torture until my family is comfortable with us." I switched on the shower and waited for it to heat up before stepping inside. Since getting back together with Jake, I'd made it my life mission to create some kind of peace between him and my family. I wasn't giving either of them up. There was only so much compromising I could do, and definitely only so much sacrificing.

I knew what it felt like to give up Jake for someone else, and it not only made me miss him, it had made me miss *me*. I wasn't the girl who gave up on someone just because someone else told her to. It took me a while to remember that, but once I had Jake back in my life, I knew there was no way I was letting go without a fight.

That's when I invented "Reconciliation Saturday." Once a month Jake and I drove to Lanton and spent Saturday and the better part of Sunday with my family. Getting Jake to Lanton the first time was hard, and there were still the odd few idiots who watched him with suspicion whenever we went into town, but he was willing to put himself through it for me.

A few seconds later, Jake joined me in the shower. He brushed my wet hair off my face as he crowded me against the cold tiles. "Baby, your dad is never going to be comfortable with us."

I wasn't sure that was true at all. "Andie came around. And Mom has too. Dad will get there."

"You again," Dad grunted at Jake.

Dad released me from his hug, kissed my forehead, and strolled toward the living room without another word to Jake.

My boyfriend stood on my parents' doorstep with a resigned look on his face. "Your dad will get there, huh?"

"In time." I gave him a look of apology and grabbed his arm to pull him inside.

"I thought I heard voices!"

We spun around to watch my mom descend the staircase with a huge smile on her face. As soon as she reached us, she pulled me into a tight hug. When she released me, she turned to Jake and cupped his cheek in her hand. "It's good to see you."

He smiled, a little of the tension leaving him. "You too, Delia."

"I made my macaroni pie in exchange for dishes duty."

"It's a deal," he agreed. Jake loved my mom's macaroni pie.

The front door flew open and Andie stepped inside, talking to the hulking figure of her husband-to-be over her shoulder. "Fruitcake? Really?"

"Yes, fruitcake," Rick said in an insistent voice as he gently nudged her inside.

Andie huffed and turned to us. "I thought the benefit of marrying an orphan was that I didn't have to put up with crappy opinions from the groom's side of the family."

"Andie," Mom admonished.

I, however, chuckled at Rick. "Good thing you've got a thick skin."

"You need it to marry a Redford sister. Right, Jake?" Rick clapped a hand on Jake's shoulder in greeting.

"Truer words have never been spoken," Jake said. "How you doing?"

"My head's bursting from discussing wedding plans but on the plus side, I've been working overtime to get a break from it."

"Liar," Andie snorted, finally coming forward to embrace Mom in hello. "He's fussier than anyone about this stuff." She pulled back on a pout. "Mom, please tell him we can't have fruitcake for our wedding cake."

I wrinkled my nose. "No fruitcake. Vanilla sponge with buttercream frosting."

"Yes, exactly!" Andie threw her arms around me like I'd just saved her from drowning.

"Why don't you have both?" Jake shrugged.

Andie and Rick stared at him a moment before looking back at each other. "He's a genius," Rick stated.

"Agreed." She grinned cheekily at me. "I'm so glad I got you two back together."

"Oh yeah, because you totally should take all the credit for that," I said.

Before we could get into an argument, Rick turned to Mom. "If baking two cakes is too much, Delia, we'll buy one."

"Don't be silly." Mom waved him off. "I can bake two. Claudia will help me."

I snorted. "I'll inform her she's been drafted."

"You all going to stand out in the hall yakking or you coming in here to watch the rerun of last Sunday's game?" Dad called from the living room.

"I thought for sure he was going to offer you a beer." I snuggled into Jake's side, trying not to be mad at my dad—and failing.

It was bad enough he talked to Rick and ignored anything Jake had to say during the game, but to get up and grab himself and Rick a beer and not get Jake one was rude. Rick had frowned at Dad, handed Jake his beer, and got up to get himself another.

Five months had passed since I'd first brought Jake home. That was five visits and Dad's reception hadn't gotten any less frosty.

I huffed out an exasperated sigh as Jake and I walked down Main Street. As soon as Jake had finished his beer, I'd practically hauled him out of the house for a walk, in the hopes that I'd cool off. "I'm sorry."

"Don't be." Jake tightened his arm around my shoulder. "Jim's just trying to make sure I'm in this for the long haul."

"You mean he's testing you?" I wrinkled my nose in annoyance.

"Yeah, I guess."

"Well, it sucks, and my dad is this close to getting my foot in his ass."

"Ach, leave it. I've handled worse." Jake's eyes swept over Hub's across the street and I saw them dim slightly with memories. It didn't help that people still looked at him as if he was something of a curiosity. "This town still freaks me out," he muttered.

I frowned. "You know you can stop coming here anytime and I'd understand."

"Nah," he looked down at me solemnly. "I think the time for running is long past." He tugged on my hand and pulled me across the street.

"Where are we going?"

Jake grinned. "If I recall, my girl has a thing for chocolate milkshakes."

Amazed, I gave him a tentative smile. "You want to go into Hub's for a milkshake?"

Hub's? One of the places where we had a ton of memories of Brett acting like an ass around us. The kind of memories that led to worse memories.

Jake pushed open the diner door, smiling back at me. "Yeah." He gave my hand a reassuring squeeze and led me inside. "Time to make new memories, Supergirl."

The End

Acknowledgements

The continuation of Charley and Jake's story has been one of the most challenging for me—the date of release was delayed because I was determined to give my readers the right conclusion to their epic romance. I hope fans of these characters feel it was worth the wait!

I want to say a massive thank you to my amazing editor Jennifer Sommersby Young. Jenn, I couldn't have done it without you. Thank you for your honesty and commitment, and your invaluable direction. Without you I wouldn't have found the heart of the story in Charley.

I'd also like to thank, as always, my brilliant agent Lauren Abramo. Thank you for helping to put Charley and Jake's story into the hands of German readers.

And thank you to Nina Wegscheider and her team at Ullstein for giving German readers the opportunity to get to know Charley and Jake!

Moreover, a big thank you to Angela McLaurin at Fictional Formats. Thank you so much for making the INTO THE DEEP series look so beautiful in ebook and print! You're a true rock star.

There are a number of bloggers who have been so enthusiastic about the INTO THE DEEP series—to name but a few, Christine Estevez, Natasha Tomic, Kathryn Grimes, Shelley Bunnell, Michelle

Kannan, Gael at Booky Ramblings, and Milasy & Lisa at The Rock Stars of Romance. Thank you ladies, and to all the other bloggers, who have been so amazingly supportive. A special thanks to Christine E!

My Street Team Club 39 deserves a huge thank you as well for their constant support. I adore you, my lovelies!

Finally, as always, thank you to you, my wonderful reader.

Live young. Live hard. Love deep.

12953802R00147

Printed in Poland
by Amazon Fulfillment
Poland Sp. z o.o., Wrocław